OMENS O[illegible]
DI[illegible]

The Basilica Diaries
Book One

Richard Kurti

Also in the The Basilica Diaries series

Palette of Blood

Demon of Truth

OMENS OF DEATH

Published by Sapere Books.

24 Trafalgar Road, Ilkley, LS29 8HH

saperebooks.com

ISBN: 978-1-80055-893-9

PART ONE

1: SACRIFICE

Rome, 1497

As the first rays of sunlight edged over the seven hills of Rome, they fell onto a pair of waxy-white feet. Strangely, the dawn light brought no warmth to the man, who didn't even stir.

The sun rose higher, waking birds, shimmering across the wild grasses, spreading a comforting red glow up the man's legs. Yet still he remained motionless.

Perhaps because he was upside down.

Or because he was deep in meditation.

Or perhaps because the man was too cold ever to feel warmth again.

A curious robin fluttered across from a nearby cypress tree and landed on the white toes. He peered at the upside-down man as if hoping for some friendly words or a few breadcrumbs.

But none came.

Unable to resist, the bird swooped down, rested on the man's nose and started to peck at the insects that crawled across his face.

Little Enzo was in a good mood considering it was so early in the morning. As the Via Collatina left the city walls, it climbed for two miles up into the farms that spread across the ridge; it meant going out of Rome was a sweat, but the journey back was downhill all the way. So even though the slopping milk churns in Enzo's hands were heavy as lead, he whistled cheerfully as he walked.

He'd only been doing the job since he turned twelve, so it was still a novelty to venture out into the countryside each daybreak and call it work. As long as he had the milk on his master's table in time for breakfast, no-one minded if he stopped every now and then to admire the view. It always put a smile on Enzo's young face to imagine the size of the giant that had taken such huge bites out of the colosseum, and smashed his angry fists into the old forum, spreading carnage and chaos. To think that a thousand years ago, Christians were still being fed to the lions in that temple of death; it was hard to imagine this was the same city.

It was only as the dusty road rounded a small copse of cypress trees, that Enzo noticed the upside-down cross silhouetted against the sunrise. He stopped for a moment, trying to understand exactly what he was seeing. Something to do with the crumbling pagan shrines that still dotted the road? Perhaps it was the start of a new barn that one of the farmers was building. Enzo knew for sure it was none of his business, but since when did that stop a young boy?

He diverted onto a narrow track, walking in a lazy arc around the inverted cross, until the low sun was behind him, falling directly onto the crucifix.

The boy froze.

His mouth dropped open in disbelief. He wanted to scream, but nothing came out. His empty stomach knotted in fear. Yet despite the horror, he was drawn closer, as if under a ghastly spell.

An elderly man had been nailed to the cross, upside down, so that all the blood ran up his body and engorged his face, swelling it into a hideous grimace. The whites of his eyes were devil-red where the blood vessels had ruptured, and lice swarmed over his face and neck. The body had been stripped of all its clothes, yet the jewellery had been left untouched: a silver chain hung limp around one ankle; gold rings clustered on the man's chubby fingers, flamboyant badges of wealth and power that were useless to him now.

The churns slid from Enzo's grip and clattered to ground, spilling milk across the dirt.

He turned and bolted towards the city gates, stumbling over rocks and screaming for help as tears of shock streaked his cheeks.

2: CRISTINA

Cristina Falchoni folded back the mahogany window shutters and watched light flood into the library. It always gave her a small pulse of pleasure to see the overflowing bookcases come to life each morning.

Five years ago this had been the elegant 'day salon' in her parents' townhouse, designed to receive guests and impress business associates. Now, despite all the scepticism she had faced, Cristina had turned it into one of the finest private studies in Rome. Of course, if her parents ever returned to the city, she would have some serious explaining to do, but there was no point worrying about hypotheticals now.

Cristina glanced at the iron verge and foliot clock on the far wall and noticed that the weight was almost touching the floor. *A day early*, she thought to herself. *Perhaps it's the damp air coming off the Tyrrhenian Sea.*

She slid open a small drawer in the bureau to reveal a dozen different winding keys of all shapes and sizes, selected one engraved with symbols of the zodiac, and carefully wound up the clock.

For a few moments Cristina gazed at the intricate mechanism, watching the pallets click against the escape wheel. She loved the steady, logical tick it made; it was the pulse of her life, and she always felt uneasy when the clock fell silent. So many people didn't understand that the silence of a library was not really silence at all; it was the sigh of a heavy book being slid from a shelf, and the gentle thud of it being placed on a lectern; it was the rustle of pages turning, and the creak of oiled floorboards as you walked to open the window. It was the sound of a curious bee who floated in, flew once around the room, then left you in peace. Above all, it was the euphoria you heard inside your head whenever disparate ideas came together.

Unlike other twenty-five-year-olds in Rome, Cristina didn't need the lascivious masked balls and raucous receptions that the city was notorious for, as she wasn't interested in capturing a wealthy husband; everything she needed was in the looming bookstacks of this library. It was the centre of her world, and today more than any other day was proof of this room's importance.

She plucked an academic robe from the back of the door, slipped it on and checked her reflection in the mirror. With black breeches merging into leather boots, and a hip-length jacket and white shirt hugging her petite frame, Cristina could have easily passed for one of the students at Sapienza University … were it not for the fact that women were still forbidden from studying. Perhaps that was why she enjoyed letting her long curly hair tumble so chaotically around her striking, pale face, feminising the academic clothes in an act of defiance. She smiled to herself, remembering all the arguments she'd had with her parents over the years; they were constantly urging her to look elegant and pretty, like the wealthy merchant's daughter she was. However, Cristina was convinced you had to dress for the place you were going to, not where you were coming from, and her eyes had been fixed on the university ever since she was a child, whether they wanted her or not.

She took a large silver candlestick from the mantelpiece and placed it on a window ledge so that it was clearly visible from the Piazza Navona below. One candlestick meant the coast was clear, two warned to stay away; this was how Cristina signalled to the university academics who risked their reputations to give her private tuition and who were notoriously wary of gossiping neighbours.

Cristina peered through the small glass panes cluttered with leading, watching the chaotic piazza closely, until she spotted Professor De Luca approaching from Via di Pasquino. He glanced up, saw the candlestick and made his way round to the servants' entrance. A few moments later she heard footsteps on the narrow service stairs, then a gentle knock. She swung open one of the bookstacks to reveal a middle-aged man with salt-and-pepper hair. "Signorina Falchoni." He gave a small bow. "Always a pleasure."

"Come in, come in." Cristina tried to usher him towards the long table, but he paused at the chessboard that was set up by the doors, mid-game.

"A moment, Cristina." His delicate fingers hovered over the pieces. "I had a thought…" With a sly smile he moved his bishop across the board, probing her defences.

Cristina studied the new configuration. "Interesting. I'll get to it later."

"But you see what I've done?"

"Right now, Professor, we have work to do." Gently she guided him away from the chessboard.

"You'll be pleased to know I've found what we were looking for." De Luca put his leather bag down on the table, slid out a large book and held it up like a relic. "Alberti's treatise on perspective. *De Pictura*. It has finally arrived from Siena. This should keep us busy until Michaelmas." He waited for a joyous reaction and was perturbed when it didn't come.

"I think we need to change the syllabus, Professor."

"Change?" he frowned. "Do you know how hard it was to acquire this book?"

"Our immediate focus now needs to be on architecture, specifically that of cathedrals. We need to immerse ourselves in the works of the master builders."

De Luca stared at her for a moment as he processed the information. Then his eyes widened. "No?"

"Yes!"

"Really? You have succeeded?"

"Not me. And not officially."

"Then how —"

"Working through my brother, we were able to plant a seed in the Pope's mind. A little discreet watering, and now His Holiness has made the decision all on his own, inspired purely by God."

De Luca stroked his goatee beard thoughtfully. "He will *really* commit to it?"

"A formal announcement will be made by the end of the week."

"Well, well." De Luca sat down. "Where will he build this new St Peter's?"

"On top of the old one. Where else?"

"And what of the immense cost? That is what has thwarted previous popes who have attempted it."

"Money doesn't worry this one." Cristina put a bottle of port and two small glasses on the table. "Pope Alexander's biggest worry is that he is a Borgia, steeped in blood and corruption. A magnificent new St Peter's is a chance to cleanse his soul. He can atone in stone. All his sins will be forgotten, and he will be remembered as the man who built the greatest church in Christendom."

De Luca poured two glasses, gave one to Cristina then raised his in a toast. "To your good health. And your stubbornness. I'm impressed."

Cristina laughed, slugged back the drink, then hurried to the far end of the table. "I've taken down all the relevant books on architecture and drawn up a list of what we still need to acquire." She handed several sheets of paper to De Luca. "I've also bought copies of the architectural plans for Florence Cathedral, and a mathematical study of Brunelleschi's Dome." She unfurled the plans and was immediately absorbed by the complex drawings.

De Luca scanned the list of required books. "Impressive. Very thorough."

"Let me know the cost," Cristina added. "I will give you the money immediately."

"Very well." De Luca folded the list and put it in his pocket. "But for the first lesson, I think we should step out of your library."

"*Out*? Why?"

"If the old St Peter's is to be destroyed, we should spend the next few days studying it, learning from it."

"But..." Cristina was puzzled. "But all our books are here. In this library. Why would we leave?"

"Because —" De Luca pointed to the open window — "the real world is out there."

3: DOMENICO

Horse's hooves clattered noisily on the dew-damp stones of Via Collatina. A more cautious rider would have slowed to avoid the risk of the horse slipping, but Capitano Domenico Falchoni felt he owed it to the murder victim to get to the crime scene as quickly as possible, and he pressed on.

It was only the guttural shrieks of the crows that pulled Domenico up. There they were, circling over the inverted crucifix with dark intent.

How often had he seen these black-hearted scavengers picking their way across a battlefield of the dead? How many of his fallen comrades had been pecked and degraded as they lay in the blood-soaked mud? As a raw recruit Domenico had tried to shoo them away, and it took several violent battles for him to realise the futility of his compassion. Wherever there was death, there were crows, and there was nothing he could do about it.

"Sir! Over here!" The voice of his burly deputy, Antonio Gilo, pulled him back to the present. Domenico spurred his horse and rode closer to the subdued group huddled around the crucifix.

At forty-two, Gilo was twelve years older than Domenico, and gritty experience had toughened him up; but rather than becoming cynical, life in the world of violent crime had helped Gilo understand his own limitations. When Domenico was promoted over him, Gilo gave no hint of resentment; deep down, perhaps he even felt relieved, and he now saw himself as the loyal protector of his boss.

"What have we got?" Domenico dismounted and tied the reins around the branch of a fallen tree.

"Put it this way," Gilo said as he shook his head, "I won't be eating breakfast any time soon."

"That bad, eh?"

"What is it about Rome that attracts all the sick bastards?" The permanent glint in Gilo's eyes took the edge off the horror.

Both men studied the degraded body nailed upside down to the cross. The skin was now grey. All the blood had drained away, creating a grotesque red stain down the stony hillside. Domenico could feel an old, familiar nausea rising in his stomach and turned away. Back on the path, two of the *Guardie Vaticane* had slung a rope across the roadway to keep curious spectators away; another guard stood next to a young boy who squatted on the ground, wiping tears from his cheeks.

Protocols. Stick to the protocols and everything could be controlled. Domenico was Capitano della Guardia Apostolica, responsible for all aspects of Vatican security. Everyone looked to him for a lead, and he had to deliver. "Right, Gilo, victim's an old man — in his sixties, maybe?"

"At least."

"Nailed to a cross in the middle of the night, hoisted upside down for the crows … terrible way to die."

"There are some sick, sick people in this city." Gilo scratched his grey, close-cropped hair.

"I think it's more than that," Domenico replied. "It's not just sick, it's a message. This is how St Peter was executed."

"Really? *Our* St Peter?"

"Exactly like this. As ordered by Emperor Nero a thousand years ago. Head down, arms outstretched."

"All right." Gilo peered at the victim's face. "So … we're dealing with a lunatic? A religious fanatic?"

Domenico studied the gathering crowd. Some looked on with horror; some clutched their rosary beads and prayed. One man was even trying to sell oranges to the spectators.

"That was the boy who found him." Gilo pointed to Enzo sitting next to a guard. "He raised the alarm."

"Going to give him a few nightmares." Domenico crouched down to examine the crucified body more closely, and his nose caught the too familiar smell of cold blood; death had its own distinctive, bitter aroma. *Protocols. Focus.* "Any idea who he could be?"

"Not yet, sir. But the rings on his fingers suggest someone important."

"Send one of the men to ask at the watch towers, see if anyone's been reported missing."

Gilo turned to the closest soldier. "You heard the chief!" The soldier hurried away.

Suddenly a shout went up from the crowd. "And the great dragon was cast down!"

Everyone spun round as an old monk in a dirty brown cowl pushed his way to the front. "The old serpent, he that is called the Devil and Satan, the deceiver of the whole world!"

A dread murmur spread through the crowd as foreboding started to bite.

"He was cast down to the earth, and his angels were cast down with him!"

"Here we go," Gilo muttered.

"Tell him if he doesn't shut up, he's going to be arrested," Domenico said testily.

"Hey! You!" Gilo strode towards the Prophet of Doom. "My day's hard enough already. Get out of here!"

While Gilo wrangled the crowd, Domenico turned to one of the guards. "Take the victim down. Put him in the morgue. Maybe there's a clue on the body."

"Yes, sir."

But just as the soldiers started to lower the crucifix to the ground, an overweight man in a uniform came wheezing up the hill. "Don't touch it!" he gasped. "You … have no … authority … here." He started to cough.

"Says who?" Domenico waited for the man to snatch a breath.

"I'm the *sergente di guardia*. This is my crime scene."

"I'm afraid not," Domenico replied.

"The murder was reported to *us*!"

"The religious symbolism of the murder makes it a Vatican matter now."

"I don't give a damn about symbolism!"

"You really want to defy the Pope?"

That shut the sergeant up, but only for a moment. "Your jurisdiction doesn't go beyond the city walls."

"Wrong again, my friend," Domenico said firmly. "It goes wherever His Holiness chooses. Wherever there are Christians. So, unless you're a heretic, I suggest you turn around and leave this to us."

A look of pure rage darkened the sergeant's flabby face, but he knew he was out of his depth. He spat on the ground, then muttered something under his breath and beat a retreat.

"Nicely done," Gilo chuckled. "What about the boy? Shall we let him go?"

Domenico glanced at Enzo, whose head was now in his hands. "Leave him to me." He walked over, crouched next to the boy and put an arm around his shoulders. The kind touch made Enzo start to cry all over again. "Hey, hey. It's over now," Domenico said gently. "There's no danger to you."

Enzo sniffed his nose clean.

"Why don't you tell me what you saw? From the beginning."

Enzo nodded and recounted everything that had happened that morning. Domenico listened closely; he didn't learn anything new, but recounting what he'd witnessed calmed the boy down.

"You did well." Domenico patted him on the back. "No need to cry. These things happen."

"It's not him I'm crying about," Enzo sniffed.

"Oh?"

Enzo pointed to the empty urns, still lying on their sides next to the crucifix. "I spilled all the milk. I'll be late back. My master will throw me out onto the street."

"I don't think so," Domenico reassured.

"You don't know him, sir! He hates missing breakfast. He has a temper."

"Here." Domenico took the boy's hand and led him back across the stony ground. He picked up the empty urns and put them in Enzo's hands. "Deputato Gilo!"

"Sir."

"Put this lad on your horse, pay for some more milk, then take him back to his master's house. Anyone gives him trouble, tell them to talk to me."

"Yes, sir."

Enzo looked up at Domenico. "Really?"

"Problem solved."

"Thank you, sir."

As Gilo lifted the boy onto his horse, Domenico turned back to the corpse that was now lying flat on the ground. Two guards were trying to remove the large iron nails that had been driven through his hands.

Flies swarmed around the spilt milk that mingled with pools of blood. What curse was on Domenico's life, that all roads led back to death? Sometimes it felt as if he had lived his entire life under the shadow of circling crows.

4: BASILICA

Cristina pushed open the heavy bronze doors of the old basilica to discover a fight in progress. Choristers and builders were jostling in a circle, jeering on two middle-aged men who were grappling with each other, swinging wildly with their fists.

"Well, this is different," Cristina observed.

De Luca's eyes went wide as he took in the chaotic scene. "Good grief!" He ran up the nave and pushed his way into the fray. "Stop this! Break it up!"

He pulled the two men apart and was astonished to see that it was the choirmaster who was brawling with one of the stonemasons. The musician's robes were torn, but he had managed to land a decent punch, and the stonemason was nursing a bloody nose.

"What in heaven's name is going on?" De Luca exclaimed, looking from one to the other. Both men ignored him. Eyes locked, panting for breath, they were steeling themselves for the next onslaught.

"Finish him off!" one of the choristers goaded.

"Smack his head in!" a builder cried back, and both men lunged towards each other again.

"NO!" De Luca screamed and threw himself between them. "Enough! This is a house of God!" His words echoed around the cavernous basilica, momentarily bringing the men to their senses. "What on earth is this about?" De Luca demanded.

Cristina looked on from the edge of the fray, amazed at how the academic took control, but then he was used to wrangling lecture halls full of boisterous young men.

"I cannot rehearse when this ignorant *stronzo*," said the choirmaster, pointing accusingly at the stonemason, "is hacking away with his chisels!"

"You want the building to fall on top of you?" the stonemason retorted. "Is that what you want?"

"Don't be absurd."

"Look!" The builder pointed to a huge crack scarring the north wall that the masons were trying to repair. "It's falling apart!"

"The basilica's been here for a thousand years," the choirmaster insisted. "I'm sure it will be all right for another hour."

The choristers jeered their agreement.

"You think I *want* to be here, patching up this ruin?" the stonemason spat furiously. "I've got a palazzo on the Tiber to finish!"

"Then why don't you do us all a favour and leave?"

"Because Cardinale Riario sent me here!"

"I don't work for him! I work for God!"

The choristers roared their approval of the put-down.

"*Testa di cazzo*!" The enraged stonemason raised his fists again.

"Come on, then!"

"Gentlemen! ENOUGH!" De Luca was out of patience. "One more punch and the City Watch will clap you both in irons!"

The prospect of facing Rome's magistrates made the fighters hesitate. De Luca pounced on the moment to turn peacemaker. "If the choir needs a little longer to finish rehearsing, a not unreasonable request, then perhaps the stonemasons deserve a little longer for lunch. An early aperitif, perhaps, then everyone wins. What do you say, gentlemen?"

It was the best compromise anyone was going to get, and both sides grudgingly dispersed. The choristers embraced their man, celebrating what they thought was a clear victory, while the stonemasons sidled away down the long, colonnaded nave to find some wine in a neighbourhood tavern.

"Hallelujah," De Luca muttered under his breath, and turned to find Cristina, but she was already over by the north wall, examining the worrying cracks. The professor hurried over to join her, picking his way through the builders' chisels.

"The mason does have a point." Cristina ran her fingers along a jagged branch of the fissures. "Judging from the colour of the stone, this crack has just opened up."

"Built on a hillside," De Luca shrugged. "The basilica's probably been shifting a little every year. I really don't think anyone should panic."

"Just because the sun has risen every day in the past, doesn't mean it will rise tomorrow."

"And yet, deep down, we both know it will."

"Perhaps." Cristina walked out into the centre of the nave, head thrown back, taking in the huge old space that was cluttered with shrines and tombs. At heart, the building was simple: a rectangle, twice as long as it was wide, with water stains running down the walls from decades of leaks that had never been repaired. Columned aisles on either side supported a timber roof that was covered in bronze plates, some of which were now falling off, and mosaics and frescoes jostled for attention.

Cristina breathed in deeply: the air was damp and aromatic from a hundred different moulds that were feeding off the rotting building. It reminded her of venturing down into the cellar of her father's villa in Frascati when she was a child.

"If the Vatican won't even pay for the upkeep of this, I really don't see that they will provide funds for a gleaming new basilica," De Luca sighed.

"They will. And they are. Because of that." Cristina strode towards to the far end of the nave, where a massive altar sat in a semi-circular recess. She tapped her boot on the flagstones under her feet. "Down there. The tomb of St Peter."

"If true," the professor observed.

"Meaning?"

"If you believe the legends."

"It's a matter of historical fact. The emperor Constantine ordered the church to be built directly over St Peter's burial site."

"And no-one has seen the grave since. They didn't build a crypt; they covered the whole thing in earth."

"What are you suggesting?" Cristina couldn't hide her tetchiness.

"You're a scholar, Cristina. Observation is everything. If St Peter's tomb is really there, why did they make it impossible to see?"

"There is no point doubting for doubt's sake." She looked up at the large gold crucifix hanging over the altar. "This man walked with Christ. 'Thou art Peter, and upon this rock I shall build my Church.' Constantine took a shovel and started the foundations with his own hands. He filled twelve bags of soil, one for each of the apostles, and it is a scandal that the heart of Christianity is now a crumbling wreck. What does that say about Western civilisation?"

"That we have no money?" De Luca suggested.

"There is plenty of money. It's just in the wrong hands." Cristina refused to accept excuses. "In the Dark Ages, when Europe was under attack from all sides, it was the Church that kept civilisation alive. The Church trained scholars, built universities, commissioned artists and anointed kings."

"Precisely," De Luca nodded. "Influence through knowledge. *That* is true power. It doesn't lie in the cold marble of a building."

"Europe needs a beacon of light." Cristina paced in front of the altar. "The Ottomans are threatening from the East; there is discontent in the northern states. This crumbling building must be replaced by a statement of power and authority."

"No, no, it's more complex than that," De Luca insisted. "Constantinople fell to the Ottomans, but the books that were smuggled out found their way here, to Rome and Florence and Venice. Learning and science flourish in the Islamic world."

"Yet the Sultan would happily unleash a bloodbath to rid the world of Christians."

"He is a politician, not a monster."

"Tell that to the villages along the coasts of Spain and Italy, where men have been snatched in Ottoman raids. Tell it to the innocent men who will die chained to oars as galley slaves. Who are whipped and beaten, then tossed overboard when they are sick."

"Have you seen our own ships?" De Luca pushed back. "You think Christian captains treat their galley slaves any better than Muslim captains?"

Cristina was not going to be caught out so easily. "Which is precisely why we need a new St Peter's. To inspire us all."

"Civilisation is about more than stone, Cristina."

"But stone is its highest expression. A cathedral is not just about architecture and frescoes, it is an expression of willpower. The fact that cathedrals are almost impossible to build is precisely the point. It urges us to reach further."

De Luca couldn't hold back a wry laugh.

"What?" Cristina demanded.

"You obviously have very little experience of working with builders."

5: PANIC

By the time Domenico arrived back at the Vatican, Rome was awash with rumours about the murder. The victim had now been identified as Count Barberini, a well-connected dandy and socialite, but that only made the case more complicated, as it put many of Rome's great and good under suspicion.

Domenico rode into the cobbled courtyard just as the guard shifts were changing, so the barrack rooms were bustling with activity. As he jumped down from his horse, a keen young lieutenant with sharp features spotted him and hurried over. "How did it go, sir?"

"Not one for the fainthearted, Tomasso."

"Sounds interesting, sir." The soldier swept a mop of black hair from his open face. "When will you be briefing us?"

Domenico handed him the reins. "Make sure he has plenty to drink. It was dusty up on the hillside."

"Yes, sir."

Domenico left his horse in the care of the young soldier and entered the labyrinthine Vatican Palace. It was a long walk to the Pope's private apartments, involving four flights of stairs and what felt like half a mile of corridors. Under normal circumstances it would have been tedious, but today it gave Domenico time to marshal his thoughts.

The perverted *modus operandi* of the murder was firing up Rome's superstitious, who saw the work of the Devil in everything from the pattern of bird droppings to the shape of a baby's birthmark. At the same time, the fact that the victim was rich and well connected gave ammunition to those who believed life in this city was defined by the machinations of the rival dynasties to win power. Was Barberini murdered because he knew too much? Or because he threatened to speak out?

Domenico sighed inwardly. As if the investigation wasn't going to be difficult enough, now he would have to deal with an endless stream of cranks, false leads and slanderous accusations.

He arrived at the Room of Pontiffs, outermost chamber of the Borgia Apartments, where one of the Pope's private secretaries was waiting to question him about his business.

"I've been summoned by the Holy Father," Domenico explained.

"In writing?"

"No. There wasn't time."

The secretary gave a disapproving sniff. Domenico focused on not reacting; he had been in these rooms countless times, yet on each occasion the Pope's inner circle treated him as if he really didn't belong. The secretary sat behind his desk and made a great show of consulting some official paperwork; Domenico was only able to keep his irritation in check by studying the new and brilliantly coloured frescoes that adorned the walls and ceiling.

Finally, the secretary beckoned Domenico to proceed through the doors into the Room of Mysteries, where another private secretary went through an identical routine. Domenico had to endure yet more bureaucracy in the Room of Saints, before finally being admitted to the Room of the Creed, a surprisingly modest chamber.

The shutters were still closed, creating an oppressive and gloomy air. Sitting behind his desk, head in his hands, was His Holiness Pope Alexander VI, Supreme Pontiff, Bishop of Rome and Leader of the Papal States.

"Holy Father." Domenico gave a respectful bow.

"Well? Are the rumours true? Is it Barberini?"

"I'm afraid so."

"Crucified? Upside down?"

"Yes, Holy Father."

"Then God help us all. The Devil is stalking the streets of Rome. Taking the souls of those who do his work." He swivelled his bulbous eyes to study Domenico's reaction.

"No, Your Holiness. I don't believe so."

"Hah." The Pope stood up and opened one of the shutters, letting a shaft of sunlight fall across his face as he gazed out onto Belvedere Courtyard.

Domenico studied the man's nose, fascinated by the way it was too long for Alexander's face, as if it had been stolen from someone else.

"Barberini certainly had a 'reputation', but he didn't deserve this," the Pope said quietly.

"No-one deserves to die in such horrific circumstances, Your Holiness."

"Tell me everything. Exactly what happened?"

Domenico gave a full account of the known facts of the murder in the calmest language he could find, ignoring the fevered speculations of the City Watch, omitting the troop of monks he'd seen hurrying towards the crime scene to flagellate themselves, and generally downplaying the sensationalist elements.

It didn't work.

The Pope closed the window shutters, sat down at his desk and picked up a rosary, which he shuffled nervously through his fingers. "Someone is sending me a message. A grave and terrible warning."

"I do not believe this is personal, Holy Father."

"Open your eyes, man!"

The sudden burst of anger caught Domenico off guard. "Forgive me. I —"

"The timing! It is too much of a coincidence. This is all connected to my plans for the new basilica."

"But no announcement has been made yet."

"Word leaks from the Vatican like water from a sieve."

"And Count Barberini had no connection to the great project, Holy Father."

"But he had done me some service. In the past. And that connects him to me. This is about me."

"I don't understand — who would be opposed to a magnificent new basilica? The construction alone will make a lot of people in Rome very rich. And think of the pilgrims it will attract."

"You are looking to the future, but many in Rome are slaves to the past. Construction cannot begin unless we demolish the old basilica, and many regard that as the most sacred shrine in Europe. To them it is hallowed ground. Yet I, a Borgia, have the audacity to tamper with it. How dare I presume?"

"Surely, Holy Father, the greater the building, the greater the glory to God?"

Alexander gave a derisive snort. "Some people, little people, cannot abide change. It terrifies them."

"The important thing is that you have the backing of the cardinals," Domenico replied.

"Perhaps."

"The Curia is as one in supporting you."

"They backed me last week, but this unnatural murder … this could change their fickle hearts."

"You have spoken to them, Holy Father?"

"It is impossible to avoid them in this place."

"And what have they said? Who do they believe is behind this?"

"The cardinals are inscrutable. As usual. But when I look into their eyes, I see fear. And if dark forces are moving against me, the cardinals will abandon me."

"Dark forces, Your Holiness?"

"I've had troubled dreams this past week. Only yesterday, as I was walking along the Western Wall, I saw a kestrel pluck a sparrow from the sky and devour it." A heavy silence descended on the room as the Pope ruminated. "Is that to be my fate as well?"

Domenico studied the Pope's mournful face, wondering if he was mentally drawing up a list of all his enemies, in which case the silence could last a long time.

"Might I suggest, Holy Father, that we treat this purely as a murder? That we don't let our judgement be clouded by superstition or fear, that we think only of men, and not of … dark forces?"

The Pope turned to Domenico and cast a withering look. "I like you. You are good at your job. That is why I made you Capitano della Guardia Apostolica. But you have no imagination."

The accusation was meant to hurt, and it hit home. But Domenico no longer had the luxury of imagination. Violent combat had taught him to keep his mind in check, to focus only on what he could change, to stick to procedures and always follow the drill, because the right protocols could get you through anything. "Forgive me, Holy Father."

Alexander shook his head in exasperation. "You cannot help being dull, but it is all the more reason to listen when I speak. It is clear to me that this dreadful crucifixion is a dire warning. The religious symbolism is too strong. A hundred and eighty-four popes have been consecrated in that basilica; martyrs and saints are buried in every nook and cranny. I decide to demolish it, and three days later a man is sacrificed just as our beloved St Peter was sacrificed. There is no doubt that this is a message I must heed."

"A message from who, Holy Father?"

"That, Domenico, is precisely what you must determine. Who … or what?" Coldness glinted in the dark eyes of the Borgia Pope. "Do it. And do it quickly. Or I will find someone who will."

6: SIBLINGS

"That's absurd!" Cristina exclaimed. "Absurd and pathetic."

"You're talking about one of the most powerful men in the world," Domenico reminded her.

"That doesn't stop him being wrong."

"At least try to show some respect."

"If I can't be honest with my own brother, there really is no hope." Cristina turned away and continued searching for a book on the shelves.

"It's not me you have to worry about." Domenico tried to sound more conciliatory. "But if you get into the habit of blurting out whatever you're thinking, you're going to end up in serious trouble. You know what Rome is like."

"Which is why I prefer to stay safely inside this library and fill my mind with learning."

"Well, the Pope communicates with God. So that doesn't leave many places to hide."

"How I would love to sit in on those 'conversations'," Cristina mused. "Especially as I assume God does not tolerate fools."

"What did I just say about keeping your counsel?" Domenico poured himself a glass of port and slumped in a chair.

Cristina watched her brother swill the drink around his glass. How different he was from her. Cautious, diplomatic, guarded Domenico; she admired him for it, and yet deep in her soul she believed it was weak not to speak out. But then, she didn't have many friends (which suited her perfectly), whereas

Domenico had risen through the Vatican ranks with astonishing speed, so who was she to judge?

"Look." Cristina took a series of books down from the shelves and laid them precisely on the table. "*The Mathematics of Circles. The Motion of Planets. A Treatise on Light and Colour.* This is how God talks to us, through knowledge and truth. He doesn't send messages through gruesome murders."

"It doesn't matter what your books say." Domenico pushed the leather volumes aside. "We are dealing with a real man. A mortal man who has fears and superstitions just like everyone else. If the Pope becomes convinced that this murder is a warning from God, who knows what he will do?"

"What do you mean?"

Domenico shrugged. "Fear pushes men down strange paths. I've seen it too often."

"But we need this Pope to succeed."

Cristina felt an old, familiar unease grip her stomach, like the last time Rome had been shaken by an earth tremor, and the solid walls of her library had quivered as if they were paper. How she hated that feeling of sudden fragility.

Trying to reassure herself, Cristina looked at all the projects lined up on her desk: newly acquired books to be studied, a sketch of how she intended to reorganise her library to create more space, a timetable for the next six months of Greek and Hebrew lessons. All this learning in the world, all this progress, and still the Head of the Church was in thrall to superstition. "Doesn't His Holiness understand that you must never give in to fear and weakness?"

"Cristina! There's no point accusing him of being ignorant. Offer him proof. *Show* him that he is wrong. Use hard evidence."

"If someone is determined to embrace ignorance, there is no helping them."

"Then kiss goodbye to your new basilica. Because that's what will happen." Domenico slugged back his port.

"That's irrational."

"But it's what will happen. The Pope will smother it before the first stone has even been quarried."

Cristina gazed out of the window at the crowds jostling through the Piazza Navona. Would the world ever be rid of ignorance? She noticed a dead fly that had got trapped between the shutters; despite the window being open it couldn't find a way out, couldn't see the gap that was right in front of it.

"If you know of a better way, Cristina, then help me solve this murder."

"My days are filled with study. From first light until dusk."

"And that's more important than bringing the guilty to justice?"

"There is nothing more important than learning." Cristina had fought this battle her whole life, and sometimes it felt as if the struggle would never end. But when she looked at her brother, just for a moment she glimpsed the little boy he had once been. She knew that haunted expression so well from their childhood; Domenico was out of his depth yet refused to admit it.

"One morning," he asked. "Just help me for one morning. Point me in the right direction."

Cristina sighed. Perhaps she could think of it as a lesson in applied logic; at least that way it would be time well spent. "His Holiness really thinks the murder was a reaction to his decision to build a new basilica?"

"Yes. And to protect the old one from destruction."

"But nothing has been officially announced?"

"No."

"So, compile a list of who knew about the decision in advance."

"There are no secrets in the Vatican," Domenico lamented. "You and I knew — should we put ourselves on the list? And who did you tell?"

"I don't think crucifixion is Professor De Luca's style."

"That's an assumption, not a fact."

"You can't seriously suspect a professor from the university?"

"Maybe."

"What time was the murder?" Cristina asked.

"After the last watch patrol. Possibly just before dawn."

"Well, that clears De Luca. He didn't know until this morning."

"Very well. One suspect down, just the rest of the city to investigate."

"Take some paper. I'll help you draw up a list of where to start."

Eagerly Domenico did as he was told.

"First thing," Cristina decided, "I will need to see the crime scene."

"That's not a good idea."

"Do you want my help or not?"

"But —"

"I need to see the crime in its context, with my own eyes, so that I can look for patterns, point to where you might find evidence," Cristina insisted.

"It's pretty brutal."

"I've dissected animals. Blood is blood," she shrugged.

"Hold that thought, Cristina. Hold that thought."

7: BLOOD

By the time Cristina and Domenico arrived the body had already been removed, but the bloodstained crucifix still lay on the ground like a gruesome, unwanted stage prop.

Gilo hurried over as he saw them riding up the dusty road, the metal on their horses' tacks chinking in the stifling air. "I wasn't expecting you back today, sir."

"My sister was … curious," Domenico replied.

"Oh." Gilo offered his hand to help Cristina dismount, but she jumped down and handed him the reins instead.

"Thank you, Deputato Gilo." She pointed to the crucifix. "Is that where the body was discovered? Or has the cross been moved?"

"Er, no. That's where it was found," Gilo replied.

"Then I'd better take a look."

"Is that wise, signorina?"

"What do you mean?" Cristina's eyes locked onto the deputy.

"Well, it's just…" Gilo could feel himself wilting under her gaze. He took a red handkerchief from his jacket and wiped the sweat from the back of his neck. "With the heat, you might come over funny."

Cristina watched him stuff the handkerchief back into his pocket and noticed that his stubby fingers were covered in small cuts that were scabbing over. "Don't worry. I'm not the fainting type." She turned away and walked towards the crime scene, feet crunching on the parched stones.

Gilo watched her disappear into the heat ripples that were rising from the baked hillside. "I didn't mean anything by it," he muttered. "Just trying to help."

"Any leads yet? Anyone see anything?" Domenico glanced over to where two Vatican guards were taking down the makeshift cordon.

"We spent the whole morning questioning people in the vicinity but haven't turned up a single witness. Not one. Which is baffling." Gilo scratched his head. "It's not exactly an easy thing to do, crucify a man. You'd think someone would've noticed."

"Have you questioned Barberini's family?"

"No wife or children. Seems he devoted his life to 'pleasures of the flesh'."

"What about the servants? Did they see anything suspicious?"

Gilo consulted his notes. "He went to bed early, drunk as usual. The servants locked up. When they woke this morning, he'd already left the house."

"And no-one heard anything in the night?"

"The servants were used to strange noises. Barberini was fond of company."

"Meaning what, exactly, Gilo?"

"He had flexible morals, sir. Very flexible."

"Which probably made him lots of enemies," Domenico speculated.

"And lots of friends as well. He liked to 'share the love', apparently."

Domenico paced over to a small, rickety table where some recovered objects had been laid out: a broken pair of spectacles, a wire garotte, a large hammer.

"They were hidden behind that boulder over there, sir. We're fairly sure the murderer used them."

Domenico studied the garotte closely, noting the dried bloodstains on the wire. Then he picked up the hammer and felt the weight in his hands. "He must have died in agony. Screaming. And no-one heard a thing." Domenico frowned. "It doesn't make any sense."

Gilo shook his head sombrely. "Unless…"

"Unless?"

"There really are 'dark forces' at work, sir."

"That kind of thinking isn't helpful."

Gilo squinted in the harsh sun as he looked over to Cristina, who was crouching beside the crucifix. "If you don't mind me asking, sir, what exactly is your sister doing here?"

Domenico shuffled evasively. "She might be able to help. She's very widely read."

"I don't see how that helps us."

"She knows about … anatomy. Wounds. That sort of thing."

"Wouldn't want her getting into any danger," Gilo said darkly.

"There are six guards up here."

"Even so."

Cristina had sensed Gilo's disapproval from the moment she arrived, but what did she care? She was used to men getting upset about a woman being somewhere she wasn't wanted. She had no time for pettiness, especially when faced with such a horrific crime as this.

And it was horrific.

Even though the body had been removed, traces of the dreadful violence were everywhere: the blood smeared down the crucifix and pooled in the dust; the holes torn in the wood from the huge nails that had been driven through Barberini's hands and feet; the hair stuck to the cross, presumably where he had struggled frantically in his final minutes. It was one thing to see paintings of the crucifixion in the tranquillity of a church, but quite a different thing to see the gruesome reality.

Cristina stood up and looked back towards the city. Who had direct line of sight? It had been a full moon the previous night; this hillside would have been bathed in light, and yet the Watch hadn't seen anything strange? They hadn't seen a group of men dragging a large crucifix out here? Hadn't seen a fat man being held captive?

The crunch of approaching footsteps interrupted her flow.

"Well? Any thoughts?" Domenico called out as he approached.

"This was an elaborate crime. It took money and organisation."

Domenico handed her a leather waterskin and she drank thirstily, then poured some over her face to wash away the dust. "You're looking for a sophisticated murderer, probably working with accomplices."

"Where do you suggest I start?"

"With the cardinals."

"What?"

"They are some of the most powerful men in Rome."

"You can't seriously think —"

"They have connections everywhere, they hear the gossip, they know all the rivalries and factions. You need to talk to them, Domenico. Find out if any of them have been behaving suspiciously."

"Very well." But Domenico wasn't convinced.

Suddenly, a cry went up. "You can't go over there! Stop!"

Cristina spun round to see a stout, middle-aged woman in plain servant's clothes marching towards them. Gilo was chasing after her in vain. "Stop! It's off limits!" He reached out to grab her arm, but the woman turned and gave him a hefty shove, sending him tumbling backwards into the dirt.

They watched in disbelief as the woman walked right up to them, lifted her skirts, then calmly urinated over the crucifix. When she was done, she adjusted her clothes and looked defiantly at Domenico.

"What?" she demanded.

"I … I think you owe us an explanation."

"Why?"

"Do you always piss on crime scenes?"

"This wasn't a crime. It was justice."

"Who exactly are you?" Domenico asked.

"I kept house for Barberini. More's the pity."

"Did he owe you money?"

"*Filo de putana*!" She spat a huge globule into the dried blood. "What he owed can never be repaid."

"I don't follow."

The housekeeper turned her fierce gaze on Cristina. "Ask her. She knows what I'm talking about."

"Me? I never met the man," Cristina stuttered.

"He was an evil old *stronzo* who preyed on us all. There weren't a servant girl in the house who was safe from his prick. His lust did nothing but spread misery. The kitchen girls whose lives he destroyed… I'd see 'em come in, bright eyes and laughing, and within months he'd stolen everything from them. It was like he ate their hearts."

Domenico looked away in embarrassment, but Cristina stared at the housekeeper. "Did you report him to the magistrates?"

"Where have you been, woman? He was rich. And we were nothing."

"But the law —"

"Don't help the poor. Anyone dared to speak up, he discarded them. Like he discarded the unwanted babies, taken up into the woods to die. And the girls who wouldn't stop crying, dumped in convents. That was Barberini. I'm glad he's dead. And I'm glad he died in agony. And I hope he burns in Hell."

"Perhaps *you* killed him." Gilo had arrived to try and re-establish his authority.

The housekeeper gave him a withering look. "If wishing a man dead is a crime, then I should've been hanged years ago. But I never laid a finger on him. None of us did. He had powerful friends. And why should we send our souls to Hell for him?"

"I'll need to take a statement," Gilo said.

"I've said all I'm going to say."

"We'll see about that." He tried to haul the housekeeper away, but Cristina grabbed her arm.

"A moment!" She took her aside. "Tell me, did you really endure all that?"

"Why would I lie?"

"People hold grudges for all sorts of reasons."

Cristina looked into the housekeeper's eyes, desperate for a denial, a confession that everything she had said was an exaggeration, a false claim to settle an old score.

But the woman looked back at her with an uncanny steadiness. "Are you a nun?"

"No. Of course not."

"Then where have you been your whole life?" The housekeeper could see that Cristina lived in a different world.

"Don't take me for a fool," Cristina said.

"Being clever don't stop you being a fool. What you need to learn can't be found in books."

"Enough! Let's go. We need a statement." Gilo bundled the housekeeper away.

"Better make this quick," she warned him. "I've got a funeral to feed."

Cristina watched Gilo lead the housekeeper along the dusty road back towards the city, stunned by the woman's capacity for unalloyed hatred.

8: CARDINALI

They found Cardinale Riario in the cavernous orangery by the western wall of the Vatican gardens, carefully tending grapevines. He looked so absorbed and peaceful that Domenico was reluctant to interrupt.

"Perhaps we should come back later," he whispered to Gilo.

"He certainly doesn't look like the sort of man who knows about murder," Gilo replied.

Even though Riario was still in his early thirties, he had the otherworldly look of a saint who had glimpsed the face of God. Domenico wondered if it was genuine, or just an image that had been cultivated as carefully as the grapevines.

"It's all right, gentlemen. You can approach." Riario beckoned them over with a benign smile. As Domenico and Gilo made their way along the path that wound between the Pope's private vines, instinctively they scrutinised Riario, watching for any signs of unease. Through family connections he had become a cardinal at just sixteen and had turned into one of the Vatican's great survivors by mastering the fraught politics of the Curia. Even though he never talked about ambition, Riario behaved as if he was here to stay, and he tended the vines with the quiet certainty of a man who knew that one day this papal garden would be his.

"Forgive the intrusion, Your Eminence." Domenico gave a polite bow.

"You've come about the Barberini murder, I assume?"

Domenico and Gilo exchanged a surprised look; no wonder Riario's star was rising.

"Are there any rumours we should be aware of, Your Eminence?"

"Plenty. The Vatican is full of them. And they all point in one direction."

"To a suspect?"

"To a cause."

"I don't quite follow, Your Eminence." Domenico frowned.

"Put your finger here, a moment." Riario instructed Gilo to hold a vine stalk to the cane while he tied some little string loops.

"Nebbiolo vines." Gilo looked at the distinctive leaves. "Unusual for this area."

"Ah! You know your grapes." Riario's eyes lit up.

"My father grew these on his smallholding. He died ten years ago, but the wines he made get better every year."

"Quite," Riario agreed. "Nebbiolo are only for those who plan ahead."

Domenico was keen to stop the conversation drifting off into tedious wine snobbery. "You were saying, Your Eminence, about the cause?"

Riario chose his words very carefully. "I am a loyal supporter of His Holiness, but the Pope's election was not without controversy."

Domenico was surprised to hear the veiled criticism. It was well known that the Borgia Pope had given Riario the Bishopric of Cartagena in return for his backing; if that didn't buy loyalty, what did? "Surely all papal elections are controversial?" Domenico ventured.

"Indeed. But few popes have such a toxic reputation as Alexander. His rise to greatness was accompanied by sharp, some would say ruthless, political manoeuvring."

"Who are we to judge His Holiness?" Domenico mused, using humility to try and draw Riario further.

"God speaks through the cardinals. Through men like me."

"And through the cardinals voting, God decreed that Alexander should be the Pope."

"Can God not change his mind?"

"Why would he, Your Eminence?"

"It is not for me to second-guess God," Riario said piously. "But there are some who are disappointed that Alexander has not changed his ways since becoming our leader. Five years is time enough for any man to reform. A Pope should not indulge his appetites without restraint."

"Which appetites in particular?"

Riario secured a final stray shoot of the vine and focused on Domenico. "Barberini arranged orgies for His Holiness the Pope. Perhaps his murder is a sign of Divine Anger."

Domenico and Gilo remained absolutely silent; if they said the wrong thing now, they risked destroying their own careers.

Riario let out a soft chuckle. "A wise reaction."

"Your Eminence, do you have any evidence for your theory?"

"A sinner is crucified upside down in the middle of the night, and no-one witnessed anything? No-one heard screams or cries for help? That is not the work of human hands."

"Do you really think God would stoop so low?"

"He sent plagues to punish the wicked. He drowned the entire Egyptian army in the Red Sea. When God is angry, no-one is left in any doubt. It appears all those who despaired at the Borgia Pope's election are now being vindicated."

"His Holiness is certainly taking this very seriously," Domenico replied. "He is ruling nothing out."

"We are all searching for the truth," Riario said modestly.

"Forgive me, Your Eminence, but perhaps you too are worried?" Gilo had chosen his moment perfectly.

"Me?" Riario seemed thrown.

"You elected His Holiness — does that not make you complicit?"

Riario looked from Gilo to Domenico, wondering about their true motives. Then he relaxed into an easy smile. "I have made my peace with God. I have nothing to fear. Whether I am punished or forgiven, I will accept His judgement with humility."

How could one argue against that? Riario had shut down any further discussion.

"Now, if you will excuse me, gentlemen, I have urgent matters calling for my attention."

Domenico and Gilo bowed and retreated from the humid orangery, wondering whether they had just encountered the Serpent, and whether the Fruit of Knowledge they'd been offered was poisoned.

9: ASTROLABE

"Riario is an idiot!" Cristina banged the table with exasperation, making her notebooks jump. "He should know better than to spout rubbish like that."

"Come on, Cristina, say what you really think." Domenico had enjoyed provoking his sister ever since they were children; when she was in full flow, she lost all her sense of humour.

"The very first Greek translation of the Old Testament contained the crucial error," she expounded. "It should have been the *Reed* Sea, not the *Red* Sea: a shallow, marshy lake rather than a huge body of water. So all along the 'miracle' had an explanation."

"There's really no point arguing about this."

"The Tenth Plague — 'every firstborn son in Egypt will die' — same thing. A mistranslation of 'first fruits', meaning crops, not children."

"Cristina, I didn't come here for a lecture."

"God is not a showman," she said emphatically. "He did not crucify Barberini."

"So where does that leave us?"

Cristina rested her forehead on the glass pane as she looked out of the window and calmed down. "What is interesting, though, is that the cardinals think the killing is a Divine Judgement on the Pope's character, but the Pope thinks it is a Divine Judgement on his decision to build a new basilica."

"Which means we are getting caught up in Vatican politics," Domenico said grimly.

"I'm afraid so. The cardinals are trying to undermine the Pope, and the Pope is trying to deflect attention away from his own failings."

Domenico hated all the grubby political games. These were men of God, spiritual leaders, and here they were trying to turn a man's violent death to their own advantage. "It's ugly," he muttered. "Really ugly."

Cristina turned to her brother. "Step away from it," she said decisively.

"I can't. This is my job."

"There are no good outcomes for you."

"The Pope is demanding answers. I can't just run away from this."

"Whatever you uncover, you will make enemies — either of the cardinals, or of the Pope. Neither outcome is good."

"Welcome to my world, Cristina. I don't have the luxury of locking myself away in a library."

"Thank God I do." She cast her eyes over the towering bookcases. "Sometimes I think this is the only safe place in Rome."

"You can't ignore the outside world forever."

"Why not?"

Domenico needed to find another line of persuasion. "You do realise all this means that your beloved new basilica is dead? It will never happen."

"That doesn't follow."

"Of course it does."

"It's illogical."

"We're way beyond logic now, Cristina."

"The new basilica has been approved."

"And it will quickly be unapproved."

"But it has *nothing* to do with Barberini!"

"Think it through. If the cardinals destroy the Pope, they will withdraw all his initiatives. If the Pope is right, he will cancel the basilica to apologise to God."

"But we've worked so hard for this. Years of planning and persuasion."

"It's finished, Cristina."

"He would seriously cancel one of the greatest building projects in Christendom?"

"This Pope will do anything to save himself."

Cristina fell silent. For one day, her dream had been alive. One day. Everything had looked so promising. How could she explain to her brother that this wasn't just about a building, about cold, dead stone? It was about defending learning and culture and art, and everything that made life worth living.

"As far as I can see, there is only one option left," Domenico said slowly.

"Go on."

"If I can prove beyond all doubt that Barberini's murder was not a Divine Judgement, that the cardinals and the Pope are both wrong, then no-one will have a reason to oppose the new basilica."

"Brave. And foolish. Publicly proving that the most powerful men in Rome are wrong…" Cristina's mind ran through the different permutations of consequences.

"Aren't you always telling me there is nothing as powerful as the truth?"

"But you risk humiliating the entire leadership of the Church."

"Not if we stick to the facts — if we prove that this is nothing more than a sordid murder, carried out by a sick and twisted man. We show the world it has nothing to do with

God, nothing to do with the Pope's character, and nothing to do with building a new basilica. That is the only way we can all win."

"It won't be easy. There is scant evidence to follow."

"Remember the housekeeper?" Domenico urged. "She said Barberini had lots of enemies. Lots of people with a motive to kill him. That's a start."

Cristina nodded; she could see the logic.

"Of course, actually assembling the proof…" Domenico glanced at his sister, waiting for her to take the bait. "That may prove impossible."

Cristina closed her eyes, painfully aware of what her brother was asking. Why couldn't she just stay here, in this room with all her books?

And then she remembered the astrolabe.

It was one of her earliest memories. On her fifth birthday, her father had taken her to the university where he had some business. Noticing that she was bored, one of the professors had shown her a beautiful clockwork astrolabe, a model of the Heavens and the Earth, constructed with a thousand tiny brass cogs and springs. The professor wound it up with a silver key, set the planets in motion, and Cristina watched in wonder as the mysterious heavenly movements danced in and out of their strange alignments. It was so complex it seemed to defy all understanding, and yet the machine followed precise rules of logic and mechanics. Every time Cristina had faced problems in her life that were so complex that they seemed impenetrable, she remembered that astrolabe. Mechanisms were always at work; the trick was uncover them and find the right key.

"Everything can be proved, Domenico," she whispered. "Eventually."

"Then you'll help me?"

Cristina scooped up all the notes and books from the long table and plonked them on the floor, leaving the surface completely clear. "Just this once, I will pause my studies until the Barberini murder is solved."

A huge smile broke across Domenico's face. He leapt up and hugged his sister. "Thank you! Thank you!"

Cristina tensed and screwed her eyes shut, trying not to give anything away. She knew how important it was for people to express their gratitude, but she wished they would stick to words and keep their arms to themselves.

She held her breath, counting the seconds, then disentangled herself. "Now," she said, pulling on a simple black overcoat, "where is the corpse?"

"In the morgue."

"Then why are we still here?"

10: POST-MORTEM

Going down the stone steps that led to the subterranean morgue was like stepping back in time to the previous winter. The oppressive, dry heat of the city was replaced by a chilly mountain dampness, for it was blocks of ice hewn from the slopes of Campocatino some seventy miles east, and packed into underground chambers, which kept this place cool.

As Domenico led the way along the dark corridors, Cristina noticed the names of some of Rome's most illustrious families emblazoned on side doors. "Seriously? They have private ice cellars?"

"It's the new status symbol," Domenico replied over his shoulder. "You're not truly rich until you have your own ice-house."

"I wonder if their guests know it's the same ice that keeps murder victims cool."

"Perhaps that's all part of the thrill." Domenico swung open a door at the far end that led into a large, gloomy cellar. The air was heavy with the smell of cold meat, but it had a pungent undertone that was deeply unappetising.

Cristina held up her lantern and saw four shrouded corpses lined up on benches against the wall; in the middle of the room, Barberini had been laid out on a table, naked and ready for inspection. Domenico gave the morgue attendant a few coins, and he shuffled off to enjoy an hour in the sun.

Cristina opened her leather bag and carefully laid out her instruments: three magnifying glasses, a set of scalpels, a cutthroat razor and a pair of surgical forceps.

"We've seized Barberini's account ledgers," Domenico said as he watched his sister prepare. "Gilo is going through them now, looking for irregularities."

"Good."

"Did he owe money? Was he being blackmailed? That sort of thing."

"How many orgies did he arrange for the Pope?" Cristina added pointedly.

"You can't help yourself, can you?"

"It could be important." She opened a book of Leonardo da Vinci's recently published anatomical drawings of the heart and vascular system, then selected a magnifying glass.

As Cristina leant over the body she could feel its coldness on her face, as if the corpse was trying to suck every last drop of life out of the air itself. Gently she placed her fingers on Barberini's grey lips; without the heat of life, the human body was a bizarre, strangely shaped lump of meat. It was curious.

She raised her magnifying glass and started to examine the body's skin, patiently working from head to toe, noting any marks or anomalies. Finally, she stood up and stretched her back. "I think he was dead before he was crucified."

"You're sure?"

"If he died on the cross, his blood would have been pumped out of the wounds. But there are blotches on his skin at key points, suggesting the blood wasn't pumped, but pooled." She offered her brother the magnifying glass and showed him how the vascular sketches related to Barberini's body. "I think he was killed, then nailed to the cross, which was then inverted."

Domenico nodded. "It would explain why no-one heard him scream."

"So what *was* the cause of death?"

"We found a garotte at the scene."

"They didn't use that to kill him. No marks on the neck." Cristine's gaze moved swiftly down the body to his wrists. "Here." She took back the magnifying glass and studied a series of faint, dark lines on the skin. "I think the garotte was used to hold his arms tight to the cross while the nails were driven through his palms."

"Which means the murderer definitely had an accomplice," Domenico added.

"At least one. I mean, could two men hoist a crucifix?"

"Possibly. But it would be tricky."

"Then it's more than likely we are looking for a gang." She handed the cutthroat razor to Domenico. "Shave his head. Look for any lesions."

While Domenico carefully scraped away Barberini's hair, Cristina hunted for incisions or stab wounds on the torso; assassins sometimes used razor-thin blades that punctured internal organs but left very little trace on the skin.

"Nothing on the head," Domenico said eventually.

Cristina frowned. "Let's turn him over."

They rolled the waxy-white body onto its front with a dull slap, and continued the search, but found nothing.

"Which means…" Cristina pulled another book from her satchel: *A Catalogue of Poisonous Herbs and their Effects on the Human Body*.

Domenico suddenly looked pale. "You do know that the Borgias are famous for getting rid of their enemies by poison?"

"I didn't. But that is interesting." Connections flashed across Cristina's mind, uncensored and dark.

Domenico recognised the unease on his sister's face. "What?"

"Nothing."

"Tell me. How bad can this get?"

"It would make perfect sense for the Pope to poison Barberini."

"No, no, no."

"If Barberini organised orgies for the Pope, he could easily have blackmailed him."

"They are just rumours."

"Barberini was living proof of the Pope's moral failings. So why not kill him in such a way that it looks like a Divine judgement, then blame his death on the decision to demolish the old basilica? That way, the Pope's reputation is protected, and he is seen as a truly God-fearing man."

Domenico stared at his sister. "You are seriously accusing the Pope of murder?"

"I'm just hypothesising."

"Well, don't. Because it could get us both thrown into jail."

"Then maybe His Holiness was merely an accomplice to murder."

"Stop! That is just as bad."

"You have to admit, Domenico, there is a brilliant elegance to the plan. Eliminate your enemies then deflect the blame onto God."

"Cristina! You have no proof of any of this."

"Not yet." She picked up the largest scalpel. "But if Barberini was poisoned, there will be plenty of evidence in his guts." As she positioned the blade over the corpse's abdomen, Domenico backed away to the far side of the room. Cristina chuckled. "There's nothing to be scared of. Dead is dead." With one clean stroke, she sliced open the body.

Barberini's bowels spilled onto the table like a tangle of writhing eels. As his stomach split open, a dreadful stench erupted and engulfed Cristina.

Immediately she gagged and clamped her hands over her mouth, trying to block out the foul stink, but it was too late. The acid was already churning in her stomach and Cristina only just managed to turn away before she retched and vomit sprayed from her mouth, splattering onto the marble floor.

She stood gasping for a few moments, recovering her composure as her nose got used to the acrid stench.

Now it was Domenico's turn to chuckle. "I assume they don't do smells in your anatomy books?"

"Very funny." She wiped her mouth, then tied a handkerchief around her nose and peered into the corpse's guts, searching for any signs of blistering or internal bleeding. Cristina worked with silently gritted teeth, determined not to show any more frailty, but just as she was making her way down to the corpse's small intestine, they heard alarmed footsteps outside.

"Sir! Sir!" It sounded like Gilo.

The door burst open and Gilo stumbled in, ashen-faced. "Come quickly, sir! The Devil is loose again!"

"What on earth's happened?" Domenico hurried over.

"A terrible thing, sir! Terrible! The monks at Sant'Onofrio. They've been struck blind."

"What? I don't understand."

"All of them! Struck blind in an instant! Cursed!"

11: DARKNESS

Fear was like a dark, jagged current running through the gathering crowd. People were squeezed onto the Sant'Onofrio steps, talking to each other in hushed voices, offering up desperate prayers, craning their necks to peer inside the courtyard.

"Make way! Clear a path!" Gilo had to push people aside to get Cristina and Domenico through. Two guards who had been placed at the gates saw them approaching, plucked them out of the melee and delivered them into the safety of the monastery.

As Cristina emerged into the once serene courtyard, she was stunned by the strange horror: thirty monks were positioned all around her as if in some ghastly living frieze of fear. Three lay on the floor, face down, sobbing pitifully; another five clung to the slender marble pillars of the cloister, too afraid to let go.

"Help us, Lord! The Devil is here!" they wailed. The remaining monks huddled under the colonnade like terrified animals, howling their despair. "We are lost! We are damned!"

All of them had been struck blind.

Cristina glanced at her brother, but he seemed paralysed by the scale of the anguish confronting him. "Domenico!"

All he could do was stare at the monks. "God help us all," he whispered.

But God seemed to have abandoned these men. Cristina knelt to comfort one who was slumped by her feet. "It's all right."

But as she reached out to touch him, he lashed out, howling, "Leave me, Satan! Leave me!"

Cristina backed away, but the monk's curse was taken up by the others.

"Leave us, Satan! Be gone!" Their pained voices echoed around the courtyard.

Cristina felt powerless in the face of such raw grief. "What do we do?"

Domenico blinked as he heard his sister's voice.

Think.

Focus.

Protocols.

But there were no precedents for this.

Think!

The bombardment at Urbino. Cannon fire raining into the town. Smashing through walls and roofs like the hand of God. What did he do then?

Domenico's mind latched onto memories of the siege and glimpsed a path through this. "Deputato Gilo! Take them back to their dormitories. Lock them in. They need to feel safe. Put a guard with each victim."

"Yes, sir!"

"Make sure they have water. Try to calm them down. And make sure no-one does anything stupid."

Gilo sprang into action organising his men, and the sheer bustle of activity seemed to break the grip of horror. Someone was in charge again, plucking the monks from their abyss of fear.

Amidst all the confusion, they found the one man in the monastery who had been spared: the caretaker, Custode Federico. Domenico led him into the quiet of the vestry and tried to calm him.

"Holy Mary, Mother of God, pray for us sinners now. Holy Mary, Mother of God, pray for us sinners now." The words tumbled from the caretaker's lips in an unstoppable mantra. "Holy Mary, Mother of God, pray for us sinners now."

Domenico sat him down and Gilo managed to get some brandy down the man's throat.

"Try to be still," Domenico urged.

"It was nothing I did. I swear!"

"No-one's blaming you."

"Everything was normal. Everything. Everything. Everything."

Gilo got some more brandy into the caretaker, who fell silent as the alcohol hit his throat.

"It's all right," Domenico reassured him. "Now —"

"It wasn't me. It wasn't me."

"No-one's blaming you. We just need to know what happened."

Three more slugs of brandy and Custode Federico was finally able to talk rationally. The bells. That had been his main job for the day. Above the chapel was a small tower with an array of bells across two levels. The lower one had got stuck, and the abbot had instructed Federico to investigate. After the top bell was rung for mass and the monks had all shut themselves in the chapel, Federico made his way up the narrow ladders to the tower.

"The headstock has woodworm, you see. Had it for as long as I can remember. But that's too expensive to replace. So all I can do is patch things up. And now part of it has sheared off and jammed the gudgeon. I don't know how many more times I can patch it up, to be honest."

"And then?" Domenico tried to keep Federico focused. "What happened then?"

"I'd been working on it for an hour, maybe, when I heard the screams." He looked down as he remembered. "Such fear

… and despair. I've never heard anything like it." Federico crossed himself.

"So you came back down…"

"By the time I arrived, they were spilling out of the chapel, wailing and clawing at the air, reaching out with their arms. I grabbed hold of the abbot. He told me to raise the alarm. And then you all came."

"Show me the chapel," Cristina said.

Federico looked at her warily. "You want to go in there? Where it happened?"

"How else can we discover the truth?"

Reluctantly, Custode Federico did as he was asked. As the doors opened, Cristina studied the space. It was a beautiful chapel, small but with an elegantly vaulted ceiling covered in frescoes. There were only a handful of windows, and those were high up and impossible to open. A single set of double doors at the west end was the only way in and out.

"Could someone have attacked them and fled?" Cristina asked.

Federico shook his head. "When they celebrate Mass, the abbot always closes the doors from the inside, so they can't be disturbed."

"They lock themselves in? That's strange."

"Years ago, when the abbot was a novice in Sicily, his monastery was raided by Saracen bandits. He gets nervous when no-one is keeping a lookout."

Cristina noticed the wine and wafers still on the altar; they had been mid-communion when the blindness had struck. She swirled the wine around the silver goblet and smelled it.

"You shouldn't touch that," Federico warned. "Not once it's been blessed."

"Do you want this crime solved or not?"

"It's not a crime, it's a curse."

"You're not really in a position to judge, are you?" She looked searchingly at the caretaker, who mumbled an apology.

A snowy-white cat was lurking in the shadows. Cristina extended her hand and kissed the air softly; a few moments later, the cat padded over and nestled itself into her legs.

"You should look away now," Cristina advised Federico. He took the hint and hurried off. Left alone, Cristina picked up the chalice and offered it to the cat, who lapped the wine eagerly. She crumbled a communion wafer into her hand; the cat sniffed it warily, then licked the crumbs. "That's it. All done."

The cat looked up at her with pleading eyes, but soon realised no more was forthcoming, and hurried over to a small patch of sunlight on the floor to make herself comfortable.

Cristina watched it closely, looking for any ill effects. The monks were blinded within minutes of starting communion, so if there had been any poison in the wine or wafers, it would have taken effect by now. But the cat seemed perfectly at ease, licking its fur contentedly.

Clearly, the chalice was not poisoned.

12: MIST

As the calmness of dusk spread over Rome, the abbot regained some composure and agreed to be questioned. Gilo guided him into the monastery office, but this room that the abbot had worked in for nearly two decades was now completely alien to him. He shuffled in cautiously, arms outstretched, hands hungrily reaching for surfaces.

"Another four paces, Padre," Gilo said, gently taking him by the arm.

The abbot stretched forwards and his fingers touched the desk; reassured, his step quickened, but his sandal caught on the chair leg and he stumbled.

Gilo caught him. "It's all right. I have you."

The abbot's searching hands found his chair and he sat down, relishing the familiar comfort of the wood on his back.

"Can I get you anything, Padre?" Domenico asked. "Some wine, perhaps?"

The abbot ignored the question. Instead, he ran his hands slowly and methodically over the surface of his desk, touching the inkwell, his quills, the monastery ledger, a crucifix, a small knife, checking everything was in its place, drawing solace from the familiar. Cristina noticed the abbot's hands — meticulously clean, with carefully trimmed nails; this was a man to whom details mattered.

"Padre, it would greatly help our investigation if we could ask you about the events leading up to..." Domenico's voice trailed off; he didn't need to articulate the horror that had consumed this monastery.

The abbot nodded as he marshalled his thoughts. "Everything was normal. Just as any other day," he began. "We'd spent our morning in study and contemplation."

Cristina was surprised at the flatness of the abbot's tone; it was as if he'd lost all interest in life.

"We were due to work on the farm in the afternoon. The gooseberries needed pruning back. But first we celebrated Mass, as we always did. It was a peaceful service… I remember feeling so close to God. And then, for no reason…" His voice faltered. "Our world collapsed."

"There must have been something that was different," Domenico suggested.

"No."

"A stranger amongst you? A noise at the doors? A dispute of some kind?"

"We are a peaceful order. We have no enemies."

"So … how were you attacked?"

"The only strange thing I can remember was the mist. A faint mist."

"You mean smoke?"

"No." The abbot shook his head. "It was like a fog that just … emerged inside the chapel. From nowhere."

"Forgive me, Padre, I don't understand."

"Have you walked along the Tiber in that hour before sunset? One minute the light is clear and strong, then suddenly a mist emerges and hangs above the water. That is what happened in the chapel, just after I had blessed the chalice. A mist."

Domenico's face creased in a frown. "How could that be possible? You were inside a building. There is no mist inside a building."

"All I can do is tell you what I saw … one of the last things I will ever see." Sadness engulfed the abbot again, and tears started to run down his cheeks. His hands fumbled in one of the desk drawers, searching for something. Cristina saw a neatly folded handkerchief next to some sealing wax and put it in his hands. The abbot wiped his eyes.

"Could the mist, or smoke, have come through the windows?" Domenico asked.

"No."

"How can you be so sure?"

"They are too high. We never open them."

"Perhaps it came from under the door?"

The abbot shook his head. "I would have seen that."

"There must be a rational explanation," Cristina insisted.

"Why?" the abbot replied.

"Because the world is not random."

"My order didn't deserve this. We are good men, punished for no reason. Do not talk to me about the rationality of the world."

Domenico gestured for Cristina to remain silent. "So, after the mist had appeared," he continued, "what happened then?"

"Then came the darkness. The mist was so serene, hanging over the altar… It was almost hypnotic. But the blindness that followed was so absolute."

"Could it have been some kind of poison?"

"It was too peaceful. It was as if God himself was becoming manifest in the chapel. And yet…" Tears filled the abbot's eyes again. "Why would God want to blind us? What sin are we guilty of?"

Domenico poured a small glass of brandy. "Here." He took the abbot's hands and placed them around the glass.

The man slugged back the spirit. “I want to curse God,” he whispered. “But I know that I must not. God is great and merciful. I know this. I have dedicated my life to Him. Every moment of the day is given over to His worship … so why has He punished us with such cruelty?”

Again, Cristina was struck by how softly the abbot spoke; his words were angry, yet he uttered them so peacefully. She didn’t know what to say in the face of such strange sorrow.

In the silence, the monastery bells started to toll. Slow, steady, mournful.

The familiar peal soothed the abbot. He folded the handkerchief, then sat perfectly still for a few moments, listening. “Custode Federico has repaired the bell. At least we have that small mercy.”

13: UNREASON

Cristina and Domenico spent the next few hours interviewing monks who had started to recover from the shock and regain some mental coherence. All of them corroborated the abbot's account, none of them could explain the ethereal mist, and none could think of any reason why their order had been so grievously punished.

In the late afternoon an eye surgeon arrived, uninvited, offering to examine the monks without charge. Cristina didn't see the point; she knew the surgeon was little more than a mountebank who pulled teeth and sold 'miraculous' elixirs that did nothing except empty the pockets of the gullible. But Domenico felt his presence might reassure the monks, so he let the examinations proceed. After much frowning and bandying of obscure terminology, the surgeon concluded that, tragically, there was nothing to be done and no cure to be had. "The entire monastery has been blinded in a shocking and mysterious act." As if that wasn't obvious.

Cristina gave the man a ducat just to get him out of the way, and he hurried off to spread news of how he had 'been called in by the Vatican to consult on divine mysteries.'

With nothing more to be done at the scene, Gilo arrived with four guards to escort Cristina to safety.

"I really don't think that's necessary," she objected.

"I think you'll find it is."

As Gilo hauled open the monastery gates the crowd surged forward, shouting a barrage of questions.

"Has there been a demonic possession?"

"When is the exorcism?"

"Will blindness spread across the city?"

"Have they prayed for forgiveness?"

Cristina recoiled under the frenzied assault and tried to back away into the monastery courtyard, but Domenico caught her and pushed her forwards. "Head down, don't say anything!"

Cristina did as she was told, but it was rough and frightening. The crowd had a manic energy that seemed to teeter on the edge of violence. She glimpsed priests offering confessions, tinkers selling charm bracelets, wild-eyed itinerant preachers heralding the end of the world, and canny children selling exotic candles 'to ward off the spirits'. It seemed as if all the odd people in Rome had been drawn to the monastery to revel in (or profit from) the suffering of the monks.

"What is wrong with them?" Cristina called out to Gilo.

"Ignorance," he replied. "Oldest sin in the world."

Suddenly a toothless woman in her sixties, her face plastered in white powder, grabbed Cristina by the arm. "It's the Jews!" she yelled. "Banish them from the city!"

"You're talking rubbish," Cristina shouted back, unable to ignore such hatred.

"I saw it in a vision! The Jews killed our Lord. Now they've turned on our Holy Brothers."

"You're deluded, woman."

"She's one of them!" the powdered woman screeched, trying to incite the crowd. "Jew-lover!"

Gilo had heard enough. "*Filo de putana!*" He lunged across and pushed the woman away from Cristina. "Leave now or be arrested!"

"You're as bad as her!" the woman spat back. "Jew-lover!"

"Last warning!"

Reluctantly the woman let go of Cristina's arm and was sucked back into the crowd.

Cristina had never felt so relieved to be back in the quiet security of her own home.

"Don't take it personally," Domenico said. "There are always a few fanatics who whip up the mob."

"All the more reason to get to the truth. And quickly." She opened her leather satchel and took out three large bundles of documents tied together with string. Domenico picked one up and saw that it was correspondence between the abbot and the various patrons and sponsors of the monastery.

"How did you get these?"

"Deputato Gilo gave them to me."

"He had no business doing that."

"Oh, he gave me these as well." Cristina pulled out the ledger books for the monastery's accounts.

Domenico was irritated that everyone seemed to be going off on different tangents; if this investigation was going to succeed, it needed to be disciplined.

"It's not his fault. I told him I was acting on your authority."

"Well, next time, ask me."

"If we do our job properly, Domenico, there won't be a next time." Cristina sat down and started to examine the letters.

"What exactly are you looking for?"

"Anything that links the monastery to Barberini."

"You really think the crimes are connected?"

"They are both violent atrocities presented as supernatural acts."

"But a high-class pimp has nothing to with a monastery. I can't see the abbot organising orgies."

"Never jump to conclusions. He has done something to make him a target. We do not live in a random world."

Domenico leaned forward and started to read over his sister's shoulder.

"You can have your own pile to go through if you want," she said tetchily.

"It's all right. I'll leave this one to you." Domenico headed back towards the main staircase. "I have to make my report before the rumours run completely out of control." He opened the door leading to the main staircase. "Make sure you lock up behind me. Just in case."

But Cristina didn't reply; she was already lost in the abbot's correspondence, searching for patterns.

14: WHISPERS

The Pope's private secretaries were like three black crows guarding the entrance to the Borgia Apartments.

"His Holiness gave me clear instructions," Domenico explained. "He is to be kept informed of all developments."

"Be that as it may, he is not available," the Lead Crow replied.

"I really think he would like to hear —"

"It is not for you to decide what the Holy Father should or should not hear."

Domenico looked from one crow to the next, searching for a fault-line, but they were as one. "Perhaps you could actually ask him if he would like to see me?"

"We already know what His Holiness thinks."

"Very well." Domenico plonked himself in a seat at one side of the corridor. "I'll wait until he comes out."

"That would be a bad idea."

"Are you really going to throw the Capitano della Guardia Apostolica out of the Vatican?" Domenico mocked. "Precisely how does that work?"

"As I was saying before you interrupted, that would be a bad idea because the Holy Father is not in his rooms at this time," the Lead Crow said calmly.

He was lying. Domenico knew this was a trick to get rid of him, but now he was backed into a corner. How foolish would it look if he waited hours and the Pope never emerged? "Why do you people always make things so difficult?" he retorted, and strode back down the corridor, trying to salvage some dignity.

Something was very wrong. As he navigated his way through the labyrinth of corridors and past the many anterooms, Domenico could feel that the Vatican was alive with rumour. Cardinals and clerks would glance at him warily; conversations changed abruptly when he came within earshot, only to resume once he had passed. The mass-blinding had sent shockwaves through the Vatican, and Domenico feared he was being lined up to take the blame.

It was a relief to get back to the noise and bustle of the guardrooms, where people were just getting on with their jobs. Weapons were being signed out of the armoury, a farrier was shoeing horses in the courtyard, soldiers were exchanging gossip and crude jokes as they handed over shift reports, and an exhausted Gilo was hastily trying to rearrange the rotas to provide security cover at the monastery throughout the night.

"What did His Holiness say?" Gilo asked.

"They wouldn't let me see him."

Gilo looked up from the rotas. "What?"

"Can't you feel it?" Domenico looked anxious. "It's in the air. They're plotting."

"What more could we have done?"

"We're still going to be blamed."

"How were we to know the monks would be afflicted?"

Domenico ushered Gilo to the far end of the room where they couldn't be overheard. "Have our sources reported anything unusual?"

By sources, he meant a handful of trusted people among the many dozens of servants who kept the Vatican buildings running smoothly; men and women who were as anonymous as the furniture they polished, yet whose ears were always open to what was being whispered.

"There has been a flurry of private meetings," Gilo admitted. "But I haven't managed to get ears inside yet."

"I wonder if the cardinals are plotting a regime change," Domenico said.

"But this Pope hasn't even been on the throne five years."

"One thing is for sure; if Alexander falls, you and I will fall with him. We will be scapegoated for losing control of the situation."

"So much for Christian charity," Gilo said darkly.

"I'm afraid we are nothing to the cardinals. Nothing. Just pawns to be tossed aside when it suits them."

Of all their sources, Domenico found the candle-wrangler the most useful. A few years earlier, he had arranged for Cristina to privately tutor Alonso's seven-year-old son; it had worked so well, the boy had won a scholarship to one of the best schools in Rome. Ever since, Alonso had been keen to repay the favour in any way he could.

As Domenico hurried down the stone steps into the Vatican cellars, he was greeted by the comforting smell of warm beeswax. He drew a deep breath, savouring the sweetness; such an improvement on the foul-smelling sheep's tallow that used to stink the place out. The Vatican burned through so many candles every day, the only way to ensure a continuous supply was to run a candle factory here in the basement. For as long as Domenico could remember, Alonso had been the head chandler.

"They look like they're for the high altar," Domenico said as he entered the dipping room, where Alonso was lowering a rack of long, ivory-coloured candles into a gently bubbling vat.

"Matching the colours … tricky. So tricky."

"Only if you're a perfectionist, Alonso. Which you clearly are."

The chandler locked the rack in place then turned to Domenico. "Don't tell me — you've come about the whispers."

"So I'm not imagining it?"

"Just about every time I entered a room today to replace the stubs, I found small huddles of cardinals."

"Anything specific?"

"Tricky for me to get close enough. So tricky."

"Perhaps it's time to replace the candles in the Archive Hall?"

Alonso gave Domenico a knowing smile. "Exactly what I was thinking."

The two men had tried this several times before and it had yielded reliable results; now they had perfected the routine.

The Archive Hall was a cavernous room, lined on either side with U-shaped alcoves formed of bookshelves. In the centre of each alcove was a cherrywood table for reading; one end of the table faced a fireplace. These alcoves were perfect for cardinals to plot as their presence here aroused no suspicion, they could meet with a number of different factions without having to visit anyone's private rooms, and it was impossible for curious rivals to loiter and eavesdrop without being seen. Each space was lit from above by a large iron chandelier comprising three concentric rings of candles, and this is what gave Alonso power. With complete impunity, he was able to unlock the pulley ropes and lower the chandeliers to replace the candles. By choosing which chandeliers to lower, he could effectively direct the cardinals to specific alcoves without them realising they were being controlled.

Up on the roof, Domenico made his way to the two lines of chimney pots that emerged through the clay tiles, one flue for each of the fireplaces in the alcoves below. What none of the cardinals realised — because none of them had ever done a day's manual labour — was that sound didn't just travel up a chimney flue, it was amplified en route as it resonated with the trapped air; plans that were whispered in the privacy of the alcoves were broadcast to the birds sitting on the chimney pots. All Domenico had to do was make sure the fires remained unlit, then co-ordinate with Alonso to know which chimney pots to were going to be 'live'.

Like all surveillance, it required patience, but after a couple of hours shooing away pigeons, Domenico started to hear voices wafting up the chimney flues.

"How many more signs do we need…?"

"People are looking to us for leadership…"

"Deposing is difficult, but not impossible…"

Domenico thought one of the voices belonged to Cardinale Orsini, but he couldn't be sure. If it was Orsini, then these threats were serious.

"If we delay, God will surely punish us as well…"

"We must find out how many are with us, and how many against…"

As the conversation ended and the footsteps faded, Domenico hurried across the roof and repositioned himself to spy on a different alcove. Eventually he heard the scrape of chairs, and more snatches of conspiracy echoed up the chimney flue.

"…strange portents. We should be afraid…"

"No-one can turn against God's will…"

It sounded like Riario, but who was he talking to? Cardinale Rovere, perhaps?

"The man is corrupted … beyond doubt…"

"We are to blame…"

"Rome will not know peace until the Borgia Pope is no more…"

15: IMPOSSIBLE

Domenico hurried up the stairs, threw open the doors to Cristina's library, and promptly stopped in his tracks. His sister had taken the monastery's ledgers (that she wasn't even supposed to have), removed all the pages from the binding, and stuck them over the bookcases. It looked as if she had decorated the entire room with ledger sheets.

"What on earth are you doing?"

"Making connections," Cristina said, searching in one of the bureau drawers.

"Then you'd better be quick, because events are overtaking us."

"Let me guess; the cardinals are panicking?"

"They are convinced these portents are punishment for electing a Borgia Pope."

"For that, the cardinals only have themselves to blame." Finally, Cristina found what she was looking for: a reel of coloured yarn.

"Blame is immaterial. Unless we can unravel these mysteries, the cardinals will depose the Pope."

"Watch," Cristina said as she picked up a small pot of binding glue and approached one of the sheets on the wall. She found a specific entry on the ledger and stuck one end of the yarn to it; then she walked across the room, unspooling yarn as she went, and fixed it to another ledger entry. She moved on again, back and forth across the room, up and down the walls, fixing the yarn to particular entries until she had spun a strange web in the middle of the library. "Do you see?"

"No." For a moment Domenico wondered if his sister had parted company with reason, then he saw the glint in her eyes and knew that she just enjoyed making him feel dull-witted. "This had better be good," he warned.

"This yarn represents the flow of money between the monastery of Sant'Onofrio and the Pope."

"So … he gave the monks money to pray for his soul. What's wrong with that?"

"Simple donations would not form such a complex pattern," Cristina replied, looking at the web of yarn. "Money flowed both ways, from the monastery to the Pope and vice versa. *And* the particular order in which they're connected matches the dates of twelve bishopric appointments across France and Spain. *And* money flowing out matches money flowing in minus ten percent. It's a consistent pattern."

"Meaning?"

"The Pope is using the monastery to disguise the bribes he receives from aspiring bishops. For each transaction, the monastery takes a fee to enrich its own coffers, then makes 'charitable donations' to various causes in Rome on a specific rotation. I suspect all of them are just fronts for the Pope."

"So, so, so…" Domenico looked at the complex tangle of yarn. "This is a map of corruption?"

"But it also proves the Pope's innocence. He wouldn't attack the very monks who are helping him disguise a corrupt income. Which means it also clears him of any involvement in the Barberini murder."

"You're assuming they're linked."

"Only an idiot would assume they're not."

Domenico kept quiet, reluctant to admit anything.

"Someone else killed Barberini and blinded the monks." Cristina walked around the yarn, studying the pattern. "Could it be the cardinals, trying to depose the Holy Father out of jealousy?"

Domenico shook his head. "Unlikely."

"But possible."

"I spent four hours at the chimney pots listening to them. There is so much distrust between the cardinals… They can exploit this crisis, but they hate each other too much ever to plan it."

"A small faction of them could do it, though. One or two working together."

"The cardinals are scared, Cristina. Genuinely afraid that this is God's wrath. To kill a pimp is one thing, but to attack a monastery? It's too much, even for them."

"Well, someone is not so squeamish." Cristina sat down at one of the desks, trying to marshal her thoughts. "Barberini organised orgies for the Pope and was murdered for it. The monks washed the Pope's illicit money, and they were blinded for it. Someone is attacking the Pope … but who?"

There was silence in the library, a deep and thoughtful silence. Only the tick of the verge and foliot clock reminded them that time was still passing.

"Maybe … what if…" Domenico took a bible from the bookshelves and leafed through the pages until he found the reference. "*If your right eye makes you stumble, tear it out,*" he read. "*If your right hand makes you stumble, cut it off and throw it from you; for it is better to lose one of the parts of your body than for your whole body to go into hell.* Matthew 5." He closed the bible. "Maybe it really is God at work. Maybe He is cleansing Rome."

Cristina shook her head slowly, emphatically, refusing even to entertain such a thought. "Absolutely not."

"Then how were the monks blinded? Explain it to me."

"The explanation is that we are dealing with someone who is very clever."

"That is sophistry."

"I believe the monks were poisoned. A toxin was released into the chapel as they prayed."

"How? The windows were sealed. You checked them yourself."

"Let's just think this through."

"Walls? Solid stone."

"Doors?"

"Closed and locked from the inside. No-one saw any smoke coming in."

"The floors?" Cristina tried to remember whether they were stone or wood.

"Stone. With no crypt underneath, just solid earth."

"It does seem impossible," Cristina mused, "but that is not good enough."

"You heard the abbot's testimony," Domenico said. "The strange mist just coalesced, like a spirit. The Holy Spirit."

"A *vengeful* Holy Spirit," Cristina replied. "Which defeats the whole point of the Divine."

Cristina could feel her mind knotting with frustration. There was an answer. Everything had an answer, but she could not see it. Now she was like that dead fly caught between the window shutters, unable to sense the current that would lead her to freedom.

"I need to think. In peace." Cristina grabbed her rosary and strode from the room.

16: FIRE

Cristina made her way to the small church of Santa Maria della Pace. Tightly packed into the neighbouring buildings, the church only revealed its presence by a colonnaded canopy that bulged out of the façade. She often came here to meditate as it was close and, being tucked away down a narrow street, peaceful.

Except for today.

As soon as she entered, Cristina could sense the febrile atmosphere. The normally empty pews were packed with men and women dressed in black, praying earnestly, rosaries clenched tightly in their fingers. The priest, an earnest man with a downturned mouth and thinning hair, moved among his congregation offering comforting words and blessings, sharing people's unease about what was happening to their city. The crucifixion of Barberini and the events at the monastery had struck fear into the population of Rome. Fear fuelled Rumour, and Rumour thrived on Ignorance; people didn't know where else to turn but the Church.

Eventually Cristina managed to find space at a shrine built into one of the arched niches that lined the nave. She sat down, eyes studying the geometric designs inlaid on the marble floor, and focused intently on her own thoughts.

If this hysteria led to the Pope being deposed, all plans for the new basilica would be scrapped, and unreason would have won. Cristina could not let that happen. And yet the atrocities did seem to defy logical explanation. How could monks in a sealed chapel suddenly be blinded? How could a man be nailed to a cross without anyone raising the alarm?

Cristina closed her eyes, her mind blocked out the world and she tried to pray for inspiration. But instead of thinking about God, her thoughts circled back to the astrolabe, that perfect image of order and reason … only now the intricate cogs and wheels had jammed, the mechanism was stuck, and she could see no way of unlocking it.

There had to be a way. There was always a way. If only she could find it.

Voices disturbed her concentration.

"Preach to us, Padre."

"Heal us."

"Comfort us."

Cristina opened her eyes and saw that some of the congregation were guiding the priest towards the pulpit.

"Lead us, Padre."

"Show us the way."

Even though no service had been scheduled, people were hungry for comfort.

The priest stood in front of the altar and cleared his throat. "*And many false prophets shall arise and lead many astray!* Matthew 24.11," he thundered, his booming voice at odds with his gaunt appearance. "In these terrible times, we turn to thee, Lord, to guide us to the path of righteousness."

"Amen."

"Hail Mary."

The murmurs of assent encouraged the priest's rhetoric.

"Lord, do not abandon us to the forces of darkness. Though we are sinners, we beg for your everlasting mercy."

"Do not abandon us, Lord," his followers echoed. "Have mercy on us."

"Evil is battering at the gates of Rome! Its talons are clawing at the city walls and destroying the tranquillity of our lives!"

The priest raised his hands in a dramatic gesture. "In its long history, Rome has battled the forces of darkness many, many times. And on each occasion, the Devil wore a different mask."

"Cast out the Devil," the congregation chimed. "Cast him out!"

"Satan appeared as the face of the barbarian hordes! He appeared as the armies of the Ottoman infidels. He appeared as heretics who deny the one true God. But with each terrible battle, Lord, you have never abandoned us."

"You are with us, Lord. You are with us."

Cristina gazed nervously at the simple people as they fell under the spell of the priest's words. Some of the older women were rocking back and forth, as if in a trance.

"No matter how profound the darkness," the priest thundered on. "No matter how black the night! No matter how deep the despair, you have never turned your back on us, Lord! And we have never lost faith in you!"

"We believe in you! We believe!"

"Now we beg for your forgiveness, Heavenly Father, and beseech you to cast the Devil out of Rome!"

"Cast him out! Cast him out!"

Then suddenly, everything changed.

Cristina heard it before she felt it — a ballooning whoosh that crackled through the air. She looked up and saw a swirling ball of fire erupt from the altar. It shot up into the curved stone roof, then exploded through the church in a burning wave of light, sweeping down the nave, searing the congregation as it passed over them.

Instinctively, Cristina pulled back, but as the wave of fire surged past, it licked hungrily at the corners of the niche, like a flailing tongue reaching out to devour her. Cristina stumbled backwards, dragging over a statue of the Virgin Mary which shattered as it struck the floor. Dancing flames snatched wildly at the air above her, then suddenly retreated as if called to heel by a tyrannical master.

The super-heated air was painful in Cristina's lungs. Gasping for breath, she stumbled out of the niche, and into a scene of pure horror.

The fireball had vanished, leaving behind a chaos of screaming and panic as people stumbled over each other to escape from the church.

Burnt victims lay on the floor, writhing in pain, skin blistering on their hands and faces. The bodies of those who were too slow lay slumped at strange angles, frozen in the moment of death. The old were crying out in pain; children were wailing in terror. The acrid smell of burning hair and scorched flesh thickened the air.

Yet strangely, the church itself was unscathed. There were no scorch marks on the frescoes; none of the wooden pews were charred. The flash of fire had been so quick and so intense, only the people had been struck down, their fragile bodies ravaged by the heat.

In a brief moment of insanity, the once peaceful church had been kissed by a terrible and malevolent force.

17: RESCUE

Domenico was nearly at the Ponte Sant'Angelo when he caught a strange, pungent smell on the breeze, but he thought nothing of it until he heard the first screams.

He stopped and listened. The noises were coming from the direction of the Piazza Navona … which was where Cristina always went when she needed to meditate.

Immediately Domenico turned back, retracing his steps with a growing sense of anxiety. As he got closer to Santa Maria della Pace, the terrified screams grew louder and the acrid smell stronger. He bolted across the Piazza del Fico, into the alley leading to the church and stopped dead, barely able to believe what he was seeing. Victims were stumbling out of the colonnaded porch, their faces blistering, hair singed and smoking, charred clothes falling from their bodies.

All the sound vanished.

The only thing Domenico could hear was the blood rushing through his ears as his body tried to block out the horror.

He forced himself to keep his eyes open, but still nothing made sense. Why were people wandering around like this?

Why were they burnt when nothing was on fire?

Was this some kind of religious ceremony?

Slowly Domenico approached the church, picking his way past the ghostly figures who stumbled around him as if in a trance, their faces contorted with fear.

He blinked once … and was back on the blood-soaked fields of Frosinone … surrounded by the tangled bodies of his friends … burnt alive when the gunpowder store exploded … blistered arms outstretched … pleading for the pain to stop…

"Domenico!"

But there was nothing he could do … nothing… He was utterly powerless in the face of the carnage…

"Domenico!"

The voice dragged him back from the harrowing tunnel of his memories.

"Here! Over here!"

He blinked again and saw Cristina staggering towards him, tears streaking her face. Domenico reached out and they clung to each other, trembling with shock. For once she didn't wriggle free, but just accepted his embrace.

"What happened?" he whispered.

Cristina tried to speak, but no sound would come from her throat.

"It's all right. You're safe now." He gripped his sister tightly; she was limp in his arms, as if all the willpower had been stolen from her. "Let's get you to a surgeon."

"No!"

"Cristina —"

"I want to go home. Just take me home."

"But you're hurt."

"Not me. I escaped. The others…" As the grief hit, sobs racked her body. "They were just praying…" she gasped through her tears. "They'd done nothing wrong."

A loud clatter of swords entered the alley. Domenico looked up and saw Gilo leading a squad of Vatican guards towards him. Thank God. Order was being imposed on the chaos.

Soldiers knew what to do when the world crumbled, how to wrestle chaos down. Four guards immediately secured the alley against further attack, while others helped the wounded to Piazza Navona where a field medical station was being thrown together. Gilo led a small squad into the church itself to confront the full horror of what lay inside.

"Get her away from here," Gilo said to Domenico as he passed.

"I need to go with you. Inside."

"No! We've got this under control," Gilo insisted. "Come back when she's safe."

"But —"

"Sir! Go! Please!"

Domenico sat Cristina down by one of the windows in her library. As he poured her a brandy, she moved the chair so that it was right next to the verge and foliot wall clock. She sat silently for a few minutes, listening to the steady tick that reassured her everything in the world was still in order … even though it wasn't.

"Drink the brandy, Cristina." Gently Domenico lifted the glass to her lips. As the alcohol warmed her from the inside, Cristina's mind started to pull into focus.

"It was the strangest thing," she whispered. "Like a pulse of fire that engulfed everything … then just as suddenly, it was gone."

"How did you avoid the flames?"

"Luck. Sheer luck." She took another sip of brandy. "It swept over us with such speed."

"But where did it come from?"

"It just appeared. From nowhere."

"Like … like a burning bush?"

Cristina shook her head. "Like revenge incarnate." She stood up and started searching the shelves for a book.

"Leave it. You should rest."

Cristina ignored her brother, took a bible and concordance down and placed them on the table. She leafed through the pages until she found the reference she was hunting for. "Isaiah 66. *The Lord will execute judgement by fire.*"

Domenico looked over her shoulder at the pages of the bible. "And here as well, see? *The Lord will come in fire, and his chariots shall be like the whirlwind, to render his anger with fury, and his rebuke with flames of fire.*"

"That is what it was like. Exactly that." But the knowledge didn't bring Cristina any comfort — quite the opposite.

"I thought you were looking for a rational explanation, not God's wrath," Domenico ventured.

"I am. But I cannot ignore the evidence. Not again."

They fell into a heavy silence, but both knew what was going through her mind.

"Please, Cristina, don't torment yourself."

"I swore, never again. Never to ignore what is in front of my eyes."

"This is completely different."

"Is it?"

"Jumping to false conclusions is as bad as being blind to the evidence, Cristina."

She nodded, but in her mind, all she could see were the tiny spots of blood on the white cotton sheets. Why had she ignored them? Why had she been so stupid? Would her parents ever forgive her?

Domenico put his arms around Cristina and held her tightly. "Don't dwell on the past," he whispered.

"I can't help it."

"Just thank God that you survived today. If He hadn't forgiven you, you would have died in that church."

"Maybe."

They clung to each other in silence as the clock ticked its steady rhythm, trying to calm two troubled souls.

18: DEUTERONOMY 29

Sleep wouldn't come.

No matter how many times Cristina adjusted the pillows, her mind refused to be still. Feverishly it kept replaying scenes from the church, trying to understand where the mysterious fireball had come from and why it had erupted with such deadly violence. Time and again she wrestled the memories down and rolled into a different position, only to have horrific images of blistering flesh creep up on her from another direction.

Clear your mind.

Think of something else, a thousand miles away. Something nice.

Cristina concentrated ... breathed slowly, deeply ... and forced her mind to think about her childhood. Yes, the summers they'd spent at the family villa in Frascati. So many warm memories.

This seemed to be working...

The rich smell of the vines teased her nose... Now she could hear the chorus of crickets that would stop and start for no apparent reason... Now she could feel the gentle breeze that blew the long grass... Sleep was finally coming.

Until she heard the faint sound of a baby crying.

The baby, asleep, upstairs in the villa.

And then Cristina saw the spots of blood. Not just three, but hundreds, multiplying as she looked at the white sheets. Spots that merged to become an angry red stain oozing down the bed and dripping onto the floor, pooling around her toes.

Panic took hold, gripping her so tightly she had to gasp for breath.

Cristina sat bolt upright in the darkness, sweating and afraid.

This was useless. She might as well get up and work, even though dawn was not yet flickering on the horizon. She lit an oil lamp and went out onto the landing. The cavernous stairwell was pitch black, with no splashes of watery moonlight to show her the way, so she held the lamp in front of her and slowly picked her way down the cold marble steps. Just as she was nearing the first floor, a breeze caught the bedroom door, which slammed shut with a startling clatter that echoed through the house. Cristina pressed on, but a few moments later, another lamp-glow appeared on the ground floor, and a young woman's voice called up the stairwell.

"Is that you, mistress?"

"It's all right, Isra. I couldn't sleep."

It impressed Cristina how alert Isra was; this was the main reason she had kept her on.

When Cristina's father had been struck down with apoplexy, her mother had taken him to their country villa to nurse him back to health. The textile business which he had spent his life building was put under the care of his foreman, and Cristina was charged with looking after the house in Rome.

As the months passed and it became clear her father was never going to make a full recovery, Cristina let most of the servants go and used the money to pay for the construction of her library. It meant she could still balance the accounts while getting the education she craved. And anyway, Cristina had simple needs. She didn't throw dinner parties or eat extravagant meals, and by closing down half the rooms, she could make do with one servant. She chose Isra because although she was only seventeen, she had the confidence of a woman ten years older and was willing to turn her hand to anything.

"Can I get you a drink, mistress?"

"No. I'm fine. Go back to bed, Isra."

"How about some warm milk and almonds?"

Now Cristina was tempted; it was exactly the comfort food she needed when the night terrors took hold. "Actually, that would be nice."

"I'll bring it up, mistress."

"Thank you. I'll be in the library."

Cristina watched as the light downstairs moved like a glow-worm into the kitchen at the back of the house. Moments later, the reassuring clatter of pans drove the silence away. Cristina felt glad that she wasn't alone in this large, empty house.

She hurried down the last few steps and opened the doors to the library. As soon as she was among her books, Cristina started to feel safe again. She held the lamp up and studied the web of corruption that still hung between the bookshelves. What a strange way to prove a Pope's innocence.

Cristina refilled the inkpot, put the lamp in the centre of the table, took a ream of blank paper from the bureau drawer, and started writing down all the known fragments of the three crimes. As each note was finished, she laid it on the marble tiles, until the whole of the library floor was covered in paper.

The doors creaked open, and Isra entered carrying a steaming beaker of milk and almonds. "You're sure you don't want this in the bedroom, mistress?"

Cristina reached out and took the drink. "I'm done with sleep for tonight. Too much to think about."

Isra looked at all the sheets of paper covering the library floor. "Seems complicated."

"And yet, when it's solved, it will seem obvious."

"Isn't it always the way?" Isra replied cryptically.

It was one of the things Cristina liked about Isra: she had a philosopher's air, and you always got the impression that she knew far more than she ever let on. Her striking looks added to the mystery — large brown eyes, black curly hair, skin that was a deep olive even in the middle of the cold Roman winters.

"If there's nothing else, mistress, I think I'll get back to my dreams."

"Sleep tight, Isra." Cristina watched her go, wondering exactly what it was the girl dreamed about. As her footsteps receded, Cristina turned her attention back to the mosaic of notes on the floor. She tiptoed through them, then started to shuffle them around, putting ideas into different clusters as she tried to find a pattern that would make sense of everything.

The biblical references leapt out at her, but the Bible had an infinite number of patterns within its pages; which one was the evidence pointing to? She tried a few different configurations, but nothing seemed to stick.

It was unlikely the perpetrators of these sickening crimes were scholars, so why not look for an obvious pattern — the Seven Deadly Sins?

Lust. Gluttony. Greed. Sloth. Wrath. Envy. Pride.

Did that help?

Barberini was a pimp, which covered lust. The monks were assisting with the Pope's corrupt finances, which could be greed. And wasn't the priest this afternoon raging about sin and whipping up fear when the fireball struck? That could be wrath.

Did that mean Rome would be terrorised by four more twisted crimes in the days to come? It was possible, and it did make sense, yet still it seemed a little too tenuous to be convincing.

Cristina put that line of thinking to one side; not forgotten, but not pursued.

She let her mind go blank, freewheeling, waiting for the ripple of an idea. Her eyes danced across the paper trail. Eventually, two words coalesced in her head: Sodom … Gomorrah.

She took down a bible and concordance and started cross-checking the verses…

The men of Sodom are wicked, sinners against the Lord… God sends two angels to destroy the city, Lot welcomes them into his home, but the men of the town surround the house and demand that he surrenders the visitors 'that we may know them.' Corrupted sexuality. Just like Barberini.

Lot tries to calm the mob, offers them his two virgin daughters 'to do to them as you please.' More depraved sexuality.

The mob refuses and tries to storm the house, when the angels strike the crowd blind. Just like the monks at Sant'Onofrio.

Lot and his family finally escape, then 'the Lord rained upon Sodom and upon Gomorrah brimstone and fire.'

Sex. Blindness. Fire.

Cristina felt the inner mechanisms of the astrolabe click into a new pattern. She smiled to herself; this felt right, it had the elegant simplicity of truth. If the murderers were recreating the fate of Sodom and Gomorrah, then maybe, if she studied the verses closely, she could predict the next strike.

And what you could predict, you could outwit.

19: CURIA

As Domenico was escorted into the Council Chamber, his eyes darted across the great carved chairs that lined each wall. Most of the cardinals were present, three of the chairs for the northern Europeans were empty, but the most notable absence was from the throne at the centre of the room.

"Is the Holy Father not coming?" Domenico asked.

"The Pope has been unexpectedly called away," Cardinale Riario replied.

"Then perhaps we should postpone —"

"His Holiness has empowered us to discuss the investigation," Riario said firmly. "The Curia will answer to the Pope."

Domenico felt as if he was walking into a trap; whatever these cardinals decided, you could be sure they would put their own interests first.

"Begin!" Cardinale Orsini commanded, his jowls trembling with authority.

"As you wish, Your Eminences, but in this instance, I am calling on the services of an expert to explain the current lines of enquiry." He signalled to the guard, who opened the door.

Cristina walked in and bowed respectfully before the Curia. "Your Eminences."

There was a stunned silence, heavy with indignation.

"Are you mocking us?" Orsini thundered.

"Not at all," Domenico replied. "But if you want a problem solved, you need to apply the finest minds. Cristina Falchoni has the finest mind I know."

"You mean your sister," Riario added pointedly.

"With all due respect, that is irrelevant, Your Eminence. She is a brilliant scholar with deep knowledge across many disciplines."

"She should be married by now. And a mother!" Orsini was playing to the more hard-line cardinals. "The Bible is clear: 'Permit not a woman to teach, nor to have dominion over a man, but to be in *quietness*.'"

Orsini's supporters chuckled at the reference.

"Is that the same Bible which describes Mary Magdalene as 'the apostle to the apostles'?" Cristina asked with apparent innocence.

Orsini's jowls shuddered slightly. "You mean the prostitute, Mary Magdalene."

"Actually, gentlemen, that is a textual error," Cristina explained. "Nine hundred years ago, Pope Gregory conflated Mary Magdalene with Mary of Bethany. A careless error that has led to widespread confusion ever since."

Cardinale Riario smiled. "I think Signorina Falchoni has just demonstrated precisely why we should listen to her."

In the grudging silence, the dissenting cardinals lowered their gazes, unwilling to lock horns with Riario just yet.

"Thank you, Your Eminence." Cristina's eyes glanced along the lines of sombre men, all clad in their scarlet capes; she took in the beautiful tapestries hanging on the walls, and the geometric gold patterns on the semi-circular ceiling. This Council Chamber was all about the theatre of power, but if Cristina stuck to logic, nothing could intimidate her. At least, that was the theory.

She cleared her throat and composed herself. "We are dealing with a highly organised and darkly motivated gang of criminals," she began. "The crucifixion, the blinding at the monastery, the mysterious eruption of fire, these are not the work of one man. Each crime was meticulously planned and precisely executed. And I now believe that they have been following a biblical script. Their template is the destruction of Sodom and Gomorrah."

"To what end?" Riario asked. "What possible motive could these criminals have for turning the Word of God against His Christian servants?"

"To intimidate. And to frighten."

"Frighten who, exactly?"

"The Pope. The Vatican. The entire Church, perhaps," Cristina replied. "As yet, the precise motive is unclear."

Cardinale Orsini shook his fleshy head. "Only a madman would attempt such a thing." His allies grunted their agreement.

"I disagree, Your Eminence." Cristina refused to be pushed off course. "A man does not have to be insane to be angry at the Church. Perhaps we are dealing with someone whom the Church has wronged."

"A heretic, then."

"Perhaps. Or perhaps just a victim."

"The Church is a force for good. Remember that," Orsini warned.

"Unless you are a Jew, or a Moor forced to convert in the torture chambers of the Spanish Inquisition," she retorted. "Every victim of torture has family, friends, people whose hearts turn to stone in the face of such cruelty."

"You are overreaching yourself." Cardinale Riario waved an admonishing finger at her. "Stick to the details of the case."

"But this is relevant, Your Eminence. His Holiness the Pope is Spanish. He built his power in Barcelona. How many victims of the Inquisition blame him for their suffering?"

"They should thank him for bringing them to the light," Orsini replied.

"You cannot torture people into salvation." To Cristina this was a self-evident truth, but many of the cardinals did not appear to agree.

"You are mistaken." Orsini slammed his fist onto the arm of his chair. "Quite mistaken. This is not the work of human hands. What we are witnessing is the Wrath of God. Here on the streets of Rome."

"God would not act like this," Cristina fired back. "Not the God I worship."

"It is not for you to decide what God would or wouldn't do." Even Riario was running out of patience with this outspoken woman. "You are straying into dangerous territory."

"This is a conspiracy of men, designed to look like the Hand of God, Your Eminences." Cristina looked up and down the ranks of cardinals. "And it seems to be working."

Domenico could feel the situation slipping out of control. The last thing he needed was a war with the Curia. He stepped forward so that he was overshadowing Cristina. "If you'll allow us to put theology aside, and return to the details of the case…"

"Very wise," said Riario.

"Regardless of who is responsible, if we work with the theory that we are now witnessing a version of the destruction of Sodom and Gomorrah," Domenico said, "then we have identified a number of possible targets for future attacks. To prevent more atrocities, I am asking for extra resources."

"How much?" Riario looked suddenly sceptical.

"We think there are twenty-five possible targets across the city. Each of those will need enhanced security and surveillance."

There was silence in the room as the cardinals exchanged furtive glances. You could always rely on the idea of spending money to rob them of the power of speech.

"The man is empire-building," Orsini finally scoffed. "He is using these tragedies to enhance his own power."

"Do not judge everyone by your own standards." The minute she said it, Cristina knew she'd made a mistake, but she couldn't help herself.

"What did you say?" Orsini flushed as he glared at her.

"Before we get side-tracked into an argument about money," Riario intervened, "I have some questions about the atrocities that have already occurred. The specifics."

"We will happily share with you everything we know," Domenico replied.

"Exactly how were the monks blinded in a closed chapel?" Riario asked.

Domenico looked to Cristina, who hesitated. "That is still under investigation."

"Ah. In other words, you don't know."

"Not yet. But we will discover the truth. In time."

"What about the ball of fire?" Riario pressed on. "Which I believe you witnessed with your own eyes, Signorina Falchoni."

"Indeed, Your Eminence."

"How did it erupt so mysteriously, then vanish so quickly? How did it burn the people, but leave the building unharmed?"

"We are still working to unravel the particular chemical reaction," Cristina admitted.

"Then let me answer instead," Cardinale Orsini interrupted. "You *have* no rational explanations, because there *are* no rational explanations. This is the work of Divine forces, and we need to heed the warnings. The only way to prevent further suffering is through penitence and prayer. We must ask for His forgiveness."

"While secretly plotting to remove the Pope?"

"Cristina! Stop!" Domenico hissed.

"A Pope who you elected just a few years ago!"

"Get this woman out of here!" Orsini signalled to the guards on the door, who hurried forward and grabbed Cristina.

"Take your hands off me!" She wriggled free and glared at the cardinals. "You latch onto these simplistic solutions, but the truth is far more complex!"

"Why go for an elaborate solution, when the simpler one works?" Riario said.

"Because it's not true!"

"You should be familiar with Occam's razor. Always select the solution with the fewest assumptions."

"Don't give me a lecture on logic! I have been studying it my whole life."

"On this occasion —" Riario stood up as he made his final pronouncement — "I must agree with Cardinale Orsini. God is punishing Rome. Only prayer, fasting and penitence can save us from more suffering. And I would advise you, Domenico Falchoni, to think carefully before you invite your sister to address this Curia again."

And that was it. Reason had lost. Cristina had failed.

20: UNREASON

The feral cats kept a close eye on Cristina and Domenico as they picked their way through the ancient ruins in the centre of Rome. Alert and quick-witted, the cats didn't mind humans roaming across their territory, especially if they brought scraps of food, but it was obvious these two were preoccupied, so the strays slunk back into the tangle of crumbling walls and carried on chasing lizards.

As they walked up the Via Sacra, away from the colosseum, Cristina kicked a stone and watched it skitter along the ancient, slave-built road. "Why won't they see reason?"

"Getting angry at the cardinals won't help." Domenico had become an expert at coaxing his sister down from the ledge of her indignation.

"How could I not be angry?" She pulled out a tall thistle that was growing from the crack in the path and started swiping the air with it. "We should all be angry when we're confronted by ignorance."

Domenico shrugged. "Living in this city, you should be used to it by now."

"Well, I'm not. And I never will be. No-one should accept ignorance."

"You underestimate its power, Cristina."

"Nothing is as powerful as reason," she insisted.

"And yet here we are, faced with baffling crimes that defy all reason. Crimes that no-one can explain."

"Because we need more time. And more resources, which the fools in the Vatican won't give us."

Domenico paused as they walked under the imposing Arch of Titus and gazed up at the carved panels celebrating the Roman conquest of Jerusalem in 71 AD. "I'm afraid you're wrong, Cristina. Ignorance is more powerful than reason."

"Ignorance didn't build this arch." She slapped the great stone pedestal and listened to the echo. "Still standing after fifteen hundred years."

"But where are they now? The mighty emperors? Roman civilisation lasted a thousand years, yet in the end it was destroyed by barbarians who had a fraction of Rome's learning. A fraction. But they still won." Domenico turned and gazed at the ruined forum that spread out below them. "They destroyed a great empire with brute force."

"And that must never happen again," Cristina said. "If European civilisation were to collapse, it would be the greatest tragedy in history."

"I agree. But that doesn't mean it won't happen."

"It will not. It cannot. We have too much learning." Cristina picked her way down the uneven path, shooing away some scrawny goats.

Domenico followed patiently, waiting for the right moment to continue the conversation; he had to time it perfectly, or his sister would bat away his words with a clever retort. He finally caught up with her sitting in the shade of the massive brick arches that were all that remained of Basilica Julia, the great Roman courthouse. "You know how much I respect you, Cristina. But sometimes … you don't always see the whole picture."

"Why do I feel a lecture coming on?" She shuffled over on the fallen stone to make room for Domenico. "Come on. Let's get it over with."

"When I was in the army, there were things I witnessed … things that no-one should ever see. And when you've lived through that, normal life is never the same again." He hesitated.

Cristina studied his face, saw his gentle eyes blink as memories flooded back. Her brother rarely spoke about his time on the battlefield. He never reminisced or told boastful tales full of heroism. Domenico had returned from the wars a changed man; everyone could see that, but no-one really wanted to talk about it.

"When enemy spies were captured, they were interrogated. I would urge them to give up their secrets voluntarily, to spare themselves. Most relented. But some … some had such a stubborn sense of duty…" Domenico turned away, avoiding his sister's gaze. "Torture isn't just about pain, it's about terror. It has everything to do with darkness and unreason. And the worst thing is, it works."

Cristina could see how difficult this was for her brother. "You don't have to go back there."

He shook his head. "They had this instrument, the Pear of Anguish. Hold it in your hand, and it was just an elegant, ingenious device: a simple bulb made from four leaves that separated as a screw was turned. And it was so beautifully made. With such precision. Only when it was put into the victim's mouth did the true horror become apparent. As the screw was turned and the leaves expanded, it would shatter the victim's skull. Slowly. From the inside." Domenico heard his sister gasp, but he hadn't finished. "The most sadistic torturers never started with the mouth. They would use it on the lower half of the body first. Not just to inflict unimaginable pain, but to instil the greatest fear. It was fear that did the work."

He fell silent, head bowed. Cristina could sense his loneliness but didn't know how to comfort him. What did people do in these situations? "I'm so sorry," she whispered.

"It was not your sin."

"You should not have had to witness that. No-one should."

"Barbarity lies behind every 'Great Victory' that is trumpeted from the rooftops and celebrated with feasts. Barbarity and violence and pain."

Finally, her brother was starting to make sense — the way he clung to order and procedure, the way he used humour to deflect any conversation that threatened to go too deep. He was a man living with raw wounds, even though they were invisible.

Domenico cleared his throat and stood up. He shook his shoulders, as if ridding himself of a bad dream, and retreated behind his official role again.

Cristina touched his hand. "You don't have to pretend with me, Domenico."

"I was just trying to make the point: reason is not the most powerful force in the world. Fear is. And if the cardinals are behaving irrationally, it is because they are human. And they are afraid. That puts them beyond the reach of reason." He straightened his jacket and walked back towards the Vatican.

21: MORGUE

Cristina didn't stir. She sat quietly in the ancient ruins, absorbing what her brother had just told her, while three stray cats with tortoiseshell coats eyed her from the shadows.

Domenico seemed so lonely in his pain, yet he refused to let anyone get close enough to help. Should she respect his loneliness? Or should she sweep her brother's defences aside and make his pain her business? Cristina felt out of her depth; perhaps if she had children of her own, it would come more naturally.

Work.

She stood up briskly, startling the cats who skittered away.

Whenever she felt lost, the only answer was to bury herself in work. The final toll from the Santa Maria fireball attack was seven dead and another twelve still receiving treatment in hospital. The bodies had been taken to the morgue, where Cristina was due to examine them in the morning. She intended to swab their burns in the hope of finding chemical residues that might explain the exact cause of the explosion, but if she started the job now, she could work late into the night until she was so exhausted, she would collapse into bed and outwit the demons of doubt that troubled her sleep.

Walking across Rome, Cristina could feel that this was a city in transition. The older quarters were a jumble of closely set buildings packed into narrow streets, with overhanging stories blocking out the sky. But turn the corner and you suddenly found yourself on a broad, straight avenue leading towards some grand piazza with an imposing obelisk as its focus. It felt like a battle between the past and the future being waged in geometry and stone, with an army of stonemasons on the front line.

But as she got closer to the city morgue, a more sinister noise started to mingle with the clatter of hammers and chisels … the chant of an angry mob.

"Give them back! Give them back! Give them back!"

Cristina quickened her pace.

"Give them back! Give them back!"

She took a shortcut through a narrow alley and emerged into a riot. A large crowd, about a hundred strong, was besieging the morgue.

"Give them back! Give them back!"

Cristina recognised Tenente Tomasso, desperately trying to control the situation with just a handful of Vatican guards, but they were no match for the mob's raw anger. A man on the front line was swinging a sledgehammer at the morgue doors, and by the time the guards had wrestled him away, the wood was already starting to fracture.

Tomasso fired his pistol into the air.

CRACK!

The crowd backed away for a moment.

"Go home! All of you!" Tomasso yelled. "This is an official building! You have no business here!"

For a few moments the unity of the mob faltered — some wanted to heed the warning, others were too furious to care.

Cristina seized her moment and pushed her way through. "Tenente!" She waved her hands in the air, trying to attract his attention. "What is happening here?"

Two guards barged forward, grabbed hold of Cristina, and half-lifted, half-dragged her to the front, where she could shelter behind the fragile line of troops.

"You shouldn't be here!" Tomasso urged.

"I have work to do."

"Please, signorina! If they knew what you were up to, they'd lynch you!"

"Give them back! Give them back! Give them back!"

The chant found its feet again, rekindling the unity of the mob.

"It's a morgue! There's nothing to steal," Cristina shouted into the melee.

"They want their loved ones back," the lieutenant explained. "The families of the dead."

"What?"

"They don't want any experiments done on them."

"I'm not experimenting. I'm trying to find out who is responsible for their murder."

"That's not what they think."

"Then tell them!"

"You tell them! They won't listen to me!" Tomasso saw that the ringleaders had commandeered a large barrow from one of the shops and were edging it through the mob to use as a battering ram.

"You're only hurting yourselves!" Cristina screamed at the crowd. "We're trying to help!"

She may as well have been yelling at the incoming tide.

The front three rows of rioters manhandled the barrow so that it lined up with the morgue entrance. They heaved it back, then with a rising cheer, rammed it hard into the doors.

CRACK!

The splits in the wood spread top to bottom. The crowd drew the cart back to make another run.

"What do we do, sir?" one of the guards yelled at the lieutenant.

"Hold the line!"

But Cristina could see that it was hopeless. "No. Let them do as they please."

"Are you sure?" Tomasso hated giving up.

"If their ears are closed, I cannot help them."

"Ooooooh!" The crowd chanted as it surged forward behind the barrow.

CRACK! This time the morgue doors split wide open, and with a triumphant cheer, the mob surged inside. Moments later, the first shrouded body was carried out, passed from hand to hand and delivered into the care of a grieving family.

Cristina could only look on, bewildered. There was something so primitive about the mob's behaviour; it was like watching a colony of ants transporting their eggs. But at least larvae had value; they were precious objects vital to the colony's survival. These shrouded bodies were dead, finished. What difference would a couple of days in the morgue make?

"What did they honestly think I was going to do?" she asked Tenente Tomasso.

"They don't think." He wiped his sleeve across his brow. "That's the problem."

It was just as Domenico said. Reason counted for nothing with these people; they were marching to a different drumbeat.

In less than half an hour, it was all over. The bodies had been taken, the mob had dissolved, and Tomasso and the guards had gone to find some wood to make emergency repairs to the doors. All was quiet again.

Cristina stepped into the cold morgue, fearing the worst, but she was surprised at how little damage had been done. None of the medical instruments had been taken, Barberini's half-dissected body lay on the slab, exactly as she'd left it, and one of the fireball victims still remained; presumably no-one had come forward to claim him.

Gently Cristina pulled back the winding sheet. The victim was an old man with a deeply lined face; his eyebrows were gone, his hair singed and his skin badly blistered. He must have been near the altar, in a direct line with the blast.

"What are you going to do to him?"

The voice startled Cristina. She spun round and saw a young man standing in the shadows. His gentle face, half-smothered by a bushy beard, was at odds with his strong body.

"Is he family?"

The man stepped forward and looked tenderly at the corpse. "My grandfather."

"I'm sorry."

He touched the old man's face, disturbed by the blistering.

"I was there as well," Cristina said. "But I was lucky."

"Nonno was a glassblower. Spent all his life working with furnaces. Never had an accident. That he should go like this..."

"Someone is responsible," Cristina said solemnly. "There is a monster loose on the streets of Rome, and I'm determined to catch him."

"How can tampering with the dead help?" The young man looked at her. It wasn't an accusation; he really wanted to know.

"There will be traces of chemicals on his body that will explain how the fireball was created."

"And how will that help you find who did this?"

"Some chemicals are difficult to obtain. It should narrow the list of who we are looking for."

"Then do what you must." The bearded man stepped back from the corpse. "Nonno would've liked the idea that he was still useful after death."

"Thank you."

Cristina started to unpack the testing equipment from her bag: thin glass tubes, six different marker chemicals in small bottles, medical forceps, and a bag of muslin swabs.

The young man watched intently, as if standing guard over his grandfather, but he had nothing to fear; Cristina worked gently and respectfully, swabbing and testing, collecting the precious data.

22: BURIALS

All seven victims of the Santa Maria church atrocity were to be buried in one ceremony, officiated by Cardinale Riario. A beautiful spot had been chosen in the Cimitero del Verano, a sprawling jumble of tombs and graves laced with rows of cypress trees, which had grown up above the ancient Christian catacombs near Via Tiburtino.

It was to be a lavish affair, paid for by the Vatican to reassure citizens that the Church was leading the fight against the evils that were terrorising Rome. Seven identical graves had been dug in an arc, and leading stonemasons were already competing for the contract to construct a grand memorial to the victims.

Cristina only went along to pay her respects to the glassblower and his family; she was worried they might be spurned because they'd allowed her to conduct an autopsy, and there was nothing sadder than a sparsely attended funeral.

She needn't have worried.

Over a thousand people had turned out for the funerals, all dressed in black, many clutching rosaries. By the time Cristina arrived, it was impossible to get near the graves, and she had to settle for a spot on a small rise on the opposite slope. As she studied the crowd, Cristina realised that it wasn't just the victims' families who had turned up, it was everyone with an axe to grind in this crisis: soothsayers and mystics, prophets of doom and politicians on the make. She'd seen many of them outside the monastery after the blinding of the monks, whipping up fear and peddling superstition.

A bell tolled in the St Lawrence tower and the crowd fell silent. A few moments later, a choir started singing and the procession made its way up the central path. First came the choirboys in their white surplices, followed by two monks swinging smoking thuribles from long chains; then came six priests who flanked Cardinale Riario. Behind them came the pallbearers carrying the seven shrouded bodies on wooden biers, each one decked with lilies. At the rear of the procession was a troop of Vatican guards in full dress uniform. The Church certainly knew how to choreograph an occasion.

Cristina could tell that Riario understood the drama of the moment, and he made sure he was at the centre of everything. He blessed each body in turn, sprinkling them with holy water; he personally read the funeral Mass, offering salvation to the victims' families, and he even appeared to shed a tear when the choir lamented the passing of so many innocent lives in mournful polyphony.

Cristina was too far away to hear any of the words, yet the distance offered a revealing perspective on the funerals. Rather than getting emotionally caught up, she started to see the whole ceremony as an elaborate dance. Each family moved centre stage as Riario chanted prayers for the souls of the departed; they wept, he comforted, they withdrew, then he moved down the line and repeated the ritual. It was like a folk dance with seven movements.

The different components of the procession all wore distinctive colours, so as the choir, priests and soldiers moved around each other, they created a fluid geometric pattern that seemed to mesmerise the mourners.

When it came to the committals, as ceremonial shots were fired into the air, the guards lowered all the coffins with a military precision that left the crowd in awe.

How primal it all was, designed to evoke strong emotions and encourage ostentatious grief.

As Cristina's gaze wandered over the crowd, it occurred to her that the murderers responsible for all this suffering might well be somewhere in this gathering, hiding in plain sight. Just like this service, the perpetrators' crimes had been meticulously planned and executed to provoke fear and wonder: the bizarre crucifixion, the mass blinding, the sudden fireball ... all seemed to defy logical explanation. Cristina was convinced the atrocities were the work of human hands, yet she understood that it was their baffling and mysterious nature that had imbued them with such terrifying power. It was why the murderers now held Rome in their grip.

A gust of wind rolled through the cemetery, making the cypress trees sway in unison. Sunlight flickered on Cristina's face as it filtered through the branches, and for a moment she was hypnotised by the fluttering glare.

She felt a movement in her mind, like an astrolabe wheel clicking a notch.

What if the perpetrators of these crimes didn't just understand how to manipulate the irrational — what if they also lived and died by it?

Normal criminals would want to escape so that they could enjoy the benefits of their sins, but what if the men she was hunting were playing by different rules? If their own behaviour was not rational, could that explain the baffling nature of the murders?

The astrolabe in Cristina's mind clicked again and she could see a planetary alignment start to form. Without waiting for the funeral service to end, she turned and hurried away.

23: FANATICS

The ugly stain on the hillside had dried to a deep brown, but even though insects had been feasting off Barberini's blood ever since his untimely crucifixion, it would take a summer downpour to wash his death clean away.

Cristina stood on the exact spot where the cross had been raised and slowly turned in a full circle, trying to deduce who could have seen what was happening on that dreadful night.

Several of the houses on the edge of the city had small windows on their upper floors that faced this way, but would anyone have been looking out in the middle of the night?

The most prominent building that faced the hillside was the watch tower at the Collatina Gate. Dead or alive, Barberini had been brought out of the city, presumably through that gate; even if the crucifix was already in place, it was inconceivable that the Watch didn't notice anything strange. Either Barberini was abducted, in which case he would have been struggling, or he left the city willingly and would have been clearly visible to the night shift. Yet they claimed to have seen nothing.

But … what if the Watch Guards were involved in the murder?

To anyone else, this would have been a bizarre suggestion, for the Watch were drawn from the Civic Militia who were known and respected for their integrity; but to Cristina it was now the most promising line of enquiry, as she was looking for answers rooted in *unreason*.

What if a fanatic had infiltrated the Watch and waited, possibly years, for the perfect moment to murder? What if he was behaving like those spies who become sleepers in enemy territory until called on to act? That someone might spend a lifetime becoming a trusted member of the Watch simply in order to murder, was an absurd idea … which was precisely why Cristina now had to consider it.

Brandishing the warrant letters that Domenico had given her, Cristina entered the Collatina Tower and asked to inspect the guard rotas for the past month. As the sergeant handed her the ledger, she noticed with distaste how sweaty his hands were.

She took the book, wiped the leather binding with her gloves, then started to look down the list of names, hoping that something would resonate.

"Any unusual behaviour among the guards?" Cristina asked the sergeant, a flabby man with too many hairs sprouting from his ears.

He shrugged. "When you've been doing this job as long as I have, nothing's a surprise."

Cristina found the page from the night of the murder and started to make a list of all the guards who were on that shift. "And these six men, they're trustworthy?"

The sergeant's eyes scanned the list. "Very diligent. Sometimes a bit too diligent."

"What do you mean?"

"I always tell my boys, what happens on shift, stays on shift. We're not paid enough to take work home, so once you've finished, leave it all behind you."

"Good advice."

"But not everyone listens."

"Oh?"

"Magrini has been off sick since the night of the murder."

"Who?"

"Young chap. Kept blaming himself in case he'd missed something."

"Well, I don't want to sound harsh," Cristina replied, "but he did. He missed a lot. An entire crucifixion."

The sergeant bristled defensively. "My men take their duties very seriously. I won't have you making scapegoats here."

"I'm just saying —"

"Well, don't. Magrini is one of the best guards I've got. Always punctual. Thorough. Honest. A decent man."

"And yet no-one has seen him since the night of the murder."

The sergeant really didn't like the way this was going. "He's a young man. And he's upset. If you had a grain of compassion, you'd understand."

"Where does he live?"

"I'm not having you disturb him at home. He'll be back at work soon enough."

"I just thought I could take him a basket of fruit, or a bunch of flowers," Cristina replied innocently. "As a mark of my compassion."

She found the house at the end of a narrow cul-de-sac, Vicolo delle Orsoline. The shutters were closed, but Cristina hammered on the door anyway. No one answered. She tried again, then called out. "Magrini! Are you there?"

Silence.

"Magrini?" No reply. Just as she was about to give up, one of the neighbours appeared at a first-floor window. "Keep it down! My husband's trying to sleep!"

"At this hour?"

"He works nights at the bakery," she scowled.

"Apologies." Cristina flashed the neighbour a charming smile. "I was just trying to find a young man called Magrini, from the City Watch. I've got a message for him."

"Well, it'll have to wait," the neighbour replied. "He's taken the family away for a few days. Out of the city."

"Where to?"

"Anywhere but Rome," the neighbour snapped.

"I thought this was his home?"

"He's not been the same since that nasty business on the hill. Holiday might do him good."

"What's Magrini like?"

"Nice family. No trouble. Good neighbours. Respectful."

"They think highly of him at the Watch."

"And he keeps his children *quiet*," the neighbour said pointedly. "Unlike some." She withdrew into her apartment and closed the window behind her.

Something wasn't right. Cristina could feel it. She pressed her face close to the downstairs shutters and peered through the gaps; it looked as if the room had been stripped bare. The front door was secured with a heavy iron lock, but there was a side gate shared with the other houses that seemed quite flimsy. Cristina leant on it, felt it flex, then kicked it sharply with her boot. The latch flicked up and the door swung open onto a small courtyard.

Cristina checked she wasn't being observed by the baker's wife, then snuck into the courtyard. The windows at the back of Magrini's house had no shutters, and she was able to peer inside. Just as she'd suspected, every room had been stripped bare. There were no clothes, no pots or pans, no furniture, no bread or wine, and no sign of any children.

Magrini hadn't gone away for the weekend. He had disappeared.

24: BLAME

Rome's streets had descended into their regular afternoon chaos as markets were packed away and the city's poorest swooped on the leftovers like flocks of hungry birds. Bruised fruit, bread that had gone stale, scraps of meat that were on the brink of going off — whatever couldn't be sold could still make a feast for the hungry.

Cristina pushed through the ragged bustle, oblivious to the daily struggle for survival that gripped so many in this city, because she was immersed in her own thoughts. If a traitor, working on the inside, had enabled Barberini's crucifixion, what did that mean for the monastery blinding? Her theory that the monks were poisoned by gas only seemed impossible if you assumed people were behaving rationally. But what if they weren't?

What if one of the monks let himself be locked in the chapel, then released the toxin and willingly sacrificed his own sight to commit the crime? Unreason and fanaticism could make sense of the impossible.

Cristina arrived at Sant'Onofrio to find that a team of nuns from the Convent of Santa Francesca Romana had taken charge of the nursing regime. These sisters specialised in working with soldiers who had been blinded on the battlefield; even when there was no hope of a cure, with the right therapies, patients could be rehabilitated and learn to live in a different way.

"It's all about their minds," Sister Ginevra said as she led Cristina across the courtyard. "Once the mind accepts, the body can adapt and heal." She was still a young woman, barely in her thirties, even though her square face and scrubbed skin made her look older. But there was nothing old about the sister's mind — she spoke quickly because she had so many thoughts to articulate. "Trauma affects each of us in different ways. None of us know how we will react until we are tested."

"I think I'd be plunged into desperate rage," Cristina confessed.

Sister Ginevra shook her head. "You'd find a way through. You're too bright to stay lost for long." She stopped and pointed to a short, round monk who was walking through the cloisters, feeling each pillar as he went, counting the paces between them. "Brother Matteo, he's already turned back to life. The ideal patient."

They watched as he walked back and forth across the cloister lawn, trying to go a little faster each time.

"He's got bruises all over his shins from tripping and stumbling, but he never gives up," Sister Ginevra said with admiration. "He's mapping the whole monastery in counted steps."

"So every bruise is a lesson," Cristina said.

"Quite."

Suddenly, Brother Matteo gave a small cry and tumbled flat out on the lawn. One of the sisters rushed over to help, but by the time she got to him, Matteo was already smiling at his mistake. "I forgot about the gulley. There used to be a bird bath there." He got to his feet, dusted down his robe, then diligently started counting paces from the gulley back to the edge of the lawn.

"Impressive," Cristina said.

"Would that they were all like that." Sister Ginevra led Cristina to a small side chapel, where a wiry monk with a shock of red hair was slumped on his knees, moaning pitifully.

"Brother Cristoforo has done nothing but kneel in this chapel and weep, begging God to restore his sight," Ginevra whispered. "But longing for something that will never return … that way lies madness."

"Have you talked to him? Explained the truth?"

"We try. We need to make him understand that there is always a way to live again. But if a man is locked in the past…"

Cristina looked at the monk's desperate face, so full of anger and pain. "You'd think monks would know better than anyone about stoicism."

Sister Ginevra shrugged. "It's one thing to talk about suffering. The beauty and dignity of sacrifice. Quite another to actually live it."

"So … what will become of him?" Cristina asked.

"If he doesn't turn —" Ginevra pointed to the far end of the monastery — "the dolorem." She led the way to a series of cells that were secured behind iron railings. One of the sisters undid the padlocks and swung open the gate.

"All quiet?"

"Not too bad this morning, Sister Ginevra."

The cell doors here were securely bolted, and the only way to see inside was through a small sliding hatch. "These poor souls have already slipped the bounds of reason." Ginevra opened the observation slot on the first cell.

Cristina peered inside and saw a tall, skinny monk crumpled on the floor, muttering incoherently; his pale arms and legs were covered in dozens of angry, blood-encrusted scars.

"Brother Giacobbe became self-destructive with grief. We found him in the kitchen, cutting his limbs."

"What?"

"He blames himself for what happened. He is convinced that his own sins have brought divine punishment. By letting his blood, he hopes to purge himself of evil."

Cristina was appalled. "But there is nothing in the Scriptures to support such guilt."

"He's not the worst." Sister Ginevra walked deeper into the gloom and slid back the hatch on the furthest cell; one of the monks had been chained to the wall, and every hard surface within his reach had been padded with blankets. His own head was tightly bound with bandages that already had traces of blood seeping through.

"You chained him? Like a prisoner?"

"For his own safety. To stop him destroying the 'demons' trapped inside his head."

Cristina stepped back and looked at the other locked doors in this gloom-laden corridor. "Will they ever get out of here? Any of them?"

There was a long silence as Sister Ginevra considered the question. "The human mind is about so much more than reason. Underneath our thoughts lies a dark reservoir of fear and memory, passion and guilt. What these men are doing…" She gazed at the locked doors. "To us it seems irrational, but to them it makes perfect sense."

"Reason twisted into unreason," Cristina mused.

"Exactly."

"Have you seen this before, Sister Ginevra? With wounded soldiers?"

"Too many times."

"And tell me — this may sound strange — do any of the monks seem … pleased by what has happened?"

"Pleased?" Ginevra was puzzled.

"Unnaturally calm. Or jovial."

"No."

"Are any of them … content that their order has been blinded?"

Sister Ginevra was unnerved by the question. "That would be evil. A true mark of the devil. Whatever their faults, these men have devoted their lives to God."

"But perhaps evil stalked the monastery that morning?" Cristina pressed.

"We cannot know the mind of God. All we know is that in the end, good will triumph. Because it is more powerful than evil. But the path to victory may be painful."

Another of the sisters hurried down the corridor, searching for Sister Ginevra; one of the monks had started vomiting and needed urgent attention.

"I'm sorry. I really have to attend to this," the sister apologised.

Cristina thanked Ginevra for her time and made her own way out. At the gates, she turned and looked back at the huddles of monks scattered around the courtyard.

Someone in here was hiding a terrible secret.

But who?

25: ALTAR

"Magic pebble, miss?"

Cristina had barely set foot outside the monastery when the boy accosted her. "What?"

"Protects you against blindness."

He was no more than ten, but he had the easy banter of a wily old market trader. His hair was slicked back, and he wore a long jacket with numerous pockets stitched on the outside.

"I don't think so." Cristina tried to walk past, but the boy dodged in front of her.

"If you've been in there," he said, pointing warily to the monastery gates, "you'll be needing some protection."

"I appreciate the thought," Cristina smiled, "but there is absolutely no risk of blindness being contagious. And even if there was, there is no such thing as a magic pebble."

The boy appeared to be listening intently.

"You see, belief in magic is a hangover from pagan times," Cristina explained, "when people had no understanding of the workings of nature. But we are in a new world now. Learning and science and reason are the defining traits of European civilisation, and magic can play no part in that. You see?"

"How about grease of a hedgehog, then?" The boy fished a small jar from one of his pockets. "Comes in two strengths."

"Didn't you hear a word I said?"

"Rub it on your forehead to ward off evil spirits." He dipped his thumb into the grease and stretched up, but Cristina backed away.

"Stop this, please!" Her patience was starting to fray.

"Won't hurt, miss. Nothing to be afraid of." He sniffed the grease and rubbed some onto his own face to demonstrate. "See? Harmless."

"And useless!"

"I'll give you a week's supply for a half-ducat."

"Enough! Please."

"And I'll throw in the magic pebble for free."

"Look, if you want to earn some money, you can run a message for me. No magic. No potions. Just a fast pair of feet."

The boy gave a disappointed sigh. "Some people have no vision."

"So, is that yes or no?"

"Very well, miss."

"Run to the Vatican barracks. Tell them that the Capitano della Guardia Apostolica needs to meet his sister at Santa Maria della Pace as soon as possible. Got that?"

The boy looked at her askance. "You mean the devil's church?"

"No. That's not what I said."

"But the fireball. The curse. Satan's breath."

"Stop repeating that nonsense!"

"Only trying to help."

"I know. But it's not." Cristina handed him a couple of coins and the boy vanished into the side-streets. Would there ever come a time when people didn't reach for ridiculous fantasies to make sense of life?

The boy's head may have been full of nonsense, but his feet were fast, and by the time Cristina arrived at the church, Domenico was already waiting for her. The building was still roped off, and a guard had been placed at each door.

"You shouldn't still be involved in this." Domenico frowned as he stepped out of the church to meet her.

"I'm not giving up."

"The cardinals aren't happy."

"The cardinals are idiots."

"But powerful ones." He ushered Cristina into the church, where her outspokenness was less likely to get them into trouble. "They're taking this away from us. The cardinals have already forced me to release Barberini's body. They don't want any more difficult questions."

Cristina walked into the middle of the nave, remembering what had happened on that strange morning … how the fire had emerged from behind the priest and engulfed innocent worshippers. She approached the large stone altar and studied it closely, running her fingers through soot marks on the carvings.

"I'm not sure we'll ever know the truth about what happened here," Domenico admitted.

"It only seems puzzling if you don't consider *unreason*," Cristina replied.

"Meaning?"

"You need to break open this altar."

"What? No. Out of the question."

"Do you want to discover the truth or not?"

"I can't go round smashing up churches!"

"You're being hysterical. I just want to open it. No smashing required."

"If the cardinals —"

"Forget the cardinals! Listen to me for once."

"That's unfair, Cristina. You know I listen to you."

"I wouldn't ask if I wasn't sure. But we need to see inside this altar."

"It would be sacrilege."

"Domenico, if this doesn't lead to a breakthrough, I will give up the investigation and go back to my library."

"Is that a promise?"

"I swear."

Tenente Tomasso managed to commandeer crowbars from a building site nearby, and with Domenico's warning to do as little damage as possible ringing in his ears, he and another guard got to work. After a few false starts and unfortunate chips, they discovered that the front panel of the altar was a single piece of stone, and carefully managed to lever it forward a few inches.

Cristina lit a candle and peered into the gloomy space. Immediately the flame flickered as it caught a draught.

"Strange," Cristina muttered. She moved the candle back and forth and saw a large cobweb hanging across two corners. "Why would a spider build a web in a sealed space?"

She pushed the candle further into the belly of the altar, scratching her forearms on the rough stone … and glimpsed a ragged hole in the floor, about six inches in diameter. "That's how the flames came through." Cristina pulled her arm back and turned to Domenico. "There's a hole in the flagstones, but it wasn't there when the altar was built. It's too rough."

She handed the candle to her brother, who crouched down to see for himself.

"How the hell did they cut that?"

"From below," Cristina replied. "It's the only way."

Domenico led the way down a narrow flight of steps into the crypt. Tenente Tomasso distributed candles to the other guards, and they all started searching the damp, gloomy spaces behind the stone tombs. Cristina and Domenico held their candles up to the ceiling, hunting for any signs of disturbance, but the vaulting looked smooth and intact.

"Let's do this another way," Cristina suggested. She disappeared upstairs for a few minutes, then reappeared. "The altar is twelve paces from the north wall, and four from the east wall." Methodically, she strode out the same measurements in the crypt, then peered up at the ceiling. Domenico held his candle up to study the plasterwork.

"Nothing unusual there. It's smooth." He turned away, but Cristina remained frozen, her neck craned back.

"Maybe it's a bit too smooth." She glanced around the space and saw an old stepladder stored next to a pile of broken chairs. "Give me a hand here."

Domenico positioned the ladder under the spot where the altar was built, and Cristina clambered up the steps. Slowly, she ran her hands back and forth over the plasterwork. "Different texture. Something's been repaired here."

"Hardly surprising. It's a pretty old church."

"Pass me the crowbar."

"I don't think that's —"

"Domenico!"

Reluctantly he passed the iron bar up to Cristina, and she started hacking at the plasterwork. The first patch crumbled away quickly, showering her in dust, but the gap meant she could now slide the crowbar behind a slab of plaster and lever off a large chunk, which crashed to the floor and disintegrated.

"There you are…" Cristina was staring at a small wooden trapdoor that had been built into the ceiling, then hidden behind the plaster.

"Let me do this," Domenico said. "It might get ugly."

She ignored him, slipped her finger into the iron loop and pulled the trapdoor open. "Candle."

Tomasso handed a light up to her.

Cristina raised the candle into the gloom and discovered a cavity between the crypt ceiling and the floor of the church above. She climbed to the top step of the ladder and poked her head into the darkness.

"Dear God," she whispered.

Curled up like a foetus, were the scorched remains of a man who had been burnt to death. Trapped in this tiny crawl space with no escape, he had been engulfed in agonising fire.

She scrambled back down the ladder and breathed deeply, trying to clear the pungent smell of burnt flesh from her lungs.

"What's up there?" Domenico asked.

"The fireball came from inside the altar … released by a murderer who was hidden between the stones … in a crawl space that became his coffin."

26: EAST

In the chill of the morgue, the body looked surprisingly serene. It was as if the man had just curled up for a nap and never awoke … except that his hair and eyebrows had been burnt away, and his skin was charred black and desiccated.

Even in this clinical setting, Domenico didn't want to get too close to the body, but Cristina was fascinated. She paced around the table, absorbing every detail of the corpse.

"With no hair or skin markings left, identification is going to be difficult." She picked up a pair of medical forceps and delicately peeled back one of the body's eyelids to check for iris colour, but the intense heat had shrivelled the man's eyeballs.

"What a terrible way to die," Domenico whispered.

"Why do you think the Church fathers characterised Hell as the torment of eternal fire?" Cristina replied. "They knew exactly what they were doing, how to play on our deepest fears."

"Would it have been quick?"

Cristina started unpacking her dissection tools. "The human body is actually quite difficult to burn. It has a lot of water. But these circumstances were very particular." Using a scalpel, she punctured the corpse's neck, then ran the blade down the centre of its chest, exposing two black, crumbling lungs. "Mercifully, in this case I think it was a quick death."

"How can you tell?" Domenico peered over her shoulder.

"He inhaled the fire. It burnt his lungs to nothing, you see? He would have died moments later." She picked up a magnifying glass and studied the other internal organs. "Even after the fireball had gone, it looks as if his body smouldered for some time. The fat from his own tissue would have acted as fuel."

"Hence the pungent smell, even hours later. The guards said it lingered all night."

Cristina stepped back from the table and studied the body from a distance. "Strange. He was burnt to death, but there are no signs of struggle. His hands aren't stretched out. His fingernails aren't torn. He wasn't trying to escape or claw his way out. There's no panic in his posture. He just curled up and accepted what was coming."

She turned her attention to the other objects that were found next to the body: the shattered remains of some large glass bottles, a leather water pouch, a scorched tinder box.

Cristina closed her eyes and tried to nudge the wheels of the astrolabe in her mind, cycling different fragments of evidence, placing them next to each other in strange combinations, hoping for a resonance.

Click.

Domenico watched the hint of a smile play across her face. "What?"

"Hypothesis. Working in secret, he entered the crypt and dug into the ceiling, making a hole through to the crawl space underneath the church floor. From there, he hacked through the flagstones above his head until he had access to the space inside the altar."

"Without anyone hearing?"

"He must have worked at night. Then he moved three glass bottles of highly flammable liquid into the space. Finally, he hid himself there with enough water and food to last until the moment was right. His co-conspirators sealed him into the crawl space and plastered over the trapdoor. Making him effectively invisible."

"What man would willingly endure that?" Domenico was struggling to keep up.

"A man with extreme beliefs."

"It must have been agony. How long was he entombed?"

"He was waiting for the perfect moment. Possibly for days, breathing the trickle of air coming down through the altar, enduring unimaginable claustrophobia." Cristina shuddered. "It must have been a relief when the time finally came to end it." She thought back to the final seconds before the explosion. "*Cast the Devil out of Rome.* Those were the last words the priest uttered. That was the trigger. The bomber heard those words, ignited the liquid and sacrificed himself in the explosion."

"It doesn't bear thinking about," Domenico whispered.

"This is the face of fanaticism," Cristina said. "A crime committed by human hands, made to look like Divine Retribution."

"Who are they, Cristina? Who are we dealing with?"

"We already have one of them within our grasp."

"We do?"

"One of the monks is not what he seems. I believe one of them set off the blinding haze and sacrificed his own sight for the cause."

"But which cause? What has turned these people to such madness?"

"Discover that, and all these crimes will be solved."

Gilo volunteered to take charge of the monastery surveillance, as he had the most experience in covert operations and didn't baulk at the gruelling hours. He handpicked his team, then drew up an elaborate rota that would give him eyes and ears inside the monastery at all hours of the day and night.

The guards went in using many guises: some were porters, some cleaners; others delivered food and wine. One man even posed as a volunteer reader to help the blind monks maintain their study of scripture.

At the end of their shift, each agent gave a full report to Gilo, who collated all the information and sifted through the daily trivia, hunting for a mistake that would give the criminal away.

On the twelfth night, they had a breakthrough.

"I believe Brother Bartolo is our man, sir," Gilo gasped as he tried to catch his breath; he had run all the way across the old Papal Gardens to Domenico's apartments in the Administration Building, where senior Vatican officials had their rooms.

"Come in, come in." Domenico wiped the sleep from his eyes and led Gilo into the small sitting area. "What's this Bartolo done?"

"Three days ago, we secretly released some cockroaches into the monastery cellars, which gave us the perfect cover to send a man in as pest control."

"Slightly contentious tactic, Gilo."

"But it gave us a reason to be there throughout the night, as cockroaches prefer the dark. Turns out, so does Brother Bartolo. When he thought everyone was asleep, he crept out of his cell and felt his way to one of the storerooms on the upper floor. Our surveillance agent followed him. He saw him rummage among the clutter and pull out a small prayer mat. He laid it out carefully, then his fingers studied a small gadget sewn into the corner of the mat. It was a compass for the blind. Bartolo rotated the mat until it faced Makkah, then he prostrated himself, and started to pray in Arabic. Reciting from the Quran."

"A Christian monk praying to Allah?" Domenico was struggling to understand.

"He's not a Christian. He's an imposter. He follows Islam. And he's a heretic."

"In a monastery?"

"The Ottomans are here, sir. In Rome, walking secretly among us. Attacking us from within."

27: PURGE

His Holiness Pope Alexander VI sat in terrible silence, brooding on the information he had just received. No one dared move — not Cardinale Riario, who was on hand to advise, not the three private secretaries, and least of all Domenico, who had just delivered the news. Everyone stood rooted to the spot, listening to the sound of the Holy Father's breathing, praying that he would remain calm.

After an eternity, Riario cleared his throat and turned to Domenico. "What motive could there be? Why would Ottoman spies murder Barberini and blind the monks?"

"As yet, we do not know, Your Eminence. We have not arrested Bartolo or subjected him to interrogation."

Riario shook his head. "I can discern no strategic advantage for the Ottomans. It makes no sense."

"We didn't want to arrest anyone until the Holy Father was made aware of the situation."

All eyes returned to the Pope.

Finally, Alexander spoke. "They are trying to destabilise my papacy. This is an attack on me."

"A rather indirect attack," Riario frowned. "Surely there are better ways —"

"Do you question me?"

"No, Holy Father."

"All my great and noble work with the Inquisition in Spain, has made me the enemy of Islam. I rooted out the plague of heresy and crushed the enemies of Christ under my foot, and now I am their target. The heathens will not rest until they have destroyed me. But they have made a grave mistake. Now they will learn what it means to feel a Pope's fury."

"Forgive me, but perhaps Your Holiness is taking this too personally." Riario spoke gently, knowing that his words would enrage. "Perhaps this is all part of a wider strategy to weaken Christian Europe prior to an invasion, or a new campaign of conquest. In which case, we should approach this problem very cautiously."

The Pope glared at Riario. "Innocent people are murdered as they worship, and you urge caution?"

"Perhaps we can better protect ourselves by infiltrating the spy ring rather than destroying it."

"And leave the criminals unpunished? What kind of justice is that for the people of Rome?"

"First use the criminals for our own ends, then punish them afterwards, Holy Father."

"By which time people will have turned against me for failing to protect them."

"I don't believe —"

"We all know what is going through your devious mind, Cardinale Riario. Everyone in this room knows that you have set your eyes on my throne."

"That is not true."

"God chose me!" Alexander's rage echoed round the room. "And you must accept that, for I have no intention of leaving this throne!" He slammed his fists down on its gilt arms. "You will have to kill me first. And then you will be damned for all eternity for daring to raise your hand against God's anointed voice."

"I beg the Holy Father's forgiveness." Riario bowed extra low. "I did not mean to speak out of turn. I was merely trying to help."

"There is only one way to help." Alexander stood up to make his proclamation. "Unleash the full might of the Vatican and destroy this pernicious Ottoman spy ring. Do whatever is necessary. Punish whoever resists. Show no mercy. Eliminate them."

When powerful men vent their rage, it is ordinary people who suffer. The City Militia surged through the immigrant quarters of Rome, targeting every business that had trade links with the Ottoman Empire and every man who had a name originating in the Levant.

There were mass arrests, doors were broken down, windows smashed and shops ransacked. Anyone who resisted or tried to run was beaten into submission. This was not a covert, targeted operation against a spy ring; it was deliberately aggressive, designed to intimidate 'outsiders' whilst reassuring 'authentic citizens' that resolute action was being taken to keep them safe.

God forbid your skin was too dark or your name too foreign-sounding; the Militia arrested first and asked questions later. Anyone who they took against was presumed guilty and would have to take their chances in the city's dungeons.

The arrest of Brother Bartolo was more civilised. Domenico took charge of the troop that entered the Sant'Onofrio monastery and reminded everyone that this was a place of worship. "One rogue monk does not destroy the sanctity of God's house."

As it turned out, Bartolo came peacefully, without a word of protest or resistance. He didn't ask why the troops were there or what he had done wrong; he didn't make excuses or declare his innocence. Just like the corpse hidden in the crawl space under the altar, he accepted what was happening as if he had always known this was how it would end.

They took him to one of the holding cells under the Vatican, where he was manacled to the wall; then Domenico told the guards to leave so that he could be alone with the blind monk.

"You know what this is about, don't you?" Domenico said.

Bartolo pondered the question. "I know that I am working for a higher authority than you."

"You mean the Sultan? In Constantinople?"

The monk shrugged. He had a handsome face, but it had been overwhelmed by a long beard that was splashed with patches of grey.

"How old are you?" Domenico asked.

"Old enough to have no fear of what is coming."

"Just answer the question."

"Forty-five."

Domenico was surprised; the beard made Bartolo look a good deal older. "And how much did the Sultan pay you to betray your fellow countrymen?"

"Not everything comes down to gold."

"To destroy your own sight … you must have been deluded or desperate."

"The truth I see shines so brightly; it has no need of eyes."

"Deluded, then."

"Believe what you will, if that makes you feel safer."

"What happened to you, Bartolo? What has twisted your soul?"

Suddenly, a key rattled in the cell door. "I am not to be disturbed!" Domenico yelled. But the lock clunked anyway, and the door swung open. He turned to see three young men calmly enter the cell. They wore identical clothes: long black cassocks, bound with a red sash at the waist. Domenico knew exactly what these men were; they had come from Spain with the Pope as part of his personal entourage. They were his inquisitors.

"This is not your business," Domenico warned. "The Vatican guards are running this investigation."

"The Pope has instructed us —"

"I don't care!"

"We'll pretend you didn't say that." One of the inquisitors stepped forward and offered Domenico his hand. "My name is Padre Gabriel. And I am taking this prisoner with me to our own facility."

Domenico studied their faces. They were all unnervingly similar, clean-shaven and fresh-faced, and he felt as if he should have authority over them. These men had never seen battle, they had never fought for their lives; all they knew was how to hide behind their vestments as they inflicted pain and suffering. Yet it was their utter lack of self-doubt that made them so dangerous. Just by standing silently in the cell, they were making it clear that if Domenico didn't step aside, he too would find himself in chains.

"Padre Gabriel, Bartolo is still a man of God. No matter what he has done."

"I warn you, Domenico. Do not pursue this."

"Let me at least try to reason with him."

"We have read the intelligence reports. This heretic was seen praying to Allah. His sin is worse precisely because it was committed within the walls of a Christian monastery." Padre Gabriel signalled to the other two, who stepped forward and unlocked Bartolo's chains.

Domenico grabbed the monk's arm. "Tell them the truth," he urged, "because these men will show you no pity."

"There's no need to say your farewells just yet," Padre Gabriel said. "You're coming with us, Domenico."

"Me?"

"To help with the questioning."

"I want nothing to do with your barbaric methods."

"No-one knows Rome as well as you. It will be quicker to discern his lies if you are present."

"I have other duties —"

"One way or another, you are coming with us." Gabriel gestured to the cell door. "Now, which is it to be?"

28: VIGILANTE

CRACK! CRACK!

"Open up!"

It sounded as if someone was trying to batter the doors off their hinges.

"Open up for the Militia!"

Cristina hurried down the stairs from her library and saw Isra standing in the hallway, water dripping from her hands onto the stone floor. She had been washing pots. "They've come for me, haven't they?"

"It's all right. No-one's taking you anywhere."

CRACK! CRACK!

"They'll break it down!" Isra exclaimed. "They're coming for me!"

"Go back to the kitchen, Isra! I'll deal with it."

"Where are the pistols?"

"Go!" Cristina bundled Isra into the kitchens at the back of the house. "Now lock yourself in!"

Cristina hurried back to the shuddering front doors.

CRACK! CRACK!

"Wait! I'm coming!" She pulled her shoulders back, drew a deep breath, then slid the bolts and swung open the door.

A red-faced soldier from the City Militia was standing there, club in hand. Next to him was an elderly woman Cristina recognised but couldn't name; she'd seen her many times on the Piazza Navona, and presumed she was a neighbour.

"What on earth is the meaning of this?" Cristina hoped an imperious tone would disguise her fear.

"Does Isra Sahin live here?" the soldier demanded.

"Why?"

"Answer the question!"

"It's none of your business." Cristina went to shut the door, but the soldier forced it open with his boot.

"Course she lives here!" the old woman spat in disgust. "She'll be in the kitchens."

The soldier pushed Cristina aside and barged into the hallway.

"No! Get out!"

"Quiet!"

"You have no right!"

"Whose side are you on?" the prune-faced woman shrieked. "Traitor!"

"Get out!" Cristina clawed at the soldier to hold him back, but he was too strong for her and pushed past, striding towards the kitchens. "My brother is Capitano della Guardia Apostolica!" she warned.

"Then you should know better." The soldier tried to open the kitchen door, but Isra had bolted it from the inside. Enraged, he started to kick the lock with his heel.

"Run, Isra!" Cristina screamed. "RUN!"

But it was too late. The frame split and the kitchen door swung open just as Isra was scrambling through the kitchen window into the courtyard.

"STOP!" The soldier lunged towards her and swung his club sharply across her legs. Isra yelled in pain and tried to kick him away, but he grabbed her by the hair and dragged her back into the kitchen.

"No!" Cristina grabbed a large kitchen knife and brandished it at the soldier. "You're not taking her!"

He stopped and looked at the knife. "Seriously? You'd stab an officer of the City Militia?"

Cristina faltered. He'd called her bluff.

"There are spies all over this city who need to be rounded up," the soldier warned. "And if you didn't have connections, I'd be arresting you as well." He flicked his club across Cristina's hand and the knife clattered to the floor. "Now step aside."

"Isra works for me!"

"Step aside. Last warning." He yanked painfully on Isra's hair, reminding everyone of his power.

"I'll get you out, Isra. I swear!"

"I've done nothing wrong, mistress."

"I know. And I'll find you."

The soldier pushed Cristina aside and dragged Isra out into the street, where the crowd gave a jubilant cheer.

"Lock her up! Lock her up!" The mob surrounded them, forming a defensive shield in case anyone tried to intervene and spoil their victory.

The old crone turned back to Cristina and spat onto the cobbles. "You're next!"

Cristina was appalled to see her own neighbours descend into savage ignorance. Desperate to know how far the madness had spread, she hurried into the neighbouring street, down Via di Pasquino, and headed towards the Pantheon.

The whole atmosphere of the city had changed. The freewheeling tempo had suddenly turned into harsh intolerance. Cristina saw squads of Militia plucking people off the streets and hauling them away; if you ran, you were guilty, if you didn't, you were arrested. And as they spread fear, the young men laughed and joked amongst themselves, drunk on their own power, unleashing their prejudice. If you were Romani, you were automatically a horse-thief; if you were a Blackamoor, you were scum.

Having seized innocent people from across Rome, the Militia withdrew to their barracks, leaving the streets completely unprotected. Gangs of looters rampaged through neighbourhoods, chanting, "Take back the streets! Take back the streets!" Ostensibly they targeted shops that sold goods from the Levant, and anyone who looked vaguely Middle Eastern; in practice, everyone who had a grudge came out to vent their rage. Hiding behind chants of "Traitors!" and "Enemies of the People!" old scores were settled and debts written off at the point of a sword.

Cristina knew the Middle Eastern traders in the Piazza dei Caprettari well; she was a regular customer of the spice traders and merchants who sold a vast array of goods from tiny shops. Now they were all shuttered up, their owners inside, praying that the riot would blow itself out.

This was the horror of unreason; once unleashed, it ran wild.

At the far end of Via Monterone, Cristina saw a group of children throwing stones at the wooden shutters of a bakery where she often bought huge slabs of Syrian flatbread. They couldn't have been more than ten years old, but they had gone feral. Wrapped in bright fabrics they must have looted from the markets, and using sticks for swords, they were laying siege to the bakery.

"God Wills It!" they screamed. "God Wills It!"

It was the battle cry of the Crusaders who'd waged war on the Holy Land for three centuries.

"Seize the Holy Grails of cakes and bread!" their leader commanded. His gang leapt on the chant.

"Cakes and bread! Cakes and bread!"

The leader picked up a metal pole and jammed it into the bakery shutters. "We are the Knights Templar of Cakes and Bread!" he declared.

"Enough!" Cristina waded into the centre of the pack and started hauling the children away from the shop. "ENOUGH!"

"Do not interfere with the Will of God!" the leader retorted.

Cristina snatched the metal pole from him and swooped it in a wide arc, driving the children away from the bakery. "Forget the Will of God. You should be worried about the whipping you'll get when I tell your parents what you've done here!"

Suddenly the Crusaders crumbled, and they were just children again, caught red-handed.

"You should be ashamed of yourselves. Behaving like animals."

Some of the younger ones looked down at the cobbles. The leader attempted a feeble defence. "Someone said they were spies."

"And you believed such nonsense?" Cristina scolded. "I get my bread here every day. They've got children. Just like you. Now get lost."

No-one moved.

"GO!" she yelled, and the children bolted in all directions.

When the street was clear, Cristina knocked gently on the shutters. "It's all right. They've gone."

From inside, she heard a faint voice. "Thank you."

"You can't stay here," Cristina warned. "More will be coming. Maybe not so young."

She heard bolts slide back, then the door opened a crack. Cristina saw the young baker clutching a kitchen knife in one hand and a rolling pin in the other. Behind him, huddled in the shadows were his wife and two small children, fear in their eyes, tears on their cheeks.

"Is everyone all right?" Cristina asked.

The baker rummaged in the shadows, picked up a large flatbread and offered it to her. "Thank you."

"No, no. Really. That's not necessary."

"Please. Take it. My name is Yusuf. This is my wife, Hana, and my children."

"Cristina." She took the bread. "Thank you. But you can't stay here." Already she could hear another mob rampaging a few streets away.

"I cannot leave my shop. This is all we have."

"Baker Yusuf, you can rebuild a shop. But these mobs … who knows what they'll do next."

29: REFUGE

How quickly the world had changed. Just a few weeks ago, the service stairs had been used to smuggle in academics who feared for their tenure because they were tutoring a woman. Now Cristina was using those same steps to save an innocent family's life.

She led Baker Yusuf and Hana to the very top of the house and offered them two of the guest rooms, but the children refused to be parted from their parents, so they all settled in a room at the back, overlooking the small well in the courtyard.

"How can we thank you enough?" The baker clasped Cristina's hands.

"I think the real question is, how can I apologise for this madness?"

"We are Christian Arabs. My wife and children, we fled to this country from Syria to find peace."

"You don't have to explain."

"We built a new life. We would never betray Rome."

"I know. This is not your battle."

"Thank you for understanding."

"You should eat. Especially your children."

Baker Yusuf smiled. "The young, they are always hungry."

"There's food in the kitchens, but my own housekeeper has been arrested."

"Is she safe?" Hana looked at Cristina with large, brown eyes. "Have you heard from her?"

"I'll search for her this afternoon."

"Then please, let us prepare a meal for you," Hana said.

"Yes, yes," Yusuf agreed. "It is the least we can do. We will cook for you."

"Well, that would be nice," Cristina smiled, "especially as my cooking is terrible."

"Then you are in for a treat."

Within minutes, the rattle of pots and pans started to fill the house as Baker Yusuf and Hana got to work, firing up the oven and opening larders.

Cristina retreated to her library. Too upset to read, she ended up staring out of the window overlooking Piazza Navona. The worst seemed to be over. There were still a few gangs of young men throwing their weight around the streets, but they were now more drunk than violent. Cristina felt sick to think about the part she had unwittingly played in unleashing this mayhem. What had started out as the pursuit of truth had ended in a wave of ugliness and ignorance washing over the city. Truth was supposed to set people free, not empower the mob.

The alluring smell of fried garlic drifted into the library. Normally it would have set Cristina's stomach racing in anticipation of lunch, but not today. How could she think about food when Isra was shivering in some dank prison?

She grabbed a jacket and ran down the stairs. Baker Yusuf heard her footsteps and hurried into the hallway, carrying a small bowl of fried halloumi. "Just a little longer."

"It smells wonderful, but —"

"Manakeesh. My wife's speciality. But these will keep you going until it's ready." He offered her the cheese.

"Keep mine warm. I have to find Isra."

"Is it safe yet?"

"It can't wait. I won't be long."

"Be careful. Please. I beg you." He wrapped the cheese in some cloth and pressed it into Cristina's hand. "For the journey. And for Isra, when you find her."

Rather than taking the shortest route to the Vatican, Cristina crossed the Tiber early and made her way through Trastevere. It was quieter here, and the narrow streets and scarcity of piazzas meant it was harder for crowds to gather and stir up trouble. As she approached the guardrooms, Gilo came out to meet her.

"Bad timing, Cristina."

"It can't wait."

"You shouldn't be here."

"Where's Domenico?"

"He's busy. We're all busy."

"They've arrested Isra. She's completely innocent."

"Who?"

"Isra Sahin. She works for me, but the mob started pointing fingers, and the Militia took her away."

Gilo looked at Cristina warily. "You can vouch for her?"

"Of course! What is wrong with everyone?"

"Can't be too careful right now."

"This is *me* you're talking to."

Gilo shrugged, and in that moment Cristina sensed a strange undercurrent. The cheerful deputy was momentarily usurped by someone else.

"You do realise you've lost control of the streets?" Cristina lashed out. "This is down to your incompetence."

"Emotions are running high."

"You were supposed to break open an Ottoman spy ring. With precision. Not whip up every bigot in the city."

"The Pope has decided this is how it should happen."

"And you all just meekly do as you're told? Pathetic."

"Go home, Cristina."

"If I'd known this is how you'd react, I'd never have helped solve the case."

"Really?" Gilo crossed his arms and tilted his head back, scrutinising Cristina. "That's a strange thing to say, when the enemy within threatens us all."

Again, that strange undertone in his words; Cristina realised that she had never actually talked to Gilo without Domenico also being there. "I need to speak to my brother."

"Out of the question. He's interrogating suspects."

"I'll wait."

"That would be pointless."

"That's for me to decide."

"He's not even here, Cristina."

"What do you mean?"

"The blind monk has been taken to another facility."

"Where?"

"I'm not at liberty to say."

Cristina's anxiety notched up again. "I don't believe you."

Gilo gave an indifferent shrug. "That's for you to decide."

"Why would they take Bartolo somewhere else?"

"Well … how can I put this? The interrogation might not be very quiet."

Cristina blinked, trying to work out what Gilo meant. Suddenly, she felt a cold shudder of recognition. "No. Not that. Domenico would never use torture."

"It's not up to him anymore."

"There has to be another way —"

"The Ottomans have brought this on themselves."

"There is no excuse for barbarity!"

"In the real world, Cristina, this is how things work."

"But it's not how they *should* work."

"I'm warning you, don't get in the way of this. Go home. Rest. I'll try to get your servant released."

"Isra Sahin," Cristina said defiantly. "She has a name."

"Whatever you say."

30: TORTURE

The only way to get through this was to get drunk.

Domenico stood in the sunlit cloisters swigging a bottle of brandy as fast as he could, but not so quickly that he would throw up. There was a neatly tended garden in the courtyard behind him, and a skylark was circling somewhere overhead, singing with abandon; two neatly painted doors set in a whitewashed wall were in front of him. It would have been the perfect spot for reflection and contemplation … were it not for the horrors that were unfolding just a few feet away.

Domenico swigged the last dregs of brandy from the bottle and waited for an alcoholic haze to embrace him. But all too soon, the door closest to him creaked open and one of the young inquisitors stepped out.

"Padre Gabriel is ready for you now." The tone of his voice made it clear that Domenico had no choice but to follow him into the cell.

The room was flooded with light from a series of windows high up in the walls, but the sun brought no cheer. This was a stark and forbidding place. Gabriel stood in the centre of the room, calm and collected, like a proud craftsman; his two associates stood either side of a wooden table to which Brother Bartolo had been securely strapped so that he couldn't move.

Bartolo was gasping for breath, his face drenched with water; a pool of his own vomit lay on the floor by the table.

As he heard strange footsteps enter, the monk cried out. "Help me! For the love of God! I know nothing of any spies."

"Quiet!" Padre Gabriel barked. Then with a smile to Domenico, "Allow me to introduce my colleagues."

"I'm not interested."

"Nevertheless, this is Padre Umberto." He pointed to a pale young man who was too flabby for his age, sitting behind a small writing desk, armed with paper and some quills. "He records everything that is said."

"Even the groans," Umberto quipped.

"And this is Padre Pietro." Gabriel indicated a more muscular monk who had rolled up his sleeves, and was responsible for actually inflicting the pain.

"Torturing a blind man dehumanises us all," Domenico said. "This has to stop."

"Brother Bartolo is not a man," Padre Gabriel replied. "He is an enemy of the state."

"No, no, no," Bartolo wailed.

"And an enemy of God."

"It's not true!"

"What if you're wrong?" Domenico locked eyes with Gabriel, but his defiance triggered immediate hostility.

"What about justice for Barberini? What about this wretch's fellow monks who were robbed of their precious sight? Have you no concern for them? Or do you only weep for the perpetrator of those evils?"

"Of course not," Domenico replied. "But —"

"Think of your own sister, very nearly killed by the fanaticism of these heathens. Does she not deserve justice?"

"She would not approve of this barbarity," Domenico looked down at the water-soaked floor. "I know that much."

"People are kept safe because of what we do in this room. Remember that." Padre Gabriel turned his back on Domenico and focused intently on the blind monk.

"Brother Bartolo, one last time: will you tell us the names of everyone who is in your spy ring?"

"I cannot," Bartolo gasped, "because it is not true. There is no spy ring. I cannot reveal what does not exist."

Padre Gabriel gave a disappointed sigh, then signalled to his colleagues.

Umberto put his quill down, and carefully placed a clamp on Bartolo's nose. When that was secure, he stuffed a rag into the struggling man's mouth. "Hush now," Umberto soothed, then nodded to his colleague. "Ready."

Padre Pietro filled a large metal jug from a barrel of water then started pouring it over Bartolo's face, drenching the rag.

Immediately the blind monk started to writhe in panic and terror. The only way he could breathe was through his mouth, but as water ran down the soaking rag and into his throat it felt as if he was drowning. Desperately he tried to swallow the water to clear his mouth, grabbing a tiny gasp of air, only for his throat to fill up again.

Domenico turned away in disgust and saw Padre Gabriel, studying the procedure with intense concentration. There was no pleasure on his face, this was work and Gabriel took it very seriously. He didn't want to kill Bartolo, but he needed to push him to the point of maximum fear in order to get a confession.

"Stop this!" Domenico demanded. "Enough!"

"Do not interrupt me!" Gabriel focused on the drowning Bartolo, waiting for the perfect moment.

Just as the monk's agonised moans reached fever pitch, Padre Gabriel gave a signal, Pietro pulled the jug away and removed the rag from Bartolo's mouth.

The blind monk coughed and retched, gasping desperately. When his lungs snatched some air, he howled with anguish. "Pity me! Have pity!"

Umberto picked up his quill and diligently wrote down the words.

"So," Padre Gabriel began in a quiet voice, "let me ask one more time. Do you confess to being an Ottoman spy?"

"No! It's not true!"

"Ah, but we both know it is."

"No."

"You are part of an advance force, sent to undermine the Papal States from within."

"No!"

"Ottoman ambition knows no bounds."

"Please … I don't know."

"Constantinople has fallen. Belgrade: fallen. Athens: fallen. Ottoman eyes are now on Venice. Or perhaps you are planning another attack on Otranto, then Rome itself. Which is it to be?"

"I don't know," Bartolo sobbed.

"Venice or Otranto?"

"I hate the Ottomans! I hate them!"

"And yet," said Gabriel, allowing himself a triumphant smile, "you were witnessed praying to Allah. You were *seen*."

Silence.

"It appears the blind monk has no answer," Padre Umberto observed, quill poised.

"Indeed," Gabriel nodded. "No answer to the most damning accusation of all."

"Please … have mercy on me," Bartolo sobbed.

"You know, this is all very interesting." Gabriel pulled up a stool and sat next to the monk's face. "Under normal circumstances, the imagination does much of my work for me. When a suspect can see the instruments of torture, his mind races ahead and weakens his spirit. But you have the blessing of blindness. Which means I have to describe more fully what will happen.

"So, unless you decide to tell the truth, we will abandon this messy water procedure, and move to a more radical approach. You will be hung upside down, with your legs apart. Then we will use a two man saw, just like the ones they use in the forests to cut logs in half. Except now, you are the log. We will start to saw your crotch, and we will work all the way through your torso until we reach you neck. And do you know what is particularly ingenious about this procedure? Because you are upside down, the blood flows to your head and prevents you from passing out until the very last moment. Ensuring maximum pain."

Bartolo wept like a desperate child. "No, no, no. I beg you!"

"This is what will happen if you refuse to talk. So let me ask you one final time: are you an Ottoman spy?"

Silence … then slowly Bartolo nodded his head.

"I cannot hear," Gabriel said. "Louder."

"Yes."

Padre Umberto scribbled down the vital confession.

"Very good," Gabriel nodded. "And are you part of a sleeper cell, working to undermine Rome?"

"Yes."

"Is this spy ring behind the atrocities that have terrorised the city? Barberini's crucifixion, the fireball, and most treacherous of all, the blinding of your fellow monks?"

"Yes," Bartolo whispered.

"Excellent." Gabriel patted the monk gently as if he was comforting a dog. "Now you can return to your cell and enjoy a little supper, knowing that when you are executed, you will meet God with a clean conscience."

They undid the straps, dragging Bartolo from the table and out of the cell.

Padre Gabriel turned to Domenico. "You see? We got there in the end. Now, all we need is a witness to corroborate his confession."

"I want no part in this." Domenico strode towards the door, but Padre Gabriel grabbed his arm.

"You do not have a choice. As Capitano della Guardia Apostolica, you need to decide who that witness will be."

"*Vaffanculo*! *Cornuto.* Choose your own victims."

Padre Gabriel tutted. "Such a disappointment that a man in your position has so little stomach for the rigours of intelligence work."

31: TRAUMA

She couldn't hold it. The tighter she gripped, the more slippery it became. Panic fumbled the precious sphere from Cristina's grasp, and it dropped…

She could only watch, powerless, as the astrolabe tumbled slowly through the air and smashed onto the floor. The casing shattered; tiny springs and cogs skittered across the room in all directions. Cristina fell to her knees, desperately trying to contain the fleeing mechanicals, but it was useless. Tiny brass ratchet wheels and regulators escaped through gaps in the floorboards; clutch wheels and pinions ran for freedom into the darkness under the huge bookcases.

As she looked at the chaos, a profound sadness filled Cristina's heart; what had once been a beautiful instrument of learning was now broken beyond repair.

And it was her fault.

She woke with a start, breathing heavily, and looked round the room, trying to get her bearings.

Moonlight fell through the window onto a washstand. She saw the armoires against the far wall and remembered that she was in her own bedroom. But even though she was awake, the heavy sense of dread from the nightmare still lingered.

Cristina rolled onto her side and plumped up the pillow, trying to get comfortable. Through the shutters, she could see a small patch of the night sky and recognised the hind legs of Ursa Major striding across the heavens. But how disappointing that it was still dark; it had taken her hours to get to sleep, and now she would have to lie here until dawn broke.

She closed her eyes and tried to calm her breathing. At least the streets were quiet now; maybe that would make it easier.

But the events of the day dragged heavily on Cristina. Her beautiful project of logical deduction had led to torture and arbitrary detention. She may have solved the crimes, but at what cost? It felt as if she had betrayed everything her life was built on.

Just as she was starting to feel a comforting heaviness creep up her limbs, Cristina heard noises downstairs — the rattle of a lock, footsteps.

She sat up, immediately alert, ears straining.

A door creaked somewhere.

People were whispering.

Had the mob returned to finish their work?

Cristina swung her feet out of bed, her eyes scouring the darkness, searching for a weapon with which to defend herself. Behind the door was a rack that held some of her father's old walking sticks. She tried each one in turn, searching for the heaviest, and settled on a gnarled blackthorn walking cane. It wouldn't be much against an armed attacker, but it would have to do.

She inched the bedroom door back, willing the old hinges to remain silent, then crept onto the landing and peered over the banister.

Two figures were huddled in the gloom, whispering, but there was something familiar about them. "Domenico?"

The spark of a tinderbox lit the wick of an oil lamp in the hallway, and a warm glow ballooned in the darkness. Domenico looked up. "I've brought Isra home."

Cristina dropped the walking cane, ran down the stairs and hugged Isra tightly. "Thank God."

Domenico looked at his sister, taken aback by the display of emotion.

"Are you all right?" Cristina brushed the hair from Isra's face. "Did they hurt you?"

The young woman shook her head but seemed reluctant to talk; perhaps she too felt awkward in Cristina's embrace.

"There were dozens of women being held," Domenico said. "I don't know if they were going to question them, or just wanted to put pressure on their families."

Cristina rubbed her hands on Isra's shoulders to warm her up. "Are you hungry? What can I get you?"

But all Isra's youthful confidence had deserted her, and she just shook her head.

"Don't worry. Get to bed. Sleep now. We'll talk in the morning."

Cristina watched Isra disappear into the kitchens, beyond which were the servants' rooms. As the door clicked shut, she turned to Domenico. "What did they do to her?"

"It's been a difficult day for all of us."

Cristina led her brother to the front sitting room and poured him a glass of wine. "What happened? Tell me."

"We got confessions. That's all I can say."

"Freely given?"

Domenico shook his head. "It was brutal. But so were the crimes they committed." He closed his eyes. "It's over now."

"What did Bartolo confess to?"

"The Ottomans want to destabilise the papacy, undermine faith in the Church. You were right. Barberini, the blind monks, the fireball ... they were deliberately staged to make it look as if God had cursed the Pope."

"And you believe his confession?"

"It bears Bartolo's signature."

"That's not what I asked."

Domenico didn't answer; he knew exactly what his sister was implying.

"A confession given under duress," she insisted, "how can it be trusted?"

"Do not make me re-live it!"

"You know as well as I do, people will say anything to stop the pain."

"Enough, Cristina! Your own evidence pointed to the Ottomans. They are guilty."

"It should have gone to trial. The evidence should have been tested in a court of law. There may have been another explanation."

"A trial would just drag the Vatican into disrepute. The orgies Barberini organised for the Pope, the money-laundering ... it would all have come out. The scandal would have been disastrous. A confession means there is no trial. We have done our job."

Cristina waited until he had finished his wine. "What will happen to them now? To the spies Bartolo named?"

"The lucky ones will be executed. The less fortunate will be sent to the galleys as slaves, and die broken-backed, chained to an oar."

"What about everyone else? All the innocent ones that were rounded up, like Isra?"

"They'll be released tomorrow. Life can go back to normal for them."

Cristina let it rest, but she wondered if Isra would ever feel normal again. Would she ever really trust the authorities, or even her own neighbours who had turned against her with such venom?

Unable to get back to sleep, Cristina washed and dressed, sorted out some breakfast for herself, then left the house. She crossed the Tiber by the Saint Angelo bridge, then walked along the riverbank until she came to the Hospital di Santo Spirito; this was where the burn victims from the fireball were being treated. Cristina spent the rest of the morning talking to the patients while the doctors changed their dressings and applied honey ointments to prevent infection.

The most seriously burned may have survived, but they would be scarred for life. As she looked at the wounds, Cristina reminded herself that this was why the authorities had taken swift, if violent action. These were the real victims.

Perhaps there was some ancient philosophy that could justify unsound methods if the end result was right. But it would be a very strange philosophy, for it would legitimise all manner of evils. Could the ends ever justify the means? She would have to do some more reading on this.

In the meantime, she had to focus on the present. The terrible crimes had been solved.

God was not cursing Rome.

The rebuilding of St Peter's Basilica would go ahead.

The worst was over.

PART TWO

32: MURDER

On the night of 14th June, a timber merchant, Giorgio Schiava, was standing guard on the banks of the Tiber, keeping watch over a shipment of mahogany that had been unloaded that evening. The barge carrying it had been delayed by an awkward customs official at Fiumicino, who'd insisted on counting every piece of wood to make sure none were being smuggled into the city. He'd found nothing out of order, but the delay meant that by the time the barge had arrived in Rome, Schiava's apprentices, who would normally unload the shipment onto carts and haul them to his yard, were fast asleep in bed.

No matter. This had happened before, and rather than get into a fight with his apprentices, Schiava told them to arrive early the following morning and move the wood then. In the meantime, he would make sure no undesirables started sniffing around his cargo.

The merchant had just lit his second pipe of the night when he heard the clatter of hooves on the Ponte Fabricio, a hundred yards upstream. He withdrew into the shadows, eyes straining in the gloom.

Moments later, a rider on a white horse appeared, accompanied by two other men on foot. A body was slung across the saddle.

Working quickly and furtively, the men hauled the body from the horse, then tipped it over the ancient brick parapet and into the Tiber. Falling head-first, it made a surprisingly small splash as it hit the water. The men watched the corpse circle lazily in the currents, then started throwing stones at it until the body sank.

Job done, one of the men slapped the horse on its flanks to chase it off. The riderless horse galloped across the bridge and disappeared into the tangle of dark streets, glad to be away from the murky business of men.

Schiava's first thought was to do nothing. He had spent half his life working shipments up and down the river, and in that time had seen dozens of bodies floating in the Tiber. Why should he bother about one more? Chances were the victim was a criminal of some sort who'd deserved no more than rough justice. Far more important to keep watch over his precious cargo of timber.

Schiava's second thought was to keep a close eye on the river currents, as bodies had a nasty habit of bobbing up again when least expected, and he didn't want trouble landing anywhere near him. Schiava made up his mind to push the corpse firmly away should it drift close, and deny all knowledge.

A few hours earlier, Giovanni Borgia, 2nd Duke of Gandia, and favourite son of the Pope, had been enjoying a lavish dinner in his honour, hosted by his mother. His brothers and closest friends were all there, and everyone parted in good spirits after an evening of the most decadent food and wine.

Giovanni Borgia never arrived home.

Just before dawn, his horse ambled back into the courtyard in front of his house without its rider; one of the stirrups had been cut.

Immediately, the housekeeper sent word to the City Watch, reporting her master missing. A search party of servants was hastily assembled and hurried out onto the streets, retracing the duke's steps, occasionally diverting via upmarket brothels Giovanni was known to frequent.

By the time the search party started scouring the riverbanks, panic was taking hold.

Schiava heard the Angelus bells chime across the city, heralding the arrival of dawn and the start of a new day. His apprentices would be arriving soon.

Yet the first voices he heard were unfamiliar. They were calling out, "Giovanni! Master! Can you hear us? Giovanni, my lord!"

Schiava's mind flashed back to the body being dumped off the bridge. Maybe the victim was more important than he'd first thought. Had he made a mistake by deliberately turning the other cheek?

Whilst keeping up the pretence of knowing nothing, Schiava offered to help the servants, and subtly guided the search party to where he had last seen the body.

Not long after, they saw a gloved hand sticking out of the water, caught up on some branches at the turn of the river.

They waded through the mud and into the murky water, disentangled the corpse, and finally managed to haul Giovanni Borgia onto the riverbank.

His throat had been slit. There were nine stab wounds across his neck, head, legs and torso. He was fully clothed in one of his finest velvet doublets with pearl buttons. A purse containing 30 ducats was still attached to his belt. This was clearly not a robbery.

While the duke's servants were overwhelmed with shock and grief, Schiava's only thought was to silently reprimand himself. If he'd acted quicker and not been so cynical, he could have retrieved the body, pocketed the 30 ducats, then reported the crime, and no-one would have been any the wiser. They may even have given him a reward for finding the tragically stricken duke.

Schiava glanced up to the heavens and offered a silent prayer, apologising for his lack of Christian compassion. But God had seen into the merchant's heart and dealt out swift justice; the profit from selling his entire load of timber would be less than the reward he could have earned for reporting the murder.

Such was the price of sin.

33: SUSPECTS

"There must be easier things to steal!" Domenico was perched on the roof of San Teodoro church, overlooking the ancient Palatine ruins.

"Have you found the missing section?" Gilo called up from the safety of the courtyard.

"Not yet!" Domenico continued picking his way across the clay tiles.

Nearly a thousand years old, San Teodoro had recently been renovated, and bronze guttering had been installed around the edges of the octagonal roof. Bronze drainpipes dropped down at regular intervals to channel the rain away, but over the last few months these had become targets for thieves. Not only was the metal easy to melt down and sell, but the theft often went unnoticed until a thunderstorm sent water splashing down the church walls, by which time the culprits were long gone.

On the far side of the drum-like building, Domenico came across the sawn remains of the guttering; this time, thieves had removed a huge arc as well as the downpipe. He spent a few minutes searching for any clues that may have been left behind, but there was nothing. This gang knew exactly what they were doing; more than likely the bronze had already been spirited away through a series of middlemen, lining everyone's pockets as it went. That was how Rome's vast black economy worked.

"Don't people care about their immortal souls?" Domenico wondered as he scrambled down the stepped roofs of the side chapels and landed back in the courtyard.

"I think they care more about their grumbling bellies," Gilo replied.

"This wasn't the work of the poor. This was a professional gang." Domenico looked up at the building. "The poor pick pockets. And they would never dare steal from the Church."

"Well, we did our job." Gilo had turned stoicism into an art. "We inspected the crime scene. All we can do is make our report."

Domenico nodded wearily. "The Church repairs something, and a few months later it just gets stolen again. I don't know what the solution is."

"Maybe the Church should stop thinking of it as theft, and start thinking of it as charity," Gilo ventured.

"Right," Domenico laughed. "Alms go to those who dare."

Suddenly, urgent footsteps were hurrying towards them. They turned and saw a pale and shaken Tenente Tomasso hurtle into the courtyard. "Sir! Come quickly!"

"What's happened?"

"The Pope's son! Murdered!"

"What?"

"His favourite son! Giovanni Borgia!"

Domenico shook his head. This couldn't be true. Who would dare raise a murderous hand against the Pope's own family? "You must be mistaken, Tenente."

"Please, sir! Come *now*!"

Tomasso grabbed Domenico's arm, forcing him to follow, and the three of them ran through the narrow streets down to the Tiber, just south of the Ponte Fabricio. With every step, Domenico felt a rising dread; wars had been started over crimes such as this, and the one thing Domenico never wanted to witness again was war.

Already, word had spread, and a ghoulish crowd was starting to gather on the riverbank. Tenente Tomasso pushed the bystanders aside, clearing a path for Domenico and Gilo to get down to the water's edge, where a body lay in the stinking mud. The militia stood silently, guarding the corpse.

Memories overwhelmed Domenico.

Hauling drowned comrades from the waters of the Mediterranean. Their ghastly pallor. Eyes open, always open, staring at you. As if shaming the living for having survived.

Shaming you. Blaming you.

Concentrate!

Domenico drew a deep breath.

Focus. Follow the protocols.

He crouched down to examine the body. Its fingers were wrinkled, and bloating had already started, so the man had clearly been in the water for some hours.

And the wounds … the savagery of the wounds.

Methodically, Gilo counted each one. "Nine stab wounds, sir. And the throat cut."

"This wasn't just murder. It was a crime of hate," Domenico said.

"I'm afraid it is definitely Giovanni Borgia," Gilo confirmed. "No mistake."

Domenico turned to Tomasso. "Has anyone told the Holy Father?"

"No-one dared, sir. We called you first."

"We need to tell him before the rumours do." Domenico glanced over to the gathering crowd. "Move them back, Tenente. Right back. To the other side of the path."

Tomasso jumped into action, glad to be able to do something to feel less helpless.

"Who would dare commit such a crime, Gilo?"

Gilo scratched his stubbly chin. "This Borgia was famous for being dissolute, sir."

"Aren't they all?"

"But this one in particular. The Duke of Gandia had many enemies."

"I knew he had fallen out with the Orsini family. But who else?"

"Well, he was having an affair with his brother's wife, for starters."

"What?"

"A secret affair, of course. But everyone knew."

"I didn't." Domenico looked at the brutalised body. "But that would explain the savagery of the wounds."

"And apparently he had a terrible row with Ascanio Sforza just a few days ago."

"Over money?"

"Money. Mistresses. Corruption. It's usually one of them. Giovanni Borgia was trouble."

"How do you tell a father the worst possible news he could ever hear? Let alone the Holy Father?"

"Well, I'm glad it's not me in charge, sir," Gilo commiserated.

"Unless you fancy volunteering for the job?"

"Not today, sir. But thank you for the offer." Keen to move on, Gilo crouched next to the corpse. "What's that?" He pointed to a lump under Giovanni's doublet. "Just above his heart?"

"Take a look."

Cautiously, Gilo popped open four pearl buttons and peeled back the bloodied doublet, to reveal a small glass phial with a cork stopper. It reminded him of the flasks in alchemists' laboratories, except inside this one was a curl of paper with writing on it.

Domenico took the phial, removed the cork and pulled out the strip of paper. On one side were written the words, *You will never catch me.* On the other, *You torture the innocent, but vengeance is mine.*

"What does it mean?" Gilo asked.

Domenico couldn't answer, because nausea was overwhelming him. His body already knew what his mind was struggling to accept: the truth was unravelling.

"What if the killer is still out there?" he whispered. "The killer we've been chasing these past months?"

"I don't understand, sir."

"Barberini. The blinded monks. The fireball."

"No, no, sir." Gilo was adamant. "This murder is nothing to do with the other crimes."

"What if he's taunting us?"

"Bartolo is in prison."

"But what if we've caught the wrong man?"

"He confessed, sir!"

"Bartolo confessed when he could bear the pain no longer," Domenico said impatiently. "Don't you see?"

"We have evidence against him. Your own sister built the case."

"What about *this* evidence?" Domenico brandished the fragment of paper they'd pulled from the body. "*You will never catch me. You torture the innocent, but vengeance is mine.* He's telling us that we have imprisoned the wrong people. That everyone we rounded up was innocent. There was no Ottoman spy ring."

"You cannot know that." Gilo was desperate to cling to what they'd achieved.

But Domenico knew in his bones that they were standing in the middle of a huge miscarriage of justice. "Cristina was right; the evidence against Bartolo was never tested in court. The real killer is still at large." The shame Domenico felt was like a physical pain. All that suffering and cruelty had been for nothing. "Mark my words, Gilo, the killings are going to continue."

"Come on, sir. You don't always have to dwell on the dark side of things."

Domenico looked at his deputy in disbelief. "What exactly is there to be optimistic about, Gilo? Aristocrats murdered, monks blinded, worshippers burnt to death as they prayed, the wrong people arrested and tortured; we have no idea who committed these crimes, no idea! And now they've murdered the Holy Father's dearest son." He pointed to the wet, waxy corpse. "Yesterday, the Duke of Gandia was one of the most powerful men in Rome. Now look at him. And tomorrow … tomorrow, it may be the Pope himself who is the target of this evil."

34: GRIEF

Pope Alexander VI crumpled to the floor as if the muscles in his legs had been severed. He didn't make a sound; he didn't cry out in pain or grief. He just crumpled.

Instinctively Domenico moved forward to help the man, but Cardinale Riario brandished a forbidding hand. "You do not touch the Holy Father unless he commands it."

"But he needs help."

"Not from you."

Of the three cardinals present, only Riario had the authority to move. Slowly he circled the grieving pontiff, then knelt next to him. "Allow me to help Your Holiness."

The Pope reached out and grasped Riario's hand, but the simple human touch unleashed his grief. Alexander wailed with a pain and sorrow that was so primal, it made Domenico shiver.

"My son. My son. My son. My beloved son." Tears ran down his contorted face; his body rocked back and forth as it tried to expel the anguish. "All is darkness now … all is darkness."

It was terrible to witness. No father deserved this, not even a Borgia.

Gently, Cardinale Riario helped the Pope into a chair. "Shall I dismiss everyone, Holy Father?"

"No."

"You should rest."

"Who did this? I want to know who is responsible! He must be punished without mercy."

"Very good." Riario took a step back, then pointedly turned to Domenico. "*Now* you may speak."

Domenico hesitated. He knew that if he got this wrong, he wouldn't last the day. "Your Holiness, the people who murdered your son … we believe they may be the same ones who murdered Barberini and blinded the monks."

Alexander blinked, struggling to understand. "But the Ottoman spies, Bartolo … they are in prison."

"It appears they might not be guilty after all. This was found on your son's body." He handed the small piece of paper to Riario, who read it, then passed it to the Pope.

"This is very disappointing," Riario said coldly.

"It is, Your Eminence."

"I thought you had evidence to prove their guilt?"

"So did we."

"And they confessed," the Pope added. "They confessed!"

"Not to us. They confessed to your own, personal inquisitors, Holy Father."

A dreadful calm descended as all eyes burned into Domenico.

"How dare you insinuate —"

"I am just trying to explain —"

"Silence!" Riario's voice echoed around the room. Everyone tensed.

Alexander took a silk handkerchief from the pocket of his robe and slowly dried his eyes. As he regained his composure, a terrible resolve settled over him. "If my inquisitors found the Ottoman spies guilty, then they must be guilty."

The pressure of the truth would not allow Domenico to remain silent. "Forgive me, Holy Father, but they were all in prison when your son was murdered."

"Then there must be more out there. Ones you have missed. Through carelessness, or negligence."

"The note implies none of these crimes had anything to do with the Ottomans, Holy Father."

"Let me repeat: if my inquisitors found the Ottoman spies guilty, then they must be guilty."

"Yet there are serious doubts about the integrity of those confessions."

"Doubts from who?" Riario said with contempt. "You?"

"At the very least, those men deserve a trial."

"It is not for you to instruct the Holy Father."

"No, your Eminence. I just —"

"Do you have children?" Alexander interrupted.

"No."

"Then you cannot possibly understand what it means to hear the words, 'Your son is dead.'"

Domenico looked at the Pope; the calmness of his words belied the haunted, broken expression on the man's face. "My heart weeps for you, Holy Father."

"That makes no difference to the pain I feel. My heart can only heal if there is justice."

"We will pursue every line of inquiry, Your Holiness. All the men at my disposal will be assigned to catching your son's killers. You have my word."

"Not enough," Alexander said. "The Ottoman spies now in jail … execute them all."

No-one dared utter a sound.

The Pope looked around the room, spoiling for a fight. "I spoke. Does no-one acknowledge the Pope when he speaks?"

Riario nodded. "If that is your wish, Holy Father."

"My wish is to kill them all. Every last one. Barberini's family want justice for his brutal murder. Honour demands it. The victims who were consumed by fire as they worshipped, need justice. And *I* am demanding justice. Someone must pay for my loss."

"Very well, Your Holiness."

"My wish is to see the skies above Rome black with smoke from bonfires as they consume these heathen monsters. Is that clear? I want the whole of Rome to see the heretics punished for what they have done to us. Innocent people have suffered and died. Justice demands retribution."

"It will be done, Holy Father." Cardinale Riario bowed low in utter obedience. What did it matter to him if the Pope was making a terrible mistake? It would only hasten the day of Riario's own accession.

It seemed to Domenico that everyone in the room had lost sight of what really mattered: the truth of the threat they were facing. "Executing the Ottomans will not put an end to the killings, Holy Father." He tried to say it as humbly as possible, but Alexander glared at him.

"Leave. And obey."

"But your own life may be at risk, Holy Father."

"I am God's voice on Earth. I am infallible. My words are infallible. Do you understand?"

"Yes."

"And I, Pope Alexander VI, Bishop of Rome and leader of the Papal States, declare that those who confessed are guilty. The only person in this room who is wrong, is *you*."

It was the most dangerous moment of Domenico's life. Not the wars or the sieges, not the duels or the diseases; this was the moment he had to survive.

The Pope could make as many declarations as he wanted; the murderer was still out there, and getting closer. But Domenico could not catch a killer if he himself was languishing in jail.

And he knew that if he answered back, he would lose everything.

So Domenico said nothing.

35: RECOIL

"Get out of my way!"

"You have to calm down, Cristina."

"Don't tell me what to do!"

"I'm your brother! Listen to me!"

"When you say something intelligent, I'll listen!" Cristina grabbed Domenico by the arms and tried to bundle him out of the way. "Let me leave!"

"You'll achieve nothing, Cristina!"

"So you're going to imprison me in my own house?"

"This is as much my house as yours."

"Let me go!" She pushed him off and lunged for the front doors, but he grabbed her cloak and pulled her back. "You'll just make everything worse!"

"I have to try."

"You think you can walk into the Vatican, bang on the Pope's door and demand the release of prisoners? You're deluded!"

"Don't ever call me that!" Cristina spun round and started pummelling her brother's chest. "Never!"

He grabbed her arms to stop the attack, but she retaliated by kicking his shins, and they ended up in a messy brawl, wrestling and clawing at each other as if they were children again. Cristina jerked herself backwards to pull Domenico off balance. As he stumbled, he reached out to grab the console table and sent the oil lamp crashing to the floor.

The shock of shattering glass made them freeze. Breathless, they looked down at the sad remains of the lamp and the slick of oil creeping across the flagstones. They heard footsteps thundering towards them; a door was flung open and Isra rushed into the hall. She looked at the broken glass, then at Cristina and Domenico with their red faces. "What on earth is happening?"

"Nothing," Domenico said with a guilty shrug.

"It's all right, Isra." Cristina straightened her clothes. "I was just leaving."

"I don't think you were," Domenico said pointedly.

"Someone has to stop the miscarriage of justice."

Isra looked at the smashed lamp. "I'll fetch a brush."

"Leave it. I'll clean it up when I get back." Cristina turned to go, but Domenico held her arm firmly.

Refusing to get drawn into the fight, Isra disappeared into the kitchen. But the hiatus had broken the momentum, and neither sibling wanted to start again.

"Please, don't do anything rash." Domenico was trying to sound conciliatory. "That's all I'm asking."

"People were tortured because of me. And I was wrong. I missed something. Some vital piece of evidence."

"It's not your fault."

"Innocent people will be executed!"

"The sentences won't be carried out just yet."

"They shouldn't be carried out at all."

"I've said I need more time for questioning."

"Domenico, they need to be set free."

"That won't happen, and you know it."

Cristina crouched down and started picking up the broken glass.

"The Pope won't change his mind unless we find out who really killed his son. I can delay the executions for a week. Two at the most. If you help me, Cristina, maybe we can still see justice done."

"Don't ask me to get involved again."

"You know these crimes better than anyone. They're all linked; we just have to find out how."

"I should never have agreed to help in the first place." She put the largest shards of glass on the table then carefully started on the smaller pieces.

"You mustn't blame yourself."

"My logic put the wrong people in prison."

"You tried your best."

"When you're wrong in a book, you just tear out the page and start again. People's lives aren't so simple."

"You didn't do anything from malice. You were simply trying to get to the truth."

Cristina winced as some glass embedded itself into her palm, immediately drawing blood. She put her hand to her mouth, sucking the wound clean.

"Here." Domenico took a handkerchief from his pocket and went to tie it round his sister's hand, but she pulled back. "Come on," Domenico said gently. "Don't be like that." He took her hand and gently wound the handkerchief around it like a bandage.

"Is Isra safe?" Cristina asked. "Will they round up ordinary people again?"

"No. They only want the people named in the confessions."

"She's changed. Since they arrested her, Isra's been very quiet."

"I'm not surprised. There are no pleasant jails in Rome." He tied the handkerchief with a knot. "Now, try to keep it dry for the rest of the day."

"It's like she doesn't trust me anymore. Doesn't trust anyone."

"You mustn't dwell on that."

"I'm not like you, Domenico. I can't just bury things I don't like. I have to make sense of them."

"Not everything in the world makes sense."

"But it should," Cristina said firmly. "It should."

After Domenico left, Isra crouched next to Cristina and together the two women swept up the last pieces of glass.

"Mistress, when will it be safe for the baker?" Isra asked.

Baker Yusuf. His family had been so quiet on the top floor, self-contained and anxious not to be a burden, that Cristina had forgotten all about them. "Perhaps they should stay another day or two. Just to be sure."

"That's good," Isra nodded. "All they want is to go home and open up the bakery."

When the oil stain had been mopped away, Cristina returned to the kitchen with Isra, and together they prepared a large tray to take up to the top floor.

As they carried the food into the room where the family were sheltering, Cristina was amazed by how ingeniously Baker Yusuf had transformed this space into a temporary home. The lines of washing crisscrossing the room had been used to divide the space into different areas, giving the parents some privacy and the children their own areas to play. A pulley had been rigged from the window to hoist water up from the courtyard, and pots of dried food had been neatly stacked; two metal racks had repurposed the fireplace for cooking.

Cristina took in every detail, wondering how these people, whose lives were so buffeted by forces beyond their control, could find such resilience.

36: CONFESSION

How wonderful it was to be twelve again.

All the worries of the adult world dissolved, and now Cristina felt only the thrill of living in the moment. She was bouncing her baby brother on her knee, delighting in his burbling chuckles.

They both knew what was coming — his favourite game: peekaboo.

"Where's Cristina gone? Where is she?"

A chortle of expectation as Aldo stared at the hands that covered her face.

"She's gone … she's gone…"

A peek through her fingers.

A giggle.

"Here I am!!"

Howls of delight.

And the more Aldo laughed, the more it made Cristina laugh. He was such a happy baby, so enthralled by the sights and sounds that whirled around him. They could have played all afternoon, but when Cristina saw him yawn, she knew it was time for his nap. This afternoon, she had been left as the baby's guardian, and she was determined that when her parents returned from the lawyers in town, they would find Aldo rested and well-fed. Everything would be perfect.

She warmed some milk on the kitchen range, carefully tested it with her elbow until it was just the right temperature, then decanted it into a bottle and sat by the window to feed the baby.

Then over her shoulder, she rubbed his back, waited for the burp, and gave Aldo one last snuggly kiss before laying him in the crib —

Her memory froze.

It always froze at that moment.

Even in her sleep, Cristina couldn't get past it.

Were they there? The tiny spots of blood on the cotton sheets?

Did she miss them?

Did she see them and ignore them?

Or did she imagine that? Were the sheets really pristine? Was she blameless?

Remember…

If only she could remember the truth of that moment.

But it was burnt out by the horrified grief that tore through the house when her parents returned…

Her mother running from room to room like a haunted soul, cloak billowing, howls of anguish as sharp as a knife on glass.

Her father wrapping his arms around Cristina, trying to break the numbing spell of shock.

Yet for years after, when her parents consoled her, was there a flicker of blame in their eyes? Did she imagine it? Did they ever really believe her, or forgive her?

The baby had been so well, so happy and strong. There was no reason for Aldo to suddenly die. No reason.

So there was always doubt.

Those tiny spots of blood on the sheets — if only someone had noticed them, there might have been time to do something.

Were they already there when she put Aldo down?

Did she miss them?

Cristina woke abruptly.

She could feel sweat on the back of her neck, hear her own rapid breathing.

She sat up, an adult again.

She was in her library, fully clothed, sitting on the chaise longue. But it didn't make any difference where she tried to sleep if she was forever locked in the circle of her own guilt. How could she stay sane if there was no peace when she closed her eyes?

She got up briskly; there was only one person who would understand the self-doubt that was wreaking such havoc in her mind.

As she entered the cloisters around the cobbled courtyard of Sapienza University, Cristina paused to soak in the atmosphere. This place never lost its magic for her. While some students hurried across the quad, heads low, deep in thought, others stood in the shade of the colonnade, joking and debating.

Did any of these young men appreciate how fortunate they were? What a gift it was to have the door to learning permanently open for you.

The future has passed here. That was the university's motto. But it wasn't true, not unless the future excluded women, something Cristina refused to accept.

Professor De Luca was pleased by the surprise visit, and while he hauled piles of books from chairs to make space for her to sit, Cristina moved her rook across the chessboard, counterattacking rather than defending against his bishop's aggression.

De Luca looked at the pieces. "Hm. You're normally more cautious." He went to move his knight, but suspecting a trap, decided to leave it until later.

Cristina watched him study the board. "Do you ever find yourself envying the chess pieces, Professor?"

"A world full of men who do nothing but fight? Rulers who define their entire existence by conquest? No, thank you. I'm happier as an academic."

"You're lucky to be sheltered by the walls of the university."

De Luca knew Cristina well enough to see that something was wrong. "The real world can be a messy and painful place." He held up a decanter. "Which is why they invented sherry."

"Perfect. Thank you."

He poured two glasses and sat opposite her.

"I wonder, Professor, will I ever be able to escape from the past?"

"You've been having the dreams again?"

"I try so hard, but … they're never far away."

"Blaming yourself for the madness of the world will only make you mad as well."

"I took a vow that summer, when I was twelve. Before God, kneeling in front of His altar, I swore that I would never succumb to careless thinking again. My family paid a terrible price, but through that I learnt that the truth of the world is revealed through tiny details that *don't* fit. Never ignore details. Those are what you need to study."

"And that is why you are such a brilliant scholar, Cristina. You are tireless and pedantic."

"So why do I keep making mistakes?"

"I'm afraid that's what it means to be human." De Luca sipped his sherry.

"Domenico was relying on me for this investigation. He trusted me. But somehow I missed a crucial piece of evidence, and now innocent people will die."

"You did not condemn them, Cristina. That was not your decision."

"I found enough evidence to implicate them, but not enough to get to the truth." She put her head in her hands. "Why am I such a failure?"

"Cristina, don't do this to yourself." Gently, Professor De Luca reached out and touched her hand. "Show me your face."

Cristina wiped her eyes and reluctantly did as she was asked.

"What you have done is nothing short of miraculous. You took emotional trauma and turned it into a formidable talent. I wish my students had even half your determination."

"But what has it achieved? Except miscarriages of justice."

"Reason is the only thing we have, Cristina. The only thing. It is the divine within us, and if we turn our backs on it, we are damned. If something has been missed in your investigation, then you must redouble your efforts, not abandon the project. Search harder, experiment with different patterns of possibility, rebuild your arguments from a different premise. But please, never give up on reason. Never."

37: SPECTACLE

It was unusual for the Vatican barracks to feel so sombre. Normally, they were full of chat as the men swapped boastful stories of lovers, gambling and excessive drinking.

Not today.

Because today, the inquisitor Padre Gabriel was briefing Domenico, Deputato Gilo and Tenente Tomasso about the mechanics of the impending executions. All the other soldiers had been told to leave the mess rooms.

"The first thing to get right is the terminology," Padre Gabriel said in a matter-of-fact way. "Never say 'burning at the stake'. It is too crude and explicit. We prefer the term 'immolation', which has more of a theological ring to it."

"Does that make it any less painful?" Tomasso asked.

"Pain is the whole point." Padre Gabriel refused to be thrown by the sardonic question. "The theatre of public execution is all about turning pain into fear, and fear into obedience. Now, the heretics will feel the most intense agony at the start of the process, so it is in those first few minutes when we hope to hear their howls of repentance. This is when the effect on the crowd is most profound." Padre Gabriel unfurled a map of the city on which he had marked seven crosses. "All the executions will take place here, in the Piazza del Popolo. That way, anyone entering or leaving Rome by the western gate will have to walk past them."

"How many will be done each day?" Domenico asked, secretly wondering how long this could all be delayed.

"Oh, no. You misunderstand. The heretics will be executed at the same time. All seven of them."

"God help us," Domenico muttered.

"It'll look as if the whole piazza is on fire," Gilo said.

"Which is precisely the point." Padre Gabriel was proud of his meticulous planning. "The choreography of the executions is key. The crowds will be able to move between the different bonfires, watching each heretic burn. It will feel to the onlookers as if they are surrounded by God's justice. Wherever they look, Holy Fires will be raging."

"But the heat and smoke … it's not safe," Domenico objected. "The crowds will be impossible to control. They'll panic."

"On the contrary," Gabriel insisted. "The crowds will be like frightened lambs. Trust me, I have much experience of this."

"In Spain, maybe. But this is Rome."

"Instilling fear is the whole point of the exercise. These heathens could be quietly executed in a prison yard, but where is the public benefit in that? The lesson that needs to be driven home, again and again, is that anyone who raises a finger against the Pope and his subjects will suffer the agonies of immolation."

Everyone stared at the map in grim silence, trying to imagine the horrors hiding behind each innocent-looking cross.

"How long will it go on?" Tomasso asked.

"An excellent question. And a surprisingly complex answer. Some of the heretics will die quickly, of shock. Some will last until they suffocate in the smoke. We hope at least three of them will survive the early stages and remain alive while flames actually engulf them."

"That's impossible," Domenico said. "No-one could survive that."

"You'd be surprised. Once the nerves are burnt, the skin no longer feels pain, and the sinner can watch his own body be consumed by fire. It's an extraordinary sight. The fat leaking from their bodies sustains the bonfire, and their clothes act like a wick. I have known people to survive for an hour. And even after they are dead and their souls have gone to Hell, their bodies can yet burn for another seven hours. The aroma of burning flesh will hang over this city all night, reminding people of their duty to God."

Suddenly, the door swung open and Cristina entered. "Domenico, we have to talk."

Padre Gabriel spun round furiously. "Get out, woman!"

She stopped in her tracks, trying to work out what was being agreed in this furtive meeting. "I'm not here to see you."

"Out!"

"It's all right." Domenico hurried over to Cristina. "She's my sister."

"She has no business being here!" Gabriel insisted. "A female has no business being anywhere near this building."

"I apologise, Padre Gabriel." Domenico hastily ushered Cristina outside and closed the doors behind him.

"What are you planning in there?" Cristina let Domenico hustle her into the courtyard, but she was not going to be silenced. "Was it the executions?"

"Cristina, why are you here?" Domenico asked impatiently.

"You can't let this happen!"

"Do you want me to burn next to them? Is that what you want?"

"No. Of course not."

"Then why are you here?"

"I've decided I will help with the investigation."

"You will?" It was the first piece of good news Domenico had heard all day.

"Let's bring these criminals to justice, and bring sanity back to Rome."

"Thank you, Cristina." He tried to hug his sister, but she quickly disentangled herself.

"Promise me you will spare the people who have been wrongly accused."

"You ask the impossible."

"They are innocent, Domenico! And you know it."

"Then their souls will find peace."

Cristina was stunned. "That's it? That's all you can say?"

"I'm afraid —"

"Never mind their souls, what about their wives and children?"

"This is out of our hands now. Please, don't make it harder than it already is."

Cristina could see how torn her brother was, a good man hopelessly cornered. "Then at least let me talk to them first."

"Why?"

"I need to question them."

"Are you going to make trouble, Cristina? Because —"

"Do you want to find the real murderers, or not? Your choice."

38: DEATH ROW

It was so dark in the cavernous undercroft, Cristina's eyes struggled to adjust. There was no natural light down here, just a few flame torches flickering in the gloom, casting a meagre glow across the rows of prisoners' cages.

She had to wait by a secure gate at the top of some stone steps while a guard searched her. In truth, Cristina was grateful for the delay as it gave time for her nose to get accustomed to the foul smell.

"What's in this?" The guard held up Cristina's goatskin, removed the cork and sniffed the contents.

"Water. To help loosen their tongues," she replied.

"*You* drink some." The guard thrust the skin at her.

"It's not for me. It's for the prisoners."

"How do I know it's not poisoned?"

"Why would I do that? What would be the point?" Cristina didn't even try to hide her irritation. "I want to talk to them."

"Maybe you want to help them cheat the bonfires of justice. Now drink."

Cristina slugged a large mouthful of water from the skin and wiped her lips. "See? Still here."

Unimpressed, the guard opened the gate and beckoned for her to descend the steps to the vault floor. "Mind you don't slip on any shit. They toss it around down there." He slammed the gate shut behind her.

Cristina picked her way down the steps, her hands feeling their way along the slime-damp walls. By the time she reached the bottom step, her eyes had adjusted enough to make out a long row of iron cages stretching the entire length of the vaults; inside each was a bloodied, broken prisoner, lying in filthy straw.

She stopped at the first cage and recognised Bartolo by what was left of his monk's habit, now reduced to tatters that clung to his broken body.

"Can you hear me?"

No response, just a rasping sound as if each breath inflicted pain.

"Brother Bartolo, I need to talk to you. I'm trying to help."

She saw him slowly, agonisingly turn his head towards her. He peered at her through swollen, bloodshot eyes. His lips quivered.

"I'm trying to get a stay of execution, pending fresh evidence. But I need to ask you some questions. Can you speak?"

She watched his lips move; with enormous effort he drew a breath and whispered, "*Fila de putana*." Then he turned his head away.

End of conversation.

"As you wish." Clinging to the cages, Cristina made her way deeper into the undercroft. Somewhere close by she could hear the agitated sound of rats, furtively scurrying back and forth across the stone floor; she braced herself, ready to kick away anything that dared latch itself onto her riding boots.

As she came to the next cage, Cristina saw a young man crumpled on the floor; black bruises covered his shoulders, and his arms hung at a strange angle where they had been pulled from their sockets. The man didn't even look up, because the slightest movement would send pain shooting through his limbs; it was less painful to let the lice crawl over his body than to raise a finger and brush them off. He didn't look as if he would appreciate being questioned.

In the next cage, Cristina saw an old woman, eyes closed, rocking back and forth as if in a trance, her lips muttering prayers in Arabic. From what Cristina could make out, it was the same verse, over and over again. Her silver hair was covered in matted blood from where she had been beaten.

"No-one will talk to you," a man's voice declared from the darkness. "You're wasting your time."

Cristina spun round, trying to make out who had spoken.

"Down here. Beyond the torch."

The voice sounded stoical rather than angry. Cristina went deeper into the undercroft until she came to a man in his late thirties, crouching on the floor of a corner cage. A black woman of a similar age was in the adjacent cell; they had managed to entwine their fingers through the bars.

"Is that water?" the man asked.

Cristina pushed the goatskin into the cage, but rather than drink, the man held it up for the woman to drink first.

"I'm trying to help," Cristina said quietly.

"They still won't talk," the man replied. "Either they're in too much pain, or they're frightened you're another trick from the Inquisition."

"I'm not. I swear."

"Why should they believe you? They have been broken. Body and spirit."

Cristina looked around at the shadowy figures languishing in their fetid cages. This was the insanity of torturing confessions from people; it had nothing to do with the truth.

When the woman had finished drinking, the man took the goatskin and drank deeply himself before handing it back.

"My name is Cristina Falchoni. I was investigating the murders before..." Her voice trailed off as she remembered the part she had played in the fate of these people. "I have some knowledge of the crimes."

"I am Halil. This is my wife, Nubia."

"You're married?"

"They arrested us together."

"I'm so sorry."

"The monk named us, but in truth we have never met him. Not that we remember."

"Yet you confessed?"

"To spare each other. It was the only way." He held up his arms to show Cristina the violent bruising and deep cuts. "They would not have stopped. Now we must look to Allah to help us."

Cristina felt sick with shame. "Rome should not have turned on you like this."

"We loved this city," Nubia said, her voice hoarse from hours of crying. "We never hid who we were. We built our lives here, respected the laws. And all for what? To be treated like vermin?"

Halil squeezed his wife's hand gently, trying to comfort her.

Cristina had no answers for Nubia. She pushed the goatskin back through the bars for them to take another drink.

"Has anyone been to see you? Family? Children?"

Nubia shook her head. "We only have each other, mercifully. Or our children would have been orphaned by your city."

"When did you settle in Rome?"

"Fifteen years ago," Halil replied. "I was a soldier in the Ottoman army. The Venetians captured me when they invaded Albania. I served five years as a galley slave, chained to the oars."

Cristina glanced at his hands. The twisted knuckles and calluses that would last a lifetime showed that he was telling the truth.

"By some miracle, I survived," Halil continued. "Eventually the Venetians set me free, and I came south to Rome. Here I met Nubia." He looked at his wife tenderly.

"Were you enslaved as well?" Cristina asked Nubia.

"By the Ottomans. I was captured in Alexandria. They made me a servant to their army. It was my job to make and serve coffee to the generals."

"I've heard of coffee, but never seen any."

"It is from Ethiopia. It is the taste of Africa." Nubia smiled as she remembered a happier time.

"Perhaps one day I will find some."

"It will come to Europe, eventually. Once you have tasted it, nothing will ever be the same. And the smell…" Nubia drew a deep breath.

"When the Christian armies liberated Otranto, they set Nubia free," Halil explained. "She came north, and we met here, in Rome."

"Between the two of you, that's quite a love story."

"Fate brought us together. Many times our lives have been in peril, but we have always put our trust in Allah."

"And now we have to trust him again," Nubia said.

Cristina looked from one to the other, astonished at their calm acceptance of such a terrible injustice. "Well, I am determined to get you out of here," she said.

"Do not taunt us," Nubia warned. "We are reconciled to death."

"Wouldn't you rather live?"

"Is that still possible?" Nubia looked at Cristina with searching dark eyes.

"I want to prove your innocence," Cristina replied, "but I need evidence. Do you have any knowledge of who has been attacking Rome with these strange crimes?"

"No."

"Is there an Ottoman spy ring?"

"If there is, they would not commit these crimes that have spread such terror," Halil said. "It would make no sense. Being a spy is about staying out of sight, about secretly gathering information. It is not about murdering and blinding people, or setting fire to churches. What sense would it make to provoke the anger of the authorities and bring down their wrath?"

"Perhaps if they wanted to frighten the Pope, to stop him building a new cathedral."

"Why would the Ottomans care what the Pope builds? If he wants to bankrupt Rome with a grand basilica, let him."

"This is nothing to do with us." Nubia shook her head solemnly. "We have both been slaves; we value our freedom more than anything. We would never raise a finger against a city that has given us refuge."

"What about Brother Bartolo?" Cristina asked. "Clearly he was not what he appeared."

"We have never heard of the man. No-one in these cages even knew he existed until they were arrested," Halil said.

"There are not many followers of Allah in Rome," Nubia explained. "We are a small community, quietly getting by. Looking out for each other. Muslims here are just as the Christians used to be in ancient Rome, before Constantine converted."

"Someone had to get Bartolo a Quran," Halil added, "teach him the Hadith, show him our customs. But no-one knew of him. No-one. Don't you think that is strange?"

Cristina could feel the wheels in her mind clicking round, trying to find a new order that would explain the discrepancies.

Nubia reached her hand through the cage and gently touched Cristina. "Can you really set us free?"

Cristina hesitated. How could she say yes, when she knew how impossible that seemed? But how could she turn her back on these good people?

"Do not promise what you cannot deliver," Nubia warned. "It is too painful to resurrect hope, only to have it snatched away again."

"All I can promise is that I will do everything I can to uncover the truth," Cristina replied. "But whether the truth will be enough to set you free … that I no longer know."

39: CLEMENCY

The city morgue was a strange place to have a picnic, but Cristina was now convinced there was a vital clue she had missed, and was determined to stay amongst the corpses until she had made a breakthrough. After a brief diversion via her house to pick up some cold meats and a small bottle of wine, she hurried towards the icehouse.

With every footstep, her mind locked deeper into its obsessive rhythm, circling the problem like a hawk.

What had she overlooked?

Which clue was hiding in plain sight?

Where were the 'blood spots' in this mystery?

If her baby brother's sudden death all those years before was to have any real meaning, it had to be now, with her absolute refusal to let the smallest detail escape unnoticed.

Two jovial carpenters were busy hanging a new door at the main entrance of the morgue. At first they had tried to salvage the old one, but it would have involved using so many iron straps that it would have made the door impractically heavy. Cristina showed her warrant letters to the guard who had been stationed here ever since the mob's attack, then entered the calm of ice and death.

She spread her picnic out on one of the tables so that she could pick at it as she worked, then carefully removed all the ice blocks that had been packed around the body they had recovered from beneath the altar at Santa Maria della Pace. Cristina pulled back the shroud — the body had not been touched since the autopsy, and the partial dissection still revealed the man's horribly burnt lungs.

Cristina paced around the slab, eyes locked on the corpse.

What was she looking for? She didn't know. She was just looking, waiting for observation to lead to inspiration.

She took a magnifying glass from her bag and started painstakingly working her way across the corpse's skin, head to toe, searching for a critical irregularity that would nudge her in a new direction.

An hour later, she still had nothing. All her focus and energy had drawn a blank.

No matter. She knew what to do; when she got stuck like this with her academic work, the best thing was to take a break and clear her mind. So she sat on one of the dissecting tables, poured herself a beaker of wine and started eating the cold meats.

As she put the bottle down, Cristina noticed the strange echo it sent around the room. She looked up and saw that the ceiling had a slight dome to it which was catching the sound. She started clicking her fingers and moving around the space, trying to see how the echo changed. Then she picked up the wine bottle and tapped the side of it with her magnifying glass, experimenting with different rhythms and echoes. Who knew that a simple picnic could yield so much pleasure?

Cristina froze.

Picnic.

Food.

Could that be it?

She looked at the corpse; she had cut open the trachea to examine its lungs, but what about food? She hadn't examined the victim's stomach.

Quickly Cristina picked up a scalpel and started cutting deeper into the neck. She moved the trachea aside to reveal the oesophagus, then carefully cut a long slit down its length. Her intention had been to work her way to the stomach and examine the contents, but she didn't get that far. On the second incision, she pulled back the folds of the muscular tube to discover an object stuck in the body tissue. Delicately Cristina cut around the margins and removed the object: it was a small, gold crucifix.

Moments before he had triggered the explosion, this man had swallowed a crucifix.

Cristina's vision pulsed as she glimpsed the enormity of the discovery. She stumbled backwards, steadied herself, then a strange gasp of laughter erupted from her mouth and echoed around the domed ceiling.

"Thank you, God," she whispered.

"And?"

"What do you mean, 'and'?" Cristina had cornered Domenico in his office and closed the door so that they could talk in private, without having to worry about the prying ears of the inquisitor. "This changes everything."

"So he was choking to death when he detonated the explosion?"

"He wasn't a Muslim. No follower of Allah would own a crucifix, let alone at the moment of their death."

"He didn't own it. He was trying to swallow it."

"Domenico! Think! He was wearing it around his neck for the whole time he was incarcerated under the altar. It gave him the strength to get through that ordeal. But when the time came to unleash the fireball, he swallowed the crucifix so that it *wouldn't* be found on his body. This man was a Christian assassin, trying to hide his Christianity. He was deliberately trying to throw our investigation in the wrong direction."

"And he succeeded," Domenico frowned.

"It proves the Ottoman suspects are innocent."

"That's a bit of a leap."

"The fireball was an attack *by* Christians *on* Christians."

Domenico shook his head. "What about Bartolo? He was caught praying to Allah. He is clearly guilty, and clearly a Muslim."

"Not necessarily. Perhaps Bartolo *wanted* to be caught praying to Allah. Maybe he was also trying to throw us off the scent."

"No, no." Domenico shook his head. "That's too far-fetched. He was seen, he was caught."

"What if that was all part of the deception?"

"You can't prove any of this, Cristina."

"But you can't disprove it. Not without further investigation. At the very least, the Holy Father must postpone the executions."

"He is adamant. There will be no delay."

"Then make him think again, Domenico." Cristina lifted her brother's face with her fingers so that he had to look into her eyes. "If the Pope wrongly executes innocent Muslims, he will make martyrs of them, inflame Ottoman aggression, and give the Sultan yet another excuse for war. Do you really want all that on your conscience?"

"You always find a way to make me feel bad," Domenico grumbled.

"It's what younger sisters do."

Cristina waited in the old basilica. Her brother said he would find her here as soon as his audience with the Pope was over; in the meantime, she could try and influence the decision through silent prayer.

But her mind was too distracted to pray for long, and she soon found herself wandering around the old building. So much had happened in these past few weeks, Cristina had to remind herself that the only reason she had got involved in the investigation was because of the urgent need to replace this basilica before it disintegrated. She paused by the most recently repaired cracks in the wall and took out her magnifying glass; fresh hairline cracks were already starting to appear in the new mortar. If Rome let this building collapse, then European civilisation would surely be the next thing to fall. The dream of a brilliant new St Peter's had to be kept alive, Cristina still believed that. But she also knew that the rebuilding could not be at any price. Justice must not be sacrificed along the way.

A door at the far end of the nave opened, footsteps hurried across the marble floor, and Cristina recognised the gait. She turned and saw Domenico striding towards her. She studied his body language, trying to guess the decision before he opened his mouth.

"Well? Did you succeed?" she asked.

"Yes. And no."

"Meaning?"

"The machinery of vengeance is rolling. The Pope's grief is demanding blood."

"Then you have to try again!"

"Six of the condemned have been given a stay of execution while we try to build a new case."

"And the seventh?"

"Bartolo is to be burnt at the stake immediately. He has proved himself to be a liar and a traitor. It is a fact that he blinded his fellow monks. His role in the other crimes is unclear, but he is guilty enough to be executed."

"It would be more useful to keep him alive for questioning," Cristina said.

"That's not how the Holy Father sees it. So that's not how we can see it."

Cristina nodded thoughtfully. "At least the others will be spared."

"For now. Not forever. I doubt we will be given more than a few weeks to uncover fresh evidence."

"It's not long enough."

"But it's the most we will get, Cristina."

40: BONFIRE

The sky was cloudless-blue, and a gentle breeze from the west brought crisp, clean air off the Tyrrhenian Sea; it was the sort of day that made you feel glad to be alive.

Unless you were going to be burned at the stake.

Domenico and Gilo arrived early at Piazza del Popolo with a troop of Vatican guards. As ever, the detailed groundwork had fallen to them, marshalling crowds, maintaining order and ensuring the spectacle ran smoothly. It meant imagining everything that could possibly go wrong, then putting contingencies in place to make sure it didn't.

The grim task of building the pyre had been given to a team of Vatican carpenters who were more used to carving rood screens than immolating heretics. Yet they tackled the job with professional diligence under the supervision of Tenente Tomasso.

"Where have you stored the gunpowder?" Domenico asked as he inspected the criss-crossed logs that would enclose the heart of the lethal fire.

"They won't let me use any," the lieutenant replied.

"What? But that's not what they agreed."

"Padre Gabriel has changed his mind, sir."

Domenico took off his helmet and scratched his head. "I thought we had left this barbarity behind."

"I know, sir. I did ask him to reconsider, but…"

"It's not your fault, Tenente." Domenico had made a point of raising this issue with the Inquisition: a small barrel of gunpowder placed between the victim's feet was commonly used to bring a swift end to the agonies of immolation, and they had agreed to let him use it for Bartolo.

"Padre Gabriel was adamant, sir," Tomasso explained. "He said Bartolo is a traitor and a heretic, and that no mercy was to be shown."

"Well, if those are our orders, I suppose we have no choice."

"Very good, sir." Tomasso turned back to the pyre and started filling the gaps between the logs with armfuls of kindling.

"Is this far enough back?" Gilo called across the piazza. He was busy rigging a rope cordon to keep the spectators at a safe distance from the fire.

"Plenty," Domenico replied. "It doesn't even have to be that far. They're not using gunpowder."

"What?" Gilo's face twisted sceptically. "Why not?"

"Let's just do as we're told and get the day behind us." Domenico spotted his sister climbing some steps onto a temporary raised spectator stand, and made his way over.

"Don't tell me the men responsible for this brutality are actually going to turn up and watch?" she asked.

"I think we both know the answer to that, Cristina." He climbed the steps and joined her on the podium. "This is for minor officials."

"No Pope? No cardinals?"

"They would never sully themselves."

Cristina scoffed. "It's one thing to condemn a man to death, quite another to inhale the smoke as his body burns."

"I could probably get you a seat up here, if you really want. As long as the wind doesn't change, it should be pretty smoke-free."

"I think I'd rather step into the fire myself than spend the afternoon exchanging small talk with petty officials."

"As you wish. Just make sure you're visible."

"Yes. Visible," Cristina said bitterly. "His Holiness and the cardinals can hide away in their marble palaces, but I have to witness the horror with my own eyes."

"Try not to dwell on it."

But she couldn't help herself. Cardinale Orsini was the man she had to thank for that; he had still not forgiven her for speaking against him in the Curia, and insisted that she watch the execution as a sombre lesson in 'the gravity of the affairs of men.'

As the sun climbed higher, the town criers set off to proclaim news of the imminent execution to every street and alley across the city; not long after, the crowds started to gather. Some came out of curiosity; others were driven by a morbid obsession. The enterprising had set up mobile stands selling food and refreshments. But many of those who came had been ordered to attend by priests in their local churches, who in turn were working under strict instructions from the Vatican. A large crowd was seen as an important vindication of the Pope's authority, and if people had to be forced to attend, so be it.

By late morning, the piazza was rammed with people caught in a strange state between fear and excitement. Finally, as church clocks across the city tolled twelve, a group of Vatican guards pushed open a corridor in the crowd to allow the procession of the condemned to enter the piazza.

The inquisitor Padre Umberto led the way, carrying a huge crucifix in front of him like military colours. Then came Padre Gabriel casting a smoking thurible on a long chain from side to side, sanctifying the execution. Even from where Cristina was standing, she could see the triumphant expression on Gabriel's face; he was loving every second of this, wielding his power over the cowering masses. What angered her most was that the inquisitors knew, just as she knew, that the real killers were still at large, and that all this theatre of suffering would not put an end to the murders.

Behind Gabriel came four more priests, all dressed in black, heads bowed in solemn prayer, rosaries wrapped around their fingers; and then came Bartolo, slumped in a crude wooden carriage. Presumably, the reason he wasn't walking was because his knees had been shattered by those same inquisitors who now affected such piety. At the rear of the procession were four more guards, beating out a solemn rhythm on their drums.

On the ground behind the pyre lay a large wooden frame with long ropes trailing from each corner. The guards dragged Bartolo from the cart and laid him out on the frame; as they tied his hands and feet to the struts, Padre Gabriel turned to address the crowd in thunderous tones.

"Pity not this man who has betrayed us all! He appeared among us as a humble Christian brother, while in secret he worshipped Allah, giving his love and obedience to a false god."

A disapproving murmur rippled across the crowd.

"Pity not this man who drew others to his dark cause, and through them procured the death of Count Barberini. Noble, gentle Barberini, not just a worthy citizen of Rome, but a man who gave so generously to so many. Pity not this man who procured the deaths of seven of your fellow citizens, consumed by fire as they knelt in prayer in God's Holy church."

By now, some of the crowd were in tears, remembering friends who had been caught up in the horror.

"And pity not this man who procured the murder of the Holy Father's beloved son, Giovanni, mercilessly stabbed to death and dumped in the Tiber like a dog!"

Grief tipped over into anger — Gabriel had the crowd just where he wanted them. He raised a flaming torch in his hand, brandishing it like a weapon. "Yet rejoice that he who unleashed fire shall now suffer its burning justice!"

A cheer went up from the crowd, then Padre Gabriel thrust the torch deep into the pyre and the kindling ignited with a roar. As flames licked in all directions, they caught the animal fat that had been smeared over the stacks of heavy logs, and within minutes the fire was raging.

Padre Gabriel held the flaming torch high above his head. "Bartolo the traitor! You have been found guilty of the most appalling crimes; now you must endure the harshest possible sentence. May God have mercy on your soul!"

The inquisitors hauled on the long ropes, hoisting the frame vertically, and swinging it directly into the flames of the bonfire.

The crowd gasped as the monk was immediately engulfed in flames. His tattered clothes ignited; moments later, his hair erupted into a ball of fire.

Bartolo screamed and writhed as he tried to free himself, but it was in vain. There was no escape. No-one was going to show him mercy, and the more he screamed, the more satisfaction Padre Gabriel seemed to feel.

Cristina couldn't bear to watch. She didn't care that Orsini's men were observing her; she refused to harden her heart and become part of the baying mob.

She turned her back on the crackle and heat of the pyre and pushed her way through the crowd. Finally, she made it to the spectator stand and hurried into the shadows underneath the wooden platform.

Just above her head, she could hear the excited chatter of petty officials as they watched Bartolo burn. The men cheered and shouted; their wives joked nervously, pretending to be unaffected by the horror.

Out in the piazza, a fresh cheer went up as each of the monk's limbs caught fire in turn, yet still the man would not die, still he would not fall silent.

Then just as the crowd was slipping towards frenzy, Bartolo summoned all his strength for one last declamation.

"CASTRO!" His voice was clear, unbroken, and it stunned the mob into silence. "Castro!" he cried out again.

Cristina stepped out from under the platform and looked towards the raging bonfire. Bartolo's head was thrown back and he was gazing up at the deep blue sky. But it wasn't pain on his face, it was euphoria, as if in those final moments he had found some kind of fulfilment.

"For Castro!" he exclaimed one last time. Then, with an agonised cry, he succumbed to the flames.

Even though no-one knew what the word meant, everyone had felt its power.

For the first time, Cristina was glad that she had been here to witness the moment. If that strange word made sense of everything for Bartolo, maybe it could do the same for her.

41: ENEMIES

Pope Alexander VI had been weeping. His eyes were red, and his cheeks damp with tears; this man, who was as close to God as it was possible to get without actually dying, could find no solace for his profound grief.

Domenico had been summoned to the Pope's private apartments, where he found the Holy Father kneeling opposite Cardinale Riario, both men deep in prayer. The loss of his son had shaken Alexander to the core: he looked vulnerable and numb, and seemed to have aged years in a matter of days.

"Was the crowd satisfied?" the Pope finally asked with a faltering voice.

"They have no reason to doubt that Bartolo was behind all the crimes, Holy Father. Your inquisitors made that abundantly clear."

"But you disagree?"

Domenico hesitated, trying to find the right words. "My only concern is for your safety, Holy Father."

The Pope turned his grieving eyes on Domenico. "Tell me the truth. Not what you think I want to hear."

"The truth can be dangerous."

"Perhaps lies are more dangerous." Alexander raised himself from his knees and sat on a wooden pew. "I believed that I was infallible. My son paid a terrible price for my hubris. Now I have prayed for humility. So, Domenico, tell me what you really think."

"I believe that Bartolo was guilty of the attack at the monastery. He blinded the monks and has been rightly punished. I also think he was part of a conspiracy that murdered Barberini, unleashed the fireball, and worst of all, killed your son."

The Pope looked down, trying to hold back his tears.

"Perhaps now is not the time," Cardinale Riario suggested.

"No. Go on," Alexander whispered.

"Do I think it is a conspiracy of Ottoman spies? No. Do I think whoever they are will strike again? Yes. Only this time, I believe they may try to kill you, Holy Father."

Alexander looked up and scrutinised Domenico. "Who would dare attack a Pope?"

"Every murder, every attack has moved one step closer to you. After your son, I believe that your own life is in mortal danger."

Alexander nodded slowly, then turned to Riario. "Show him."

Riario handed Domenico a sheaf of papers. "I have helped His Holiness compile a list of names. Together we have combed through his diaries and letters. Everyone on that list is someone who believes they have a reason to hate the Pope."

Domenico looked at the papers: page after page of powerbrokers in the Papal States and Spain — financiers, bishops, even a few mistresses. "These are all his enemies?"

"The Pope does not have enemies," Riario corrected. "He is God's authority on Earth, a man of peace and love. But there are people who, in their twisted minds, may have created a deluded reason to hate His Holiness."

Domenico focused on the list. He knew exactly what lay behind Riario's meticulously chosen words. No-one became the most powerful man in the Church without lying, cheating and double-crossing. Add to that the infamous Borgia ruthlessness, and you had a deadly elixir.

"Everyone on that list could be involved in the conspiracy against His Holiness," Riario emphasised. "Naturally, their animosity is baseless, but their delusions make these people dangerous."

"I understand, Your Eminence."

"What resources do you need to investigate them?" the Pope asked.

"Time. And money."

"Whatever money you need, you can have. But time … that is a luxury we do not have."

"The Holy Father will be temporarily moving his residence to Castel Sant'Angelo," Riario explained. "It is the most secure building in Rome, and given the multiple threats he is facing, the best place for him to remain safe. A small group of trusted advisors will continue to have access to the Holy Father, but such seclusion is not sustainable in the long term. The Pope cannot hide from the world forever."

"There will be more executions at the end of this month," the Pope pronounced. "By then, either you will have found the perpetrators and broken open this conspiracy, or we will execute the Ottoman suspects we already have in jail."

"That eventuality would be to save face," Riario elaborated. "But be under no illusion, Domenico: should that happen, your services would no longer be required."

Domenico arrived back in his office to find his sister waiting for him. "Finally, the Pope has given us the vital leads." He handed Cristina the papers. "He certainly has no shortage of enemies."

Cristina's eyes scanned the list, searching for one name in particular. "Nothing about Castro."

"Who knows what Bartolo was thinking as he died? It doesn't matter now."

"You're wrong."

"The people behind this conspiracy against the Pope are somewhere on that list." Domenico pointed to the papers. "I would stake my life on it."

"But it's not your life that's at stake."

"It is my career, though. And I know that any useful information Bartolo had was tortured out of him. The list is where we need to focus our investigations, Cristina. Help me with that."

But her instinct was telling her not to ignore 'Castro'. It was whispering in her ear, and she had learnt a long time ago not to ignore that quiet but insistent voice.

Why did Bartolo use his dying breaths to utter that word three times? And the look of peace on his face in those last moments … it meant something. It had to. "Give me the resources to investigate on my own. Let me find out what Castro means."

"This is no time for wild theories. We have to focus everything on these suspects." He took the papers back from Cristina and laid them out on the table. Then he dipped a quill in the inkpot and started annotating each line, deciding who should be investigated most urgently.

Cristina understood where her brother's manic energy was coming from — throwing himself into work meant that he didn't have to confront the demons haunting his own soul. And yet she remained convinced that the truth lay elsewhere. "In that case, will you give me papal warrants guaranteeing safe passage?"

Domenico looked up. "Why? Where are you going?"

"You work on the Pope's list; let me try to unravel the mystery of Castro. By the end of the month, we'll know which of us is right."

The old sibling rivalry never went away, and Cristina knew that playing on it was the quickest way to get exactly what she wanted.

42: CASTRO

How could a six-letter word be so vexing?

Cristina started with the obvious: Latin. Castro, derived from the verb *castrare*, 'I punish' or 'I purge'. That would certainly fit, the condemned man using his dying breaths to rail against a world he had waged war on.

But why declare it three times?

Three was very biblical; Peter denied Christ three times, Christ was tempted three times, three kings travelled from the East.

It was a possibility.

Cristina noted it down and allowed her mind to switch to a different tack. Could it be a code? Was Bartolo secretly communicating to supporters who had infiltrated the crowd at his execution?

She tried substituting letters for numbers, but nothing leapt out; there were simply too many permutations.

What about anagrams?

SATROC. CROTSA. RACSTO. OSTRAC. CRASTO. This could go on for hours. Maybe come back to this line of thinking later.

Cristina dipped her quill into the inkpot and held it over a clean sheet of paper. A single drop of black ink fell and made a blob as she concentrated.

Could it be a family name?

Or a street name?

Or the name of Bartolo's lover?

Or the name of a constellation of stars?

So many questions, and each one drawing Cristina deeper into a maze of branching possibilities.

By the time Isra knocked on the door and entered with a tray of supper, the library was awash with books and papers spread across the floor. Isra said nothing; there was little point. When her mistress was in a research frenzy, it was best just to let her get on with it and try to make sure she remembered to eat.

Isra cleared a small space on the table and laid out the food. But just as she was picking her way back to the door, trying not to step on any books, she noticed that all the sheets of paper had the same heading: CASTRO.

"Oh, I haven't been there since I was a child," Isra said.

Cristina looked up. "What did you say?"

"Castro. It's a small town in the south."

"It is?"

"On the coast. Are you planning a trip there?"

Cristina grabbed the ladder, slid it across the bookstacks, and scrambled up the rungs to consult an *Atlas of the Italian Peninsula*. Urgently she flicked through the pages. "You're right. How did you know that?"

"I was born in the south."

"You never said."

"You never asked." Isra was uncomfortable as Cristina's gaze locked onto her. "Sorry to interrupt, mistress." She moved for the door.

"Wait!" Cristina slid down the library steps and put the atlas on the table. "I don't want you to be frightened of me, Isra."

"No, mistress."

"What happened, the indiscriminate arrests, that was appalling. All I've tried to do, from day one, is get to the truth. To catch the killers behind these dreadful crimes."

"They said you are person who blamed an Ottoman spy ring for all the troubles."

"It was a theory. Just a line of inquiry."

"A theory that put me in jail, mistress. Put hundreds of us in jail."

"That was not my decision, Isra. How can I control what our leaders do?"

"But I've heard you talk about the Ottoman threat from the East. In this very library. How they want to destroy Europe. The Ottoman devils. Barbarian invaders."

"That's just language."

"Words have power. Words put innocent people in jail."

"I know. And I've tried to explain —"

"How many of the Sultan's subjects do you think want to wage war on Europe? Yes, there are ruthless people in his army, urging him to war so that they can loot and plunder. But most ordinary people, they just want to live in peace, like ordinary people everywhere. It is the leaders and their lust for power who twist the world out of shape. But it is people like me, with darker skins and no money, who always pay the price."

Cristina stared at her housekeeper, astonished at the diatribe. She'd never heard Isra talk about anything but domestic arrangements. "You're right," she said quietly. "I'm sorry."

"You are? Really?"

"I had half a theory. But the partial truth can be more damaging than no knowledge at all." Cristina put her hand on the atlas. "That is why I need to head south, to Castro, where I hope to uncover the full truth about this aberrant monk and the conspiracy he was part of. Let my actions be my apology, Isra."

"Thank you."

"I intend to set off first thing in the morning," Cristina said briskly. "So I'll need you to hire a strong horse from the stables on Via Labicana, just behind the colosseum. You know them?"

"Yes, mistress."

"Tell them I'll need it for two weeks, maybe more. And he must have plenty of stamina. While you do that, I'll pack a small bag. You'll have to look after the house while I'm away, of course. Make sure Baker Yusuf and his family don't go back to their shop until it's absolutely safe."

"I'm afraid I can't do that, mistress."

"Why not?"

"Because I'll be coming with you."

Cristina looked at Isra and blinked. "What? No."

"Yes, miss. I'll be coming with you to Castro."

"I don't need a housekeeper on a trip."

"With all due respect, you won't last a day on the road. Not on your own."

"Because I'm a woman?" Cristina retorted. "Now who's generalising?"

"Mistress, all you really know is in this room. The world out there is a different animal."

"So everyone keeps telling me."

"Then maybe you should start to listen."

"The best way to learn something is to throw yourself into it."

"Please, let me be your guide. I know the south."

"Thank you for the offer, Isra; it's very sweet. But I need you here, looking after the house."

"I think you're making a mistake, Signorina Falchoni."

"That's how I learn, by making mistakes and correcting them."

"But the road is not as forgiving as a library. Sometimes there are no second chances."

43: PARTNERS

The horse looked enormous standing in the courtyard behind the kitchens, but Isra had made good use of its height by renting extra saddlebags for the journey. Just as she secured the last strap, Cristina emerged from the house, stopped abruptly and gazed at the gelding, wide-eyed. "This was what the stables recommended?" she said, trying to hide her apprehension.

"He's called Amadeus. They said he's perfect for a long journey."

"Good, good. Well, that's just what I need. Perfect." Cristina wandered around the horse, bracing herself.

"I've already packed a set of clothes, a blanket, and some water, miss."

"You'll need to find room for these as well." Cristina handed Isra another bag. "Maps, star charts, and a compass."

"What about food?"

"Too bulky. I'll find some inns along the road. Buy food as I go."

"With the money you've hidden in your leg-wallet, I assume?"

Cristina looked taken aback. "How did you know about that?"

"Every thief on the road knows about leg-wallets, mistress. You'll probably be robbed before you make the first night, and once they've got to your legs, who knows where they'll stop."

Cristina looked a little pale, but defiantly pulled a pistol from her jacket. "That is why I'm taking this."

"Have you ever fired one, mistress?"

"It's basic physics. If soldiers can use them, I'm sure I won't have any trouble."

"Indeed. But basic arithmetic is that bandits never work alone. If you kill one, the others will get you while you reload."

"This is no time for pessimism, Isra."

"You shouldn't be travelling alone, miss."

"We've already discussed this —"

"The best way to hide your money is to split it into three. One third goes in your boot — if anyone tries to get it, you kick them in the face. One third goes in an empty water bottle, and one third goes in the secret pocket I've sewn into your jacket."

"What? There is no —"

"Left hand side, mistress."

Cristina unbuttoned her jacket and peered inside; hidden in the lining, disguised by the seams, was a beautifully sewn pocket. "That is impressive, Isra. Thank you."

"A pleasure."

"And thank you for the advice."

"How long do you think the journey will take?"

"Well," Cristina began, "an average horse can cover fifty miles in a day. But Amadeus looks far from average, so —"

"Six days, mistress," Isra interrupted. "It'll take you six days to get to Castro. Five if there's no rain."

"Right. So there we are. You knew all along."

"And does your route go through bandit country, miss?"

"I have Letters of Safe Passage from the Vatican."

Isra gave a wry smile. "The people you need to worry about can't even read."

"Which is why I have the pistol," Cristina insisted.

"No, mistress. These are the weapons you need." With a clatter, Isra unfurled a leather roll, revealing an assortment of swords and daggers, which she started to fix to the horse's saddle straps.

"Shouldn't they be hidden?" Cristina asked.

"The best way to win a fight is to turn up with so much weaponry, that your opponent runs away rather than fights. That's how the generals do it on the battlefield. That's what you need to do on the road."

Cristina watched as Isra secured the last of the weapons. Amadeus now looked more like a war horse, with blades glinting all over his body.

"Very good, now he's ready." Isra helped Cristina into the saddle and handed her the reins.

"Thank you, Isra. I appreciate all this. I really do."

"Have a good trip, mistress." Isra smiled and raised a hand to wave farewell.

But Cristina didn't move. Her mind had started to page through the worrying possibilities of the next few days. What if nothing went as smoothly as she had imagined? What if she couldn't fight off the bandits, or find a tavern before nightfall? She had read about flash floods that washed away herds of animals, and travellers who became so disorientated in the southern wilderness that they ended up wandering in circles for days.

"Everything all right, miss?"

"I don't suppose," Cristina began. "Would you …"

"Would I…?"

"Would you still like to come with me?"

Isra thought for a moment. "Do you really want me to?"

"You clearly know more about life on the road than I do. It's logical that you should come."

"But do you *want* me?"

"Yes. I do."

"All right, then."

"Good. Excellent." Cristina suddenly looked a lot more relaxed. "So, if you take the rest of the day to get yourself ready, we can set off at first light tomorrow. How does that sound?"

"No need, miss. I took the liberty..." Isra crossed the yard and swung open the alley gates to reveal another horse that was already loaded up for the journey, right down to the shining weapons. "This one's for me."

Cristina looked from the horse to Isra, then back again. "Am I really so obvious?"

"Not obvious, mistress, just logical. Always logical."

They left Rome by the Porta Latina in the south of the city, and followed a track to the Via Appia, the ancient Roman road that would take them all the way down to Brindisi. The surface was made up of giant cobblestones, overgrown with weeds, and the horses had to tread carefully to avoid stumbling.

"You know, this road was one of the Roman Empire's greatest engineering achievements," Cristina said as they passed some crumbling monuments. "They drained marshes, built bridges, cut through hills. It was their golden link to the Empire in the East."

"So everything the Caesars plundered came back along this road?" Isra observed.

"That's one way of looking at it. But then, this was also the road St Paul was led along when he came to Rome in chains."

Soon they arrived at a stretch that was lined for mile after mile with the decaying tombs of long-dead Roman centurions. "I wouldn't like to be here when all the ghosts come out," Isra whispered. "There must be hundreds of them."

"Not from these." Cristina pointed to the tombs. "They were all heading for Elysium. But the ones who were executed here…"

"They executed people here?" Instinctively Isra glanced at the sun to check how much daylight they had left.

"Spartacus's army of slaves was crucified along the entire length of the Via Appia. All six thousand of them. I doubt they found much peace."

As the horses climbed a gentle incline and Rome receded into the mist, the rawness of the open countryside started to press heavily on both women, and by the time they arrived at the Catacombs of San Callisto, even Cristina felt the cold presence of the dead.

"I'm glad you're here, Isra," she said.

"So am I, mistress."

44: ROAD

They made swift progress south. The importance of the Via Appia across the centuries meant it was reasonably provided with inns where travellers could eat and lodge. When none was available, Cristina and Isra found refuge in monasteries that still believed hospitality was their Christian duty.

For mile after mile, Cristina never ceased to be amazed at Isra's worldliness. Almost by instinct, she seemed to know who to trust and who to avoid, which shortcut would help and which would lead to trouble; she understood the horses and knew when they could be pushed, and when they had to rest; perhaps most useful of all, Isra could read the clouds and predict with uncanny accuracy when the weather was about to turn.

As they left the bustling city of Lecce to start on the final leg of the journey, Cristina realised she had to initiate some changes. "Why did it take a three-hundred-mile trip to make me realise that I don't pay you nearly enough?"

Isra laughed. "You pay what anyone else in Rome would pay a seventeen-year-old housekeeper. A little better, actually."

"But you're so much more than a housekeeper, Isra. And I never saw it."

"Well, how much would you like to pay me?"

"*You* name the price."

"What? I can't do that, mistress."

"How much do you think you're worth?"

Isra rode in silence for a few moments, considering the offer. "I just need enough money to be free. And safe. That's all that really matters."

"Good answer."

"I'll leave it to you to convert that to ducats. There must be a book with some tables."

Cristina smiled. "Are you mocking me?"

"Me? No. Never."

They rode on for a few miles, passing small groups of demobbed soldiers making their way north from the coast, and the odd herdsman looking for work.

"What happened to you, Isra? Where did you learn how to survive?"

"It's a long story, mistress."

"We still have twenty miles."

Isra studied Cristina. "What if you don't like what you hear?"

"I'm hardly in a position to judge."

For a few minutes they listened to the steady clatter of the horses' hooves on the rough stones.

"The year before I was born, the Ottoman army invaded from the sea and took the city of Otranto." Isra's calm words were at odds with the violence they recounted. "Their plan was to march on Rome, back along the road we've just travelled. So they executed every man in the city. Anyone who refused to convert to Islam was beheaded as well. The Ottomans killed twelve thousand people. Five thousand more were sold into slavery.

"My mother was one of the lucky ones. She survived because she was beautiful. But she was forced to marry a Janissary commander, one of the elite Ottoman troops. Her choice was death, or marry and accept the new order. She chose life. The following year, I was born. But when I was just a few months old, the Pope called for a Crusade to recapture Otranto. Those Ottomans who weren't killed in battle were driven back into the sea. My mother was left behind, with me. Only now she was seen as a collaborator. She hoped that time would heal old wounds, but it didn't. She was spurned; we both were. No other children would play with me. Life became impossible. When I was five years old, we fled the city.

"We belonged nowhere, caught between two worlds, rejected by both. So we lived off the land, here…" Isra pointed to the immense, barren landscape that surrounded them. "This was our home. We learnt how to find food and water from nothing, how to use the weather as our friend, how to track animals, how to outwit enemies."

"What a strange existence," Cristina mused.

"I have happy memories of it. But it couldn't last. When my mother fell sick, when we really needed people, no-one would help us. No doctor would touch her. And when she died, I couldn't bear to carry on that life without her. It was too lonely. So I headed north, walking along the road you know so much about. I went to Rome in search of a new life, and you hired me, and everything felt safe again."

Cristina felt too humbled to say anything. She could never have imagined that her young housekeeper had lived through so much trauma. She reached out and clasped Isra's arm. "I'm so sorry."

"For what?"

"For not knowing. For never asking. For what you had to endure."

"Don't be sorry, mistress. That was my education."

"I can't imagine running from everything and facing the wilderness. My life has been so … safe. I don't think I'd have had the strength to survive."

"You would've found a way, I'm sure of that."

"Outside my library, I'm lost. As everyone keeps pointing out."

"But inside your library, you are the most courageous person I know. That's why I know you could survive, miss. Because you have courage."

As the road curved left and started to climb, they saw the outline of Castro slowly emerge from the haze; it was tightly packed inside girdling walls, with gates that were locked shut at night. At its centre were the ruins of a square fort, with white buildings clustered around it like barnacles. The two women pulled up their horses to take in the sight.

"Well, we made it, mistress."

"Now the hard work really starts."

But Isra seemed hesitant to move forward. "What I told you, there's no need for anyone else to know. People can react in strange ways."

"I understand, Isra. But in return, you must do something for me."

"Anything, mistress."

"Stop calling me mistress. My name is Cristina."

Isra laughed. "That may take some getting used to."

"Then you'd better start now." Cristina jabbed her heels into Amadeus's flanks and led the way towards Castro.

It was one of the strangest towns Cristina had ever ridden into.

The limewashed buildings, bright in the hard sunlight, were huddled around narrow alleys that twisted up a low hill to the ruins of the fort. Overhangs made the streets gloomy, while the cracked plaster and missing bricks added an air of desolation. A couple of women, dressed all in black, shuffled furtively between the buildings; somewhere a window shutter was banging in the breeze, but apart from that, everything was quiet.

Cristina and Isra dismounted and walked their horses towards the fort. From there you could look across the glittering blue of the Ionian Sea, or peer over the low cliff to the narrow beach below. It was a beautiful setting … so why did it feel strange?

A stray dog with three legs scampered over to inspect the new arrivals. Isra patted him on the head and fished the remains of a biscuit from her pocket as a treat.

"Where is everyone?" Cristina said quietly. "Shouldn't they all be busy at this time? Hard at work?"

Isra nodded. "More to the point, where are the men? I've only seen old women."

Cristina slowly turned on her heels. One old woman was standing on the flat roof of her house, beating the dust from a rush mat; another was laying out some sheets to dry in the sun; a third was asleep, balanced precariously on a stool in the shadow of the church porch.

"You're right," Cristina said. "This is a town full of old women."

"No men, and no children," Isra nodded.

"Why on earth was Bartolo thinking about this place in his final moments?"

45: GHOSTS

Cristina found the village priest in his study behind the chapel, finishing off the last crumbs of a late lunch. Padre Ugo was the first person under thirty they'd set eyes on since entering Castro.

"Visitors!" He was delighted to see two unfamiliar faces. "Come in, come in. Can I offer you some wine?"

It was a welcome relief after the dust of the road, and Cristina and Isra made themselves comfortable in the small, sun-drenched room. The shutters were wide open, letting a gentle breeze carry the calming sound of the sea into Padre Ugo's study. Cristina licked her lips and tasted the salt; the priest smiled. "It gets everywhere." He handed her some wine. "Salt is the taste of Castro."

They clinked glasses, introduced themselves and exchanged small talk about the journey, but Cristina was careful not to reveal too much, just in case.

"Does the name Bartolo mean anything to you?" she finally asked, while Padre Ugo topped up their wine.

"Bartolo…" He frowned, trying to recall the name. "Why?"

"We're hoping to trace his family. He moved to Rome many years ago."

"Bartolo, Bartolo … no. There's no-one here by that name."

"But maybe there was in the past?" Cristina pressed.

"There could have been. I've only been here five years." His face opened into a grin. "I'm still the new boy."

"What on earth is a young priest doing in a village full of old women?" Isra asked bluntly.

"They sent me here to try and heal things. But it's a slow job."

"Heal things after what?" Cristina asked.

Padre Ugo ran his fingers through a thick mop of black hair. "That's a difficult story."

"We have time."

"A generation ago, Barbary corsairs came from the sea and stormed this village in the middle of the night. They kidnapped every adult male in Castro, loaded them onto ships and sailed to the Levant. They sold them as galley slaves to the Sultan's navy. Not one man ever came home."

"When was this, exactly?"

"Thirty-two years ago."

"And the village still hasn't recovered?" Cristina didn't understand.

"They tried." Padre Ugo nodded. "They prayed and new men moved here, started to rebuild, raise families. Then seven years to the day after the first raid, the corsairs returned, and committed the same atrocities. They abducted every man and boy. That was when the village died. From that moment, no one wanted to build a life in Castro. Everyone lives in fear of the devils returning."

"And have they?" Isra asked.

"Not yet. But the threat is enough. The Ottomans have cursed this village."

Isra went very quiet; she understood the fear that lay behind the priest's words. But Cristina was already thinking ahead. "Can we see the church records, Padre? The Bartolo family could well have been here before the raids."

"Why is it so important?" Padre Ugo was suddenly hesitant. "We're trying to move forward, not rake up the past."

"Because it could save lives. In Rome. Right now."

The priest frowned. "I don't see how our small village has anything to do with Rome? It's not possible."

"That's exactly what we're trying to find out. And we have papal warrants to prove it."

"Very well. Finish your wine."

They did as they were told, then Padre Ugo led them into the main body of the church. They walked down the nave, with its thick stone pillars supporting a line of squat arches, until they came to a side door leading to the sacristy. The priest led them inside and dragged a large, iron-strapped trunk from under a table. He unlocked it and lifted out four leather-bound ledgers. "A new parish book is started every ten years, so if the Bartolo family was ever here, they'll be in one of these."

Cristina picked up each of the ledgers in turn, feeling the patina of salt on their musty covers. Even as she flicked through the pages, she could read the plight of this community from the changing pattern of entries. The two older ledgers were full of births, marriages and deaths, jostling for space; the newer ones had just a few sparse entries, neatly recording the burials of old women with depressing regularity. There had been no births to record for the last ten years; Castro was in a death spiral.

Isra, Padre Ugo and Cristina took a ledger each, and started a painstaking search, entry by entry, line by line. Eventually, they picked up the trail.

"Here." Isra pointed to a slightly smudged line of writing. "Battista Bartolo. Born 1452."

Cristina leafed back through the years, her eyes scanning the entries. "And there's more. Look … a sister, his parents, two uncles. This was definitely his home."

"Surely Battista could have told you that himself?" Padre Ugo said.

"Bartolo is dead."

"Oh." The priest crossed himself. "God rest his soul."

"Yes … but which God?" Isra said as she closed the heavy ledger.

"What do you mean?"

Cristina didn't want to risk scaring Padre Ugo with talk of heresy. "We need to question someone who might remember the family," she said. "Any suggestions?"

Padre Ugo turned away and looked out through a gap in the shutters. "I'd rather you didn't distress my parishioners. I'm trying to help them."

"And we're trying to catch a murderer," Isra retorted.

"But you said Bartolo was dead. How can —"

"He was part of a much deeper conspiracy," Cristina replied. "A web of deception that has now put the life of the His Holiness the Pope in danger."

"The Pope?"

"So you understand the importance of this."

Padre Ugo sighed. "The evil of abduction ripples down the generations. When the strongest and brightest are stolen, all you're left with is a shell. And broken people."

"We're not here to hurt anyone," Cristina reassured him. "All we're searching for is knowledge."

Padre Ugo looked at the two women. "Maybe the oldest of the women will remember … but please, be gentle with them."

Isra led the way down some narrow steps to the harbour. "Mind your footing. Some of them are loose," she called over her shoulder.

"Shouldn't we start in the village square?" Cristina tried to catch up, but she went too fast, stumbled, and had to grab onto a tree.

"Careful!"

"There won't be anyone down here, Isra."

"The most talkative old women are always by the water."

"Why?"

"It just is that way," Isra shrugged. "Where do you think the term fishwife comes from?"

"That's just a colloquialism. It's nothing to do with real fish."

"So let's put it to the test."

"What on earth could connect talkative old women to fish?"

"Perhaps they're drawn to the sea to commune with ancient Gods of Water. Or to see the ghosts of their dead ancestors sailing into the sunset. Or maybe they just like to haggle a good deal for supper."

"Are you mocking me again?"

"No. Never. As if."

They scrambled down the last few steps and emerged from the shade of the trees onto a small quayside. The sunlight bouncing off the stones was so bright it stung their senses. Through squinting eyes they saw a line of derelict buildings stretching along the waterfront that had once been small houses and workshops. They peered into the first one, which was completely empty except for a couple of lizards resting from the heat.

"Looks like the whole village moved up the cliff for safety," Isra said.

"Imagine being too scared to sleep in your own home."

They walked towards a small jetty improvised from huge boulders that had rolled down the cliff centuries ago and found a new resting place in the water. Sitting on the tallest rock, staring out to sea, was an old woman with grey hair and wrinkled, weather-worn skin.

"She's a possibility," Isra whispered.

"Good luck with that. She looks like she really doesn't want to be disturbed."

Isra gave a cheerful wave as she approached. "Beautiful afternoon."

The old woman ignored her.

Isra noticed the woman's eyes were locked on a tiny fishing boat in the distance that was slowly making its way back to the shore. "You think he's caught any bonito?"

"She," the old woman said. "My daughter."

"Ah. Nice."

They watched the boat for a few minutes before Isra tried again. "How long has she been out?"

"Sunrise."

"Long day. Must have a good catch, though."

"We'll see."

"Is she on her own?"

"That's why I'm here. Never let her out of my sight."

Fear. It was everywhere in this village.

Cristina wondered what the old woman would do if Barbary corsairs suddenly appeared on the horizon; she would be helpless.

"I don't suppose," Isra said, trying to sound casual, "you remember a family with the name Bartolo? A little boy, perhaps?"

"Who wants to know?"

"His dying thoughts were of this village," Cristina explained. "We're trying to discover why."

"Was he in trouble?"

Cristina and Isra exchanged a wary glance.

"He was. But he's at peace now," Cristina replied.

The old woman shook her head. "He was never at peace. Not since he turned thirteen. They destroyed him." She spat on the rocks as if getting rid of a foul taste.

"Can you tell us about it?" Cristina asked.

"I'm keeping watch."

Isra looked at the little boat which didn't seem to be getting any closer. "Your daughter will be a while yet. There's barely enough breeze to catch the sail."

"So you know about sailing now?"

"No, but I can see you do."

For the first time, the old woman turned and looked at Isra and Cristina. "I don't talk to strangers."

"Very wise." Cristina glanced at the woman's hands, the bitten nails betraying the permanent anxiety beneath her tough exterior. "But people are dying because of Bartolo. We're just trying to put an end to it."

"There will never be an end," the old woman replied. "That's the horror of what they did that night." She beckoned for Cristina and Isra to sit down on the rocks. "Listen. And you might understand…"

46: ABDUCTION

The first victim was a fisherman.

Vito had sailed two miles out from Castro, hoping to catch up with a school of tuna he'd glimpsed the previous evening. Diligently he tacked back and forth, eyes scouring the deep blue waters, searching for distinctive, tell-tale ripples on the surface. A lifetime on the sea had taught him that concentration was the key to being a good fisherman, so he focused and waited.

Perhaps if he'd looked up, Vito would have realised that he was no longer the hunter, he was now the prey.

They came straight out of the sun, two small rowing boats hiding in the blinding glare. In a well-practised pincer movement, they slipped either side of the innocent fishing boat and slung grappling hooks which locked deep into its hull. Escape was now impossible. Vito was a prisoner of the Barbary corsairs.

They commandeered his boat and sailed directly back into the sun, until they came to three black galleys, sitting long and low in the water, sails down, sixty massive oars emerging from each of the ships like waterborne porcupines.

As they drew close, Vito recoiled at the foul miasma coming from the ships; it was the smell of sweat and shit, of blood and death. It was the smell of galley slaves. The corsairs laughed at Vito's squeamishness; they had long since become inured to the stench.

Deftly they swung the fishing boat to the stern of the lead vessel and tied it off to a mooring ring on the galley's hull. Vito was bundled up some steps and onto the deck.

Two hundred lost souls stared up at him in silence.

Their faces were as haunted and broken as their spirits, their legs were manacled to long chains that ran the length of the galley, their hands rested on the massive oars, four men chained to each bench for an eternity of pain.

The Barbary pirates shouted an order to Vito, but he didn't understand. Immediately two guards started to push him towards one of the rowing benches that was a man short.

"No! NO!" Vito struggled to break free. He knew that if they chained him to that bench, his life would be over.

The guards whipped him across the back with their canes, but the pain only made Vito more desperate. He lashed out, kicking and screaming, refusing to become one of the damned souls with dead eyes.

The timekeeper gave a weary sigh. He knew trouble when he saw it, and the last thing he needed was a hysterical novice upsetting the other slaves. Calmly, he drew a long, glinting scimitar from its sheath; the two guards let go of Vito's arms and stepped away.

This was Vito's moment. If he could make a dash for the side and jump over the deck rail —

His mind didn't even finish the thought. There was a soft swoosh of metal cutting through the warm air, and a moment later Vito's head was sliced clean off his body. It tumbled to the deck with a thud, and rolled among the shit and piss that swirled around the rowing benches.

The galley slaves didn't even flinch.

One of the corsairs made a joke as they tossed the headless body over the side. They didn't care about him; all they really wanted was his boat.

The captain and his pilot clambered into the little fishing boat and sailed back towards Castro to scout the coast, hunting for the best landing spot. From the village, it simply looked as if Vito was busy fishing the bay. Children playing on the beach waved at the tiny silhouette, little suspecting that they were waving at Death.

As the sun set, the guards strapped cork gags into the mouths of all the galley slaves to prevent them from crying out a warning to the villagers. Silence and stealth were as deadly as swords.

When darkness enveloped the sea, the galleys made their move, a hundred and eighty oars pulling the ships swiftly towards the sleeping village.

As soon as the galleys slid onto the sandy beach, the corsairs leapt from the decks and swarmed into the village like a stain spreading across the innocent white buildings.

Doors were kicked in.

People were dragged, naked and confused from their beds.

Women who screamed were silenced with fists or swords, whatever was quickest. It was the men the raiders wanted, men and boys.

Screams echoed from all corners of the village, dogs howled and barked, but nothing could stop the relentless surge of violence as the corsairs dragged people away.

The church bell started tolling to raise the alarm — someone had broken free. Immediately six thugs diverted towards the church, kicked open the doors and hacked the man to death where he stood. As an extra touch, two of them hung his body from the very rope he had used to sound the alarm. The others smashed and desecrated the altar, stole the silver crucifix and chalice, and laughed as they defecated on a statue of the Virgin Mary.

Thirteen-year-old Bartolo's childhood was shattered when the door to his home burst open and two men with dark skin and wild eyes dragged his father away. He tried to fight them off, but they punched him in the face until his nose exploded in blood and his senses became groggy and confused.

Bartolo yelled out, clinging to his father's legs, desperately trying to stop him being taken, but it was hopeless. Hands grabbed the child and threw him out of the front door, where another man scooped him up and dragged him away through the streets.

Desperately the young Bartolo screamed, but everywhere he looked he saw only horror, as neighbours and friends were roped and beaten and forced down narrow streets towards the sea.

The air filled with the cries of women, helpless against the pitiless cruelty of rapists and murderers.

As the streams of fear and misery converged on the beach, Bartolo saw one of the galleys pull away from the shore. Dozens of men were being beaten into submission and loaded onto the remaining ships.

Bartolo's father knew that once they were on those galleys, they would never return; they would live and die chained to an oar. Desperate to save his son, he flung his head back, smashing his captor in the face, then wriggled free and scrambled across the beach.

"Bartolo! Run!" He hurled himself at the thug holding his son, and they collapsed into the sand, wrestling and punching.

Other corsairs arrived, swords drawn, shouting at Bartolo's father as they tried to drag him away, but he refused to give up. "RUN! Save yourself!"

Swords flashed; the blade cut deep into Bartolo's arm.

The boy didn't scream. He was too afraid. Too shocked. He stared at his own arm hanging limply, blood spurting from the arteries.

His captor looked at the child in disgust. Damaged goods. Useless. How could he pull an oar with one arm?

Furious, the thug lashed out with his boot, kicking Bartolo in the face. The boy slumped backwards in the sand, his vision swimming.

"Run, Bartolo! Hide!" It was his father's voice, getting fainter as they dragged him away, still trying to protect his son.

The boy hauled himself onto his knees and looked up. The two remaining galleys were now sliding out into the harbour as the last of the corsairs bundled their precious human cargo on board.

And then they were gone, vanishing into the night as quickly as they had arrived.

Leaving a village of wailing women.

Leaving Bartolo's life in tatters.

Everything was destroyed in a few minutes of horror that could never be undone.

47: WOUNDS

The old woman fell silent and wiped her eyes with rough fingers. Even after all this time, the wounds in her heart were still tender.

She turned away and looked out to sea, but now Cristina realised that the woman wasn't looking at her daughter at all; she was gazing beyond the silhouette of the little fishing boat to the distant horizon, perpetually braced for the appearance of long shadows, low in the water, that signified Death was returning.

"You can't imagine what it does to people. To a place. To never feel truly safe again." The old woman glanced at Cristina. "Your cities, with all their fine buildings … you think they're so strong. But they could vanish like that." She snapped her fingers with surprising energy, all her pain channelled into one gesture.

"I know what it means to lose everything," Isra said quietly. "And I know the sadness that never truly lifts."

The old woman looked at her, studying her closely. Cristina felt something flow between the two women, something mysterious, like two wounded spirits recognising each other as they passed along a dusty road. It was a moment that Cristina could not be a part of … not yet.

"What happened to Bartolo?" she asked, trying to steer things back into the world of reason.

The old woman nodded. "His mother bound his wounds with a sheet, picked the boy up, and walked ten miles to the Benedictine monastery at Castiglione. One of the monks there was a surgeon. She prayed as he operated. They saved the boy's life, and his arm. It was a miracle. But God exacted a high price."

"What do you mean?"

"Bartolo never returned from the monastery. He told his mother that he wanted to devote his life to God. To give thanks by taking holy orders." The old woman frowned. "That's what he said."

"But the truth?"

"His mother never saw Bartolo again. She died a broken woman. What did she have to live for? Sometimes God demands too much of us."

Suddenly, a young woman's voice called out from the water. "Bonito! Two of them."

"How big?" the old woman called back.

"Huge!" She held one aloft as it wriggled out its last moments.

"Beautiful!" The old woman gave a toothy smile.

They watched as her daughter pulled the boat towards the stone jetty, dropped the sail, and tossed a line to her mother.

"Who are the strangers?" she whispered, her green eyes locked on Cristina and Isra. "Trouble?"

"Curious, that's all."

"Just what we need in Castro — two more women."

"They're not staying. They're city people." The old woman reached into the boat and pulled out the first of the fish, huge and glistening in the sun. "Nice work."

Cristina and Isra knew they were no longer wanted; they were just in the way.

"We should get to the monastery today," Cristina said as they walked back up to the main square. "Castiglione's not far."

"It's too late." Isra glanced up at the sun which was already dropping in the sky.

"If we water the horses and leave immediately, we can make it."

"Too risky. Let's set off at first light."

"Bartolo's mother did it in the dark. On foot. We have horses."

"She was desperate. And lucky."

"Do you really want to stay the night in this village? They clearly don't want us here."

"Cristina, I thought you brought me along to give advice."

"I did, but —"

"So listen to me. Someone will rent us a room for the night, give us a bowl of soup. Then we'll be fresh in the morning."

"The answers are close, Isra, I can feel it."

"Then they'll still be close in the morning. And we'll be rested."

"I don't need rest!" Cristina complained like an impatient child. "I need answers."

By now they were back at the main square, where their horses had found some large clumps of wild grass to chomp on.

"You really want to ride two tired horses across unfamiliar countryside in the dark?"

"If we leave now, we'll be there by sunset."

Isra sighed. "So the choice I have is, do as you say, or listen to you complain all night?"

Cristina laughed. "I wouldn't have put it quite that way, but yes."

Isra picked up the reins of her horse. "Well, at least you're honest."

"Thank you, Isra. It's the right decision."

"We'll find out soon enough."

48: FERAL

This was a wild and deserted landscape, punctuated with sprawling olive trees and boulders left over from some bygone age, yet Cristina and Isra made good progress along the dusty road, their horses seemed happy and they met no other travellers. As the outline of the Benedictine monastery at Castiglione crept into view on the distant horizon, Cristina felt vindicated in her decision to press on. Keen to avoid the impression that she was gloating, she shared the deductions that were swirling round her mind.

"You know, Isra, I think everything Bartolo confessed under interrogation was a lie."

"Everything? Really?"

"That final cry as he burnt to death … I think that showed his true heart. Having his father taken in such violent circumstances … he never recovered. It gave him a lifelong hatred of the Ottomans. Bartolo would never convert to Islam; it's unthinkable."

"But he was caught praying to Allah," Isra replied.

"What if that was an act? Designed to bring down the Pope's wrath on the Muslims in Rome? And what if his confession about an Ottoman spy ring was all a fabrication?"

"Why would he do that?"

"To trigger the persecution of Muslims. And it worked."

Isra frowned. "So Bartolo blinded Christian monks to whip up hatred against Muslims?"

"I believe so. And he recruited other Christians to his cause, to commit more murders and create a wave of fear."

"And these fellow conspirators murdered seven Christians in the fireball attack just so that the Ottomans could be blamed?"

"It makes sense."

"I don't think it does," Isra objected. "It's too extreme."

"But it worked. All through the city, Muslims were arrested and thrown into jail."

"Then why go on to murder the Pope's son?" Isra replied. "That happened when Muslims were already in jail, so it pointed to their *innocence*."

"I admit, that doesn't fit the pattern," Cristina frowned. "Not yet."

"Maybe the crimes aren't linked after all."

"They are. I can sense it."

"That's a bit vague, Cristina."

"There must be more to this than Bartolo. Another layer which I can't see. Because right now, my theory is only half-right. Which isn't good enough."

"Half is still better than nothing."

They rode on in silence for a few minutes, listening to the steady beat of the horses' hooves cut through the chorus of cicadas; they felt a growing chill in the air as the sunlight dwindled.

"You know, what I really can't understand," Isra said, "is how a Christian could murder the Pope's son."

"It's puzzling," Cristina agreed. "In effect, it's an attack on the Holy Father himself, and that is an attack on the whole of Christendom."

"So, if the murderers aren't Christian, and they aren't Muslim, then who are we looking for?" Isra pondered.

Cristina looked at the monastery on the horizon. "The answers have to be in there. We need to understand what happened from the time Bartolo arrived at the Benedictines as a child, to the time he travelled to Rome. What's in those missing years? Understand that, and maybe we can finally solve these crimes."

Without warning, Isra pulled her horse to a stop. "What's that?" She peered into the gloom at a bundle of rags in the road just ahead of them.

"Has someone dropped it?" Cristina asked.

Suddenly the rags moved and uttered a sound, like a boy sobbing.

"It's a child," Cristina exclaimed. "He's in trouble."

She started to dismount, but Isra pulled her back. "Don't."

"What do you mean?"

Isra turned in her saddle, studying the long shadows cast by the trees and boulders all around them. "We should keep going."

"But there's a child in distress."

"I'm not so sure."

"Isra! We have to help."

"Ride past. As quickly as the horses will go."

"I'm not leaving him!"

"Bad enough we're out here with the light failing —"

"He needs our help."

"Ride past. Don't stop. Don't look back."

Cristina looked at her, aghast. "But for the grace of God, that could have been you."

"That's how I know to ride past."

"You're wrong." Defiantly Cristina jumped down from her horse and approached the crying child. "Hey, hey," she said gently. "What happened? Are you lost?"

The boy didn't look up; his face remained buried in the crook of his arm as he wept. He couldn't have been more than eight years old.

Cristina crouched down. "We're not going to hurt you. We just want to help."

The boy was so quick, Cristina didn't stand a chance. One hand grabbed her hair, the other pressed a dagger to her throat. He lurched to right, threw Cristina off balance and sent her tumbling into the dirt.

Isra leapt down to help her friend, when suddenly the shadows all around them started to ripple as one scrawny youth after another broke cover — this one from the ditch, that one from behind a tree, another from the shadow of a rock, until Isra was surrounded by a gang of feral boys.

"Going somewhere?" the leader taunted. He looked about sixteen, and was dressed in a motley array of military kit that had been pilfered over the years. His face would have been handsome, were it not for the deformed stub in the middle of his face that was once a nose. Isra knew exactly what this meant: even though he was young, this boy had fallen foul of the law enough times to have his nose cut off by the magistrates. He was bad news.

"Leave us alone, and you won't get hurt," Isra bluffed.

"Oooh, we're scared!" Noseless roared with laughter, which set the others off.

"Scared! Scared!" They shrieked with over-excited glee. "Scared! Scared!"

Isra looked from one boy to the next, trying to assess her chances. Most of them seemed to be twelve or thirteen years old, and there was a clear hierarchy; the more senior ones had daggers in their belts and a full set of clothes, while the junior ones had to make do with wooden clubs and patched-up rags.

"You've had your fun, now we'll be on our way." Isra tried to get back to her horse, but one of the boys rushed forward and swung a heavy staff across her knees, knocking her to the ground.

"Punish her!" the leader commanded. "Punish!"

As the gang surged forward, Isra rolled onto her back and pulled out a small dagger hidden in her boot. She kicked one of the boys away as he swung at her, then scrambled to her feet, slicing the air with her knife to keep everyone back.

But there were too many, and they were too fast.

"Over here!"

"No! Over here!"

"Behind you!"

They taunted her as she spun this way and that, trying to keep them at bay.

"Owww! Owwww! Owwww!" one of them started to howl like a wolf, and the others took up the yell.

"Owww! Owwww! Owwww!"

And now they'd surrounded her, brandishing their weapons in her face, too many to fight off. Isra thrust her dagger at the youngest, hoping to break through, but another two leapt onto her back, pulling her hair and scratching her face.

She bit their fingers, but two more grabbed onto her legs, trying to haul her off balance. The children may have been small, but they were vicious and quick.

Just as Isra began crumpling under the attack, a loud whistle cut through the air and the children all backed off.

Cristina turned and saw Noseless sitting on top of her horse, with his two deputies astride the other.

"Thanking you kindly for the gift horses." Noseless gave a mock bow.

"You can't leave us out here!" Isra protested. "We'll die!"

Noseless shrugged. "You would've left us. 'Ride past,' you said. 'Ride past. Don't stop. Don't look back.'"

"Yeah, yeah!" the gang taunted, mimicking his indignation. "Ride past! Ride past!"

"You would've left a poor, helpless child, all alone on the side of the road."

"Go to hell!" Isra spat.

"Charming." Noseless signalled to his deputies, who started unstrapping the swords from the horses' saddles and distributing them to the other children.

"What about me?" the small boy who had been holding Cristina yelled.

"Wait your turn!"

"No!"

"Shut it!"

"No! Won't! I fooled her, and I wanna big sword." Desperate not to be left out, the boy let go of Cristina and rushed to the horses to grab a weapon.

"Idiot!" Noseless yelled.

Cristina scrambled to her feet and ran to Isra's side. "What do we do?" she whispered.

"I wish I knew."

They watched the gang fan out in front of them, testing the weight of their newly won weapons.

"Nice blades." Noseless raised the finest sword above him like a medieval knight. "Now, we just need some practice." He lowered the sword until it was pointing directly at Cristina and Isra. "Can't have these two pigs telling tales on us."

"Kill the pigs!" a deputy yelled, and the chant was taken up by the others.

"Kill the pigs! Kill the pigs!"

"Oink! Oink!"

"Kill the pigs!"

As the boys encircled them, Cristina took Isra's hand. "I'm sorry I didn't listen to you."

"We have to run," Isra whispered. "As fast as we can."

"Where to?"

"Away from the road. Stealing our horses is more important to them than killing us."

"But —"

"NOW!"

Isra yanked Cristina's arm and dragged her off the road into the scrubland. "RUN!"

The two women bolted into the gloom, feet stumbling over bushes and rocks.

Behind them the wild children howled with delight at the prospect of a chase.

"Kill the pigs! Kill the pigs!"

Cristina glanced over her shoulder and saw the feral shadows leaping after them, arms thrashing the air, swords glinting in the dying light.

"They're not giving up!" she screamed at Isra.

"They will!"

A stabbing pain shot through Cristina's lungs as she gasped for air, but sheer terror kept her feet moving.

Ahead of her she could see Isra hurtling through the scrub. Behind her the wild boys were howling in a blood-frenzy. "Kill the pigs! Oink, oink! Kill the pigs!"

"We're not going to make it!" Cristina yelled.

"Over here!" Isra had veered to the right and was waving frantically at Cristina. "Come on!"

Cristina stumbled towards her, tripping and falling, then scrambling to her feet again.

"Kill the pigs! Kill the pigs!"

Suddenly Cristina felt Isra's strong hands grab her and haul her forwards. The ground beneath them disappeared. For a moment, they fell. Then they landed in some soft dirt.

"Don't breathe! Quiet!"

Even though her lungs were screaming for air, Cristina clamped her hands over her mouth and held her breath.

As her eyes adjusted to the gloom, she realised they were in a dry gully with overhanging banks. Silently they crawled further along the gully, away from the gang, so that when the boys arrived at edge of the bank, Isra and Cristina were already fifty feet away.

The gang looked up and down the gully.

"They can't be far," one of them said.

"Who cares?" another sneered. "Let the wolves get them."

Then they all started howling like wolves again, trying to summon a pack of the hungry predators.

Another whistle from the road summoned the gang back. "Pull out!" Noseless yelled. "Let's go!"

The boys obeyed, swinging their swords at every bush they passed as they made their way back to the road.

"I'm sorry," Cristina whispered.

"We're still alive."

"No thanks to me. We should've stayed the night in Castro."

"It's too late for that." Isra looked around, trying to assess their situation.

"So … what now?" Cristina asked.

"Well, truth be told, now we're in a very bad place."

49: GULLY

The gully provided perfect cover, allowing Cristina and Isra to hike in the direction of the Benedictine monastery whilst remaining out of sight from the road. Even though they hadn't heard horses' hooves or shouts from the feral gang for some time, it was better to be cautious. Who knew what strange hiding places there were out in this wilderness?

The moon was a waning crescent, giving the two women barely enough light to pick their way along the uneven gully floor.

"I know what you're thinking," Cristina said.

"No you don't."

"You're thinking, 'I tried to tell her. But she wouldn't listen.'"

"Actually, I was working out how much money you'll owe the stables if we get back to Rome."

"When we get back," Cristina corrected.

"And how much all the weapons were worth. And how much it'll cost to buy two new horses for the journey home."

"Yes, but thanks to you, we still have money." Cristina held up the spare water bottle and shook it, listening to the rattle of gold coins. "Not to mention the ducats sewn into my jacket, and the goldsmith's notes in my boots. I hope you followed your own advice as well?"

Isra glanced over her shoulder. "I don't have any money to hide. Never have done."

"But you're the one who told me —"

"That was the knowledge of a thief, Cristina. From the wrong side of the law."

"Oh."

In a sudden eerie moment, the sky lit up with a series of brilliant flickers that turned night into day. Cristina glimpsed a line of distant hills etched against the sky.

"Good job we stayed out of sight down here," Cristina said.

But Isra was busy counting as she trudged along the gully. When she reached fifteen, a booming rumble swept over them. "Storm's three miles away. We might still make it to the monastery."

More sheet lightning shimmered above them.

"Isra, if there's a storm, won't this gully fill up with water?"

"Judging from the lightning, it's probably a dry storm."

"Probably. But not definitely?"

BOOM! The next wave of thunder hit them.

"Sounds like a big one," Cristina said anxiously. Looking along the length of the gully, she could see that the muddy walls had now become much steeper, with an overhang that was impossible to climb. "I really think we should try and find a way out. Just in case."

"Even if there is a downpour, how fast can water travel?" Isra replied. "The worst of it will fall on the hills about two miles to the west, so that's how long we've got until —"

They heard a gentle whoosh, and seconds later water was running past their feet. It was shallow, but it was fast.

Isra looked down, baffled. "That shouldn't happen."

A menacing roar started to build further up the gully, getting louder with alarming speed. Cristina and Isra looked up at the impossibly high banks, then back over their shoulders as a foaming white wall of water surged towards them.

"Oh God!"

It hit them so fast, they didn't have time to think. Suddenly there was neither up nor down. They were tumbled around and slammed from one bank to the other, like bits of flotsam.

Cristina tried to gulp in some air, but immediately her mouth filled with foaming, muddy water. Her hands flailed wildly, trying to grab hold of a root, a rock, anything … but she was being washed down the gully too fast and everything slipped through her fingers.

A heaving surge of water overwhelmed her and plunged her under the surface. Cristina retched, which only drew the water deeper into her lungs.

And then the terror started.

There was no way out of this. She wasn't going to survive. The water was unstoppable. She was going to drown in a gully in the middle of nowhere.

THUNK!

The trunk of an olive tree slammed into the back of her head like a battering ram. She felt searing pain and her vision reeled. She could feel her scalp splitting open.

Desperately her arms reached out, trying to catch the floating tree as it sped past. Her fingers grabbed onto it and held tight as the tree pulled her along the gully with terrifying speed.

She managed to tilt her head above the water just enough to gasp in some air. But up ahead the gully narrowed, making the water churn even more wildly. And now the tree started to swing round.

"No!"

It wasn't going to make it through the gap. Desperately she tried to turn it back, but the water was out of control. Cristina braced for impact.

CRACK! The tree jammed into the narrow banks and wedged fast.

Her face was thrown into the trunk. Pain split across her nose. Cristina tried to hold on, but her fingers were losing their grip. The force of water tore her away from the trunk and threw her further downstream.

It was over. That tree had been her last chance. Now the waters would swallow her up.

She stopped fighting. Her body went limp. She had lost this battle. The flood was too strong.

Despair started to creep across her mind. She knew that she was going to drown. And with acceptance, came a sense of peace.

Finally, the struggle was over. Part of her felt sad … but there was also relief. Perhaps this was what Divine forgiveness felt like. Maybe death wasn't so bad after all…

A violent force grabbed hold of Cristina's arms. She writhed to free herself, but the force hauled her up out of the raging water.

She opened her eyes.

A man was standing over her, screaming at her, but all she could hear was the water cascading in her ears. She focused on his lips.

"Are you alone?" he was screaming. "Are you alone?"

"Isra!" she gasped. "Save Isra!"

The man yelled at some other figures on the bank, who ran back up the gully to where the tree was wedged. Cristina saw them lie down on the bank, each man gripping onto the next man's legs, enabling the one at the front to lean down into the torrent, arms wide like a hermit fishing for his supper.

A few moments later she heard the man shout instructions, and the others hauled him back; in his arms, he held the half-drowned Isra.

Cristina staggered along the gully bank towards them, dropped to her knees and scooped Isra into her arms. "Breathe! Breathe!" She shook Isra and slammed her fists into her back. "Open your eyes! Breathe!"

Isra retched and coughed up a lungful of muddy brown water, then choked in some air.

"Thank God," Cristina cried. "Thank God." She closed her eyes and held her friend tightly.

When Cristina snapped open her eyes again, everything had changed. She and Isra were huddled in blankets around a campfire. Someone had tied a makeshift bandage around the cuts on her head. A few feet away the gulley was still a raging torrent of water, but out here it was warm and calm.

"I said it would be a dry storm." Isra held out her palm. "See? No rain. At least not here."

Cristina looked around, blinking. "What on earth happened?"

"God bless the Benedictines." Isra looked towards a small enclave of olive trees, where a group of six men were gathered with their horses.

The tallest of the monks saw that the two women were talking, took a flask from one of the horses and walked over. He was dressed in a black woollen robe, and prayer beads jangled off the leather belt around his waist. "Some brandy to warm you up?" He offered them the flask.

"Please." Isra took it and swigged the spirit down, relishing the warmth trickling into her body.

"Thank you for rescuing us," Cristina said. "I thought we were dead."

"You'll feel better once your clothes are dried and you've had a good meal," the monk smiled. "We've sent word back to the monastery to prepare rooms." He bent down and inspected the dressing on Cristina's head. "I think it's stopped bleeding. That's good."

"How did you know we were out here?" Cristina asked. "It's the middle of nowhere."

"We come out whenever there's a bad storm, just to make sure the goats don't get drowned in the gullies." He pointed to some trees, where a dozen goats were contentedly nibbling shrubs.

"Well, the goats are cleverer than us," Cristina remarked.

"The storm was miles away," Isra said in her defence. "We should have been safe."

"You're not wrong," the monk replied. "But those hills are full of caves that hold the water. As soon as it rains up there, water is forced out through boreholes down on the plains."

"I don't understand," Isra frowned.

"No-one does. Not anymore. Centuries ago, Berber herdsman farmed these lands. They built an irrigation system to harness the storms. It was brilliant. But when they were expelled, the channels and gullies were neglected, and the whole system became unstable."

Cristina looked at the torrent of water barrelling through the gulley. "Berber herdsmen did all that?"

"Impressive, isn't it?" the monk replied. "But it wasn't enough to stop them being driven out of the country."

Cristina nodded wearily. "Some things never change."

50: RESTLESS

For a thousand years, Benedictine monks had been giving refuge to weary travellers and lonely outcasts, so the brothers at the monastery of Castiglione knew exactly how to look after Cristina and Isra. They were given a small, sparse room each, with a bed and a bowl of water. Simple robes were provided while their wet clothes were taken away to be cleaned and dried. Even though it was well past suppertime when they arrived, one of the monks still managed to rustle up some soup and bread.

Cristina and Isra felt safe wrapped in the great stone arms of the monastery. Its walls were three feet thick, and it resembled an imposing castle, only without the fortifications and architecture of violence. It was solid, permanent and centred; the small sparrows that fluttered around the high vaulted corridors added a sense of peace.

No wonder Cristina slept soundly. It was the first time she had enjoyed truly deep sleep since leaving Rome.

The following morning, after prayers at Terce, she and Isra were taken to Abbot Arcali's study, a plain room dominated by a heavy desk, which looked out across the arid landscape stretching to the coast. Arcali was in his fifties; he had worked hard all his life and it showed in his sinewy body, but his eyes were still young and alert, eager for knowledge.

Cristina told him about the series of crimes that had shaken Rome, and the imminent threat to the Holy Father himself. All the while Arcali listened closely, without interrupting. As he concentrated, he ran his fingers absentmindedly through the grey hairs of his tonsure.

"If we can piece together the missing years," Cristina concluded, "we should be able to unravel this mystery and protect the Church from further attacks. But the key is to understand what happened to Bartolo between arriving here as a boy and joining the monastery in Rome as a man."

"I was afraid this day would come," Arcali said thoughtfully.

Cristina and Isra exchanged a wary glance. "Then something did happen here? Something strange?"

Abbot Arcali nodded. "I remember Bartolo arriving as a thirteen-year-old boy, clinging to life. I was young myself and had only been here a few years. But that night … the pain and grief that afflicted the boy and his mother… They were in shock, struggling to understand how their lives could have collapsed with such speed.

"But the child was strong, and with patience and herbal ointments, we healed his body. He asked to join our order, to give thanks to God for sparing him, so we taught him to read. He learnt how to study the Bible, and about the sacrifice and service that are at the heart of the Benedictine order."

"And he was a good student?" Cristina asked.

"In some ways, exemplary. He was an intelligent boy who absorbed everything we told him. And yet…" The abbot hesitated, as if reluctant to betray a personal secret.

"Did he ever talk about his father?" Cristina prompted. "Or the attack on the village?"

"He could not move beyond it," Arcali replied. "In truth, Bartolo had a heart filled with rage and pain. And we failed him."

Cristina could see that the sadness still weighed heavily on the abbot.

"Didn't the discipline of monastic life help?" Isra asked. "I thought that was how troubled souls heal."

"It is. But every now and then…" Abruptly the abbot stood up. "Let me show you something. Come. Follow."

Arcali led them along cavernous corridors to a wing of the monastery that contained individual cells where the monks slept and meditated. He stopped by a door at the far end. "This used to be Bartolo's room." Arcali swung open the door to reveal a storeroom, stacked high with barrels of olive oil, salt and dried fish.

"And?" Cristina didn't understand what she was supposed to notice.

The abbot rolled a barrel aside to reveal some graffiti scratched into the stone with a knife. "This is what obsessed Bartolo."

Cristina crouched down to read the phrases:

Destroy all who would destroy love.
Fight those who fight against you.
Purify the soul through the fire of vengeance.

"The self-righteous conviction of a young man," Cristina noted.

"Oh, no. This is beyond conviction." Arcali slid two large crates aside to reveal an entire wall covered in carefully etched hatred:

To compromise with evil is to cut your own throat.
The sword of justice is covered in blood.
To hate is to live.
Kill the Heathens.
Kill. Them. All.

It was shocking. Even after all these years, the carvings had not lost any of their vehemence.

"He covered the whole room with his 'maxims', as he called them."

Isra rolled aside a barrel on the opposite side of the room, revealing yet more words of hatred.

"Time didn't heal him?" Cristina studied the abbot's face.

"Time made it worse." Arcali seemed to crumple as he recalled those dark months. "His hatred of Ottomans and Muslims increased as the years passed. He struggled with the concept of forgiveness. Grief burned away all his compassion." He gazed at the wall of words. "We haven't been able to use this room since. Only for storage. The hatred is too poisonous."

"Did you expel him from the order?" Isra asked.

"We never give up on a troubled soul. But he gave up on us." Arcali sat down on one of the barrels of salt. "A traveller arrived one night in need of shelter. He said he was an artist, a painter, who was studying light and landscape as part of his apprenticeship. But he was not what he appeared. He stayed for a week, and all the time I had an uneasy sense that he was hunting for something. Or someone. When he spoke to the brothers, he would question them deeply, as if probing their hearts. It wasn't long before he fastened onto the young Bartolo. They would pray together, work in the monastery gardens, study in the library side by side. Then one morning, he vanished, and Bartolo had gone too. We never heard from them again."

"Did you ever discover who the stranger was?" Cristina asked.

"About ten years later, an inquisitor from Madrid visited Castiglione as part of his investigations. He told us about a secret and dangerous sect, the Evangelicals of Light. Their method of recruiting people was to send out disciples to remote parts of the land, searching for troubled souls."

"Perhaps Bartolo needed more devotion than he could find here," Isra suggested.

"He did." Abbot Arcali nodded gravely. "But the Evangelicals of Light practise devotion to God through violence against His enemies. Extreme violence."

51: RADICALISED

"This is a beautiful room." Cristina stood in the middle of the monastery's archive chamber, admiring its simplicity. Eight reading lecterns were arranged in a circle. Around them, an octagon of freestanding bookcases stretched up to the ceiling. "It is exactly my kind of space."

Abbot Arcali beamed with pride, even though it was a mortal sin. "Long after I am gone, this chamber will be alive with learning and thought."

"You don't have that many books, though," Isra observed.

"But that's what I really like." Cristina ran her hand along some of the empty shelves. "The optimism. All this space for new books, new knowledge. It's a building for the future."

Arcali took out a leather folio of documents and one of the newly printed bibles that had recently been shipped from Nuremberg and put them on a lectern. "I was unable to stop thinking about Bartolo, and what had become of that troubled soul, so I pressed the inquisitor until he revealed that they had captured some secret correspondence in Madrid, setting out the philosophy of the Evangelicals of Light." Arcali untied the folio and took out a bundle of letters covered in dense handwriting. "I had them copied."

Cristina studied the pages: there were masses of strange mathematical calculations cross-referenced to footnotes and appendices. "What numerical system are they using?" she asked.

"It took us two years to unravel. It's a complex mathematical analysis of the dimensions of the Temple of Solomon." Arcali opened the bible to 1 Kings. "Here … the dimensions of the

Temple are laid out in precise detail. But the Evangelicals believe they are more than measurements; they believe they're a message from God, encoded into the temple. And they are convinced that they alone have been chosen to understand."

"But you have broken their code?"

"If I'm right, for the Evangelicals the measurements set out the timescale for the whole of human existence, from the first act of Creation to the final flames of Revelation."

"Ambitious," Cristina observed.

"And worrying." The abbot pointed to a paragraph on the final page of the letters. "Look, here … they believe that Western Civilisation will end in the year 1500."

Isra breathed in sharply. "That's just three years away."

"Don't worry." Cristina shrugged. "Every time a new century dawns, someone believes it will be the end of the world. This is nothing new."

"But we are not just in any century," Arcali warned. "This is the midpoint between two millennia. If the prediction is true, it would make us the very last generation." He pointed to the final paragraph. "*Christendom must be purified before the Day of Judgement.* That's what the Evangelicals believe. The crimes that you are investigating, they could all be part of this philosophy of cleansing."

Cristina wasn't convinced. "That's quite a leap of the imagination."

"And why can't the description of the temple be just that, a description?" Isra asked. "Sometimes there is no hidden meaning."

"Then explain why the Bible sets everything out in such precise detail." Arcali turned to chapter 6.2 and started to read. "Length: threescore cubits. Breadth: twenty cubits. Height: thirty cubits. Further down, exact dimensions of the porch, precise locations of the doors. And the statues: *In the oracle he made two cherubim of olive wood, each ten cubits high. And five cubits was one wing of the cherub, and five cubits the other wing of the cherub … and for the entering of the oracle he made doors of olive wood: the lintel and door posts were a fifth part of the wall.* And so it goes on, verse after verse of dimensions. Why such detail if it is not a message from God?"

Cristina ran her fingers over the letters … and suddenly felt the astrolabe in her mind click into a new pattern. Now she could see it: buildings were not just buildings to the Evangelicals, so it made perfect sense that they would do everything to stop the demolition of the old St Peter's and destroy all plans for a new one. These crimes had started when the Pope had made his decision: that was the trigger. For zealots like the Evangelicals, a Borgia Pope was bad enough, but that he would presume to demolish Rome's most sacred building was an anathema.

Cristina studied the abbot closely. "How can we infiltrate the Evangelicals?"

"No, no, no. You need to leave them well alone."

"If we don't stop them, no-one will."

"They cannot be stopped," Arcali insisted.

"Then they will go on killing," Isra replied.

"We cannot let that happen, which is why we need to understand everything about them," Cristina urged.

"I forbid it!" Arcali exclaimed, then immediately regretted his temper. "Forgive me for shouting."

Cristina smiled. "Your vehemence tells me that you do know a way to find them."

"No."

"Then tell me, why was the inquisitor visiting your monastery in particular? Was he hunting one of them down?"

Arcali looked uneasy.

"You are too honest to lie, Padre. Your face gives your heart away."

The abbot busied himself putting the bible back on the shelves.

"Is there an Evangelical cell close by?" Cristina pressed.

"Even if there was, they would not speak to you. Their radical views do not tolerate women."

"Now I really do want to meet them."

"If something happens to you, I cannot have that on my conscience." Arcali seemed genuinely concerned.

"We are responsible for ourselves," Isra objected.

"I'm only trying to protect you."

"Thank you, but we are grown women," Cristina replied. "We don't need your protection."

Arcali sat down, outmanoeuvred. "Very well. On your own heads be it. The inquisitor came to Castiglione to question a hermit," he said.

"Which hermit? Where does he live?"

"In the caves on Marble Ridge, just south of here. No-one knows when he arrived. Some say he is a holy man; some say he is a devil. The inquisitor believed that he had run away from the Evangelicals of Light and had been in hiding ever since."

"And he's still there? In the caves?"

"I don't know. This was many years ago. But even if the hermit is still alive, you will find no answers there. When the inquisitor tracked him down and questioned him, he said his mind was in pieces and he had sunk into madness. That was then; the hermit would be an old man now."

"On the other hand," Cristina replied, "pretending to be mad in order to avoid being tortured by the Inquisition, that would be an extremely sane and intelligent strategy."

"Can you direct us to Marble Ridge?" Isra asked.

"When you talk to fanatics, your mind risks being changed forever," the abbot warned. "And not for the better."

"I have no fear of dangerous ideas," Cristina said calmly. "They can always be defeated by the truth."

"I wish I shared your optimism."

Isra gave the abbot a sympathetic smile. "Padre, if you don't help us find the caves, we will just keep on searching, and keep on falling into gullies, and you will have to keep on rescuing us. Isn't it quicker just to tell us what you know?"

Arcali looked from Isra to Cristina. "When does stubborn become foolish?"

"When it's anyone but us," Cristina smiled.

52: CAVES

Cristina gave the Benedictines a good price for two horses and saddles; the animals were young and strong, and she hoped that the stables in Rome would accept them as a fair replacement. While she was tacking up, Isra tried to persuade the monastery blacksmith to make them a couple of daggers for protection, but he resisted all her charm and pestering, and insisted that his vows forbade him from becoming an arms supplier. Abbot Arcali gave them ample food and water, beautifully packed for the journey, and a set of rosary beads each. "God will protect you," he said as they set off, although the worried expression on his face suggested that perhaps he wasn't convinced.

As they left Castiglione behind and rode deeper into the barren landscape, Cristina started looking around anxiously. "Do you think that gang will hunt us down again?"

"Why would they?" Isra shrugged. "They think we're already dead. Drowned, or savaged by wolves."

"Good. That's one less thing to worry about."

"Of course, there might be other gangs," Isra said mischievously.

"Well, I'm not stopping for anyone this time," Cristina replied. "No matter how innocent they look."

They ate while still riding south, but as she tried to break the bread in two, Isra felt something hard inside the loaf. Carefully she dug into the dough and discovered a small dagger. She unfurled a note that had been wrapped around the blade. "*Only to cut the cheese and meat*," she read. "Well, well, a gift from the blacksmith after all."

Cristina laughed. "How to maintain your vows in the real world. That's my kind of monk."

By late afternoon they arrived at a limestone ridge that looked exactly as Abbot Arcali had described: the smooth rockface was streaked with rust-coloured veins, creating the impression of marble, and halfway up it was pockmarked by a series of dark caves. As there was no obvious path to the top, Cristina and Isra tied their horses to a lone tree and started scrambling up the scree slopes.

By the time they reached the first cave, their faces were covered with dust, and their hands with small cuts. Cristina looked out over the vast, hostile landscape: swallows were swooping on the air currents, searching for cracks and ledges in which to build nests, and high above two vultures circled, patiently waiting for death to make them a gift.

Isra made her way to the right-hand side of the cave and tried to peer round the rock wall into the next opening. "This is going to be difficult," she said. "To get from cave to cave, we must scramble along that." She pointed to a narrow, crumbling ledge that ran along the sheer face of the ridge.

Cristina peered down at the drop. "It's not very forgiving." She wandered into the gloom at the back of the cave, exploring the craggy walls, and soon discovered a small connecting tunnel that linked some of the chambers. "Must have been bored out by water over the centuries." She ran her hand along the ceiling — it was damp from the trickling moisture.

Moving in single file, Cristina and Isra made their way through the branching crawl-tunnels, deeper into Marble Ridge.

"Hello?" Cristina called into the labyrinth, listening to the echo of her voice decay in the gloom.

"No welcome in the hillside for us," Isra whispered.

Cautiously they picked their way from cave to cave, until they started to find signs of human habitation: the remnants of fires, small piles of animal bones, some strange patterns daubed on the rough walls like childish paintings. Yet still there was no sign of the hermit.

"He must move around depending on the weather," Isra guessed.

They moved ever deeper into the rockface, eyes straining in the gloom, until eventually they heard a faint groan.

"What was that?" Cristina whispered.

They held their breath and listened.

"Urgghhhh…"

It sounded like a man in pain.

"Don't be afraid!" Cristina called into the darkness. "We're going to help you."

They crept forward, closing in on the sound, until they entered a cavern illuminated by a thin shaft of sunlight that had somehow punctured through the dense layers of rock above.

An old man was lying on his side, his wild grey hair and unkempt beard framed a face that was twisted in pain, and although he stared straight at Cristina and Isra, he didn't react to them.

"Urrrghhh … huuuuhhh."

"He's delirious," Isra said. "He must be sick."

"We're not going to hurt you," Cristina reassured.

The hermit's eyes swivelled as he wavered on the edge of consciousness. Cristina edged forward and knelt next to him; she reached out and laid a hand on his shoulder, but the moment she touched his skin, the hermit howled in pain.

"Sorry! I'm sorry!" Cristina peered through the rags and filth that covered the hermit's body, looking for any obvious wounds. When she crept round to the other side, she saw a huge abscess in the middle of his back, red and tight and impossible for him to reach.

"It's pressing on his spine. He must be in agony."

Isra winced. "He can't even lie on his back."

"Light a fire in one of the outer caves. We have to operate."

Isra looked alarmed. "Have you done it before?"

"No. But I've read about it. And right now, he doesn't have a choice."

Isra gathered some dried twigs and dead branches, and quickly got a fire going, fanned by the steady breeze flowing through the caves. When the heart of the fire was roaring hot, Cristina slid the blade of the dagger into it.

"What does fire do to the knife?" Isra asked.

"No-one is quite sure. But the Greek physician Galen was famous for his care of wounded Roman gladiators, and he always boiled his instruments before operating."

"Interesting," Isra nodded. "And this is one use of the dagger the Benedictines can't complain about."

After a few minutes, Cristina withdrew the blade from the fire and positioned herself behind the hermit's back. "A moment of discomfort, then it will be over."

"Urggh."

"Try to remain still."

Perhaps it was just as well that he was delirious.

Cristina drew a deep breath, then with a swift, confident movement she sliced the abscess open. A foul stench billowed from the wound, and Isra recoiled in disgust. The hermit screamed in agony then slumped forward, motionless.

"It's done," Cristina said.

The hermit didn't respond.

"Have you killed him?" Isra whispered.

"Please, show a little faith."

"He looks dead."

"Isra, fetch the honey from our food parcels."

"You can't seriously be hungry after smelling that?"

"It's the best thing to put on an open wound. Helps healing and prevents more infection."

"How old was this Galen when he died?"

"Eighty-seven."

"Honey it is, then." And Isra scrambled back down the scree slope to the horses.

53: EVANGELICALS

The hermit came round just as Cristina finished tying off the improvised bandages.

Immediately he started to struggle. "Get away from me!"

"It's all right."

"Leave me alone!" He lashed out with his fists. "Be gone!"

"You were going to die!"

For a moment the hermit paused, his face creased in concentration. "Who are you?"

"You had a terrible infection on your back. We operated to remove it."

He shook his head. "You are the Devil!"

"No!"

"And on her forehead was written, 'Babylon, mother of prostitutes and Earth's abominations!'"

"We healed you! Look!" Cristina pointed to the bandages. "We saved you."

The hermit ran his fingers over the dressing, trying to piece together what had happened. "I was sick…"

"You were going to die. But if you rest, you'll recover."

He gazed at Cristina as humility slowly replaced fear. "You helped me?"

"Of course."

"No-one ever helps me."

"Well, we did."

The hermit struggled to understand. "Few come to these caves. Those who do, abuse me." He reached a hand behind his back, touched his skin and was relieved that there was no shooting pain. "Thank you," he whispered.

"You must get sick often," Isra said, looking at the squalor in the cave.

"This was not the first time. But it was the worst. I must endure insects that bite and rocks that scratch…" His voice petered out as he scrutinised Cristina and Isra. "Why did you *really* help me?"

"We want to ask you some questions," Cristina began.

"No!" Fear and paranoia swept over the hermit again. "I never told them anything, I swear!"

"Be calm."

"I've said nothing to them! I'll say nothing to you!"

Cristina grabbed his arms. "Who do you think we are?"

"They've sent you, haven't they? It's them!"

"Who?"

"The Evangelicals of Light."

"No. I swear."

"Liar! I never betrayed any secrets. I just want to live out my life in peace."

"If you want peace, then you'll need medicine." Isra picked up the bottle of honey and held it in front of the hermit's face. "Answer our questions, and this is yours. Otherwise…" She put the honey back in the saddlebag.

"You are cruel," the hermit scowled. "Just like all the others."

"So cruel we saved your life," Isra replied.

"You saved me to torment me!"

"All we want is to talk. Ask you some questions. Is that really so terrible?"

"We are not from the Evangelicals," Cristina added. "No-one will ever know you've spoken to us. This is as secret as the confessional. You have my word."

The hermit shook his head. "Once you swear allegiance to them, you can never be free again. That's how they work."

"Well, this is how we work." Cristina reached across, took the bottle of honey from the saddlebag and placed it in the hermit's hands. "It's yours. Whether you talk to us or not. But if you want to stop more people suffering and dying, you'll tell us what you can about the Evangelicals."

The old man clasped the bottle tightly, watching Cristina and Isra withdraw to the outer caves.

As they waited for the hermit to make up his mind, Isra kept herself busy warming up some meat and cheese over the fire. They ate in silence, enjoying the dying light as the sun slipped lower in the sky. When they were done, they lay back and watched the stars emerge in the gloaming.

"Why did you give away the only thing we had to bargain with?" Isra asked Cristina.

"There's an age-old puzzle that philosophers argue about. Which of these is true: 'People must be treated harshly because they do bad things.' Or, 'People do bad things *because* they are treated harshly.'"

"Isn't that just a fancy way of asking which came first, the chicken or the egg?"

"Except you can't build a moral philosophy on eggs. The point is, what is more powerful: forgiveness or revenge?"

"I know what feels better," Isra replied.

"But that doesn't answer the question."

They stared up at the darkening blue for a while longer, then Isra turned to Cristina. "What do you believe?"

"Have you ever seen malice or hatred in a new-born child? All they want is to love and be loved. Yet somewhere, that wisdom gets forgotten."

"Suffer the little children." The voice emerged from the darkness, startling Cristina and Isra. They turned and saw the hermit sitting on a boulder in the gloom of the cave.

"How long have you been there?" Isra asked.

"A lifetime."

"Come and warm yourself by the fire," Cristina offered.

The hermit shook his head. He didn't even make eye contact; he wanted to talk as if this really was a confession. "The Evangelicals were supposed to be about love. They wanted to renew the Church. Distribute its wealth. Expel the cardinals and bishops from their palaces, and give the money to the poor. If He was with us now, Christ Himself would lead the revolution. That is what drew me to the Evangelicals, to make a better world."

The hermit seemed easier in his soul, remembering what it felt like to be part of a noble cause. Then his face darkened again. "But their methods … the cruelty of their methods … nothing had prepared me for that. They will sacrifice anyone. They were going to sacrifice me. But I didn't want to die. I was too young. Why would God create this world if He wanted us to perish?"

The hermit's question hung unanswered in the gloom.

"You rebelled against the Evangelicals?" Cristina asked.

"They brook no dissent," the hermit said. "All I could do was run. And hide. And that has been my life ever since."

"Surely they would forgive an old man," Isra said. "How many years has it been since you left them?"

"The Evangelicals never forgive."

"Are they operating in Rome?" Cristina asked.

"They are everywhere, and they are nowhere. Wherever the Church has built palaces and cathedrals, it has made itself a target. But exposing the Evangelicals … that is an impossible task."

"Nothing is impossible," Cristina said. "Not if you're determined enough."

"The Evangelicals are not like other sects. They do not have a hierarchy. They infiltrate others. They hide in plain sight. You know them without knowing that you know them."

His ominous words resonated with the contradictory evidence troubling Cristina's mind. "I knew a man who infiltrated the City Watch," she said. "He was a dutiful soldier for many years, until the moment came to crucify a sinner. I knew a man who blinded himself to make it seem as if the Devil was stalking Rome. And another who burned himself alive to spread terror."

"Then you have known the Evangelicals," the hermit warned.

"The men I am hunting now have murdered the Pope's son, and set their sights on the very highest target in Christendom."

The hermit looked at Cristina with dread. "You are tangled in a nest of Evangelicals. They will destroy you. If you want to live, do not return to Rome. Run and hide."

"I have to return. I cannot live in a world defined by fear."

"Then you must look where you trust the most. Suspect those who are closest. The power of the Evangelicals is to abuse the bond of trust. Those who you love will betray you. Remember that, and maybe you will survive. Maybe."

54: RETURN

It astonished Domenico how much paper had flooded into his office in just two weeks. Gilo's diligence was admirable: he and his team had compiled comprehensive lists of every enemy Pope Alexander had made on his climb to power, opened a dossier on each one, conducted nearly a hundred official interviews, and cross-referenced the answers on thousands of pages.

It was impressive. But it was also overwhelming, and there were times when Domenico secretly wished his deputy could be a little lazier.

"I wonder if St Peter made as many enemies," Tomasso said as he clattered into the room and put down yet another document crate.

"Who are those for?" Gilo asked.

"Jilted mistress number six."

"His Holiness certainly gets through them."

"I've got another three boxes downstairs to bring through," Tomasso said, and he hurried off to fetch them.

Domenico picked up a bundle of the fresh documents and flicked through them, skim-reading the transcripts. "We need to get lucky soon, or the Pope will die of old age before we finish collating the evidence," he said.

"It really shouldn't be this way," Gilo sighed, looking at the mountains of boxes. "Anyone who becomes Pope should lead by example."

"Whoever got rich and powerful without sinning?" Domenico replied.

"Well, if it's any comfort, I've roped Padre Gabriel in to do some of the donkey work."

Domenico looked up uneasily. "The inquisitor?"

"Needs must."

"I really don't like him, Gilo."

"With all these people to investigate, I thought —"

"I don't want him anywhere near this."

"Sir, the Inquisition may be monsters, but they do have experience in smoking out enemies."

"You didn't see what he did to Bartolo … and the pleasure he took from it."

Gilo shrugged. "I can get the files back from him, if you'd prefer?"

"No. It's done now. Leave it. Maybe this way he can redeem himself a little."

The two men made themselves comfortable and divided the new transcripts between them; perhaps this was the day they would break the case.

Riding back into Rome was strangely confusing for Cristina. She had expected it to have all the warmth and familiarity of a homecoming, where you feel secure because everything is known. Instead, she found her senses overwhelmed by all the noise and movement, and the sheer number of people in the city.

"What's the matter?" Isra asked, sensing her unease.

"I think I've spent too long in the wilderness." Cristina rode slowly through the busy streets, but her eyes darted from person to person with a manic energy. In the past she had always felt completely in tune with the rhythm of Rome, but now everything felt too complex. She looked at the vast array of goods being sold in the shops as if noticing them for the first time; she was confused by the variety of fashions people wore and the richness of their fabrics; above all, she studied the faces of the crowds who thronged the streets. In the past, they had just been people she jostled past to get to where she was going, but now she wondered about each one… What was in their past? What had brought them to Rome? What story was each one living?

"The stable manager has nothing to complain about," Isra said as she led the way into Via Labicana, "but he'll complain anyway."

The comment broke Cristina's reverie. "Why? What do you mean?"

"They love finding fault. That's where their profit lies."

And so it proved.

Patiently Isra explained how they had been ambushed and robbed, but that these were younger, stronger horses, and more than fair replacements. The groom sighed and tutted and shook his head.

"I'm not happy about this," he grumbled. "Not happy at all."

"Do you think we wanted to get robbed?" Isra replied.

"You should've been more careful."

"And you were there?"

"I'm just saying. A man can say, can't he?"

Cristina tried to ease the building tension. "I think you'll find these horses are in excellent condition. Worthy replacements for the animals you've lost."

"We'll see about that," came the surly reply.

The groom started to inspect the horses with great pedantry, determined to find fault somewhere. He gazed into the animals' eyes, looked up their nostrils, pulled back their lips and checked their teeth, then he ran his hands all over their bodies and legs, feeling for the slightest lump or bump.

Frustrated by the lack of fault, he had one of the stable lads walk the horses back and forth so that he could study their gait.

"I don't like the way they've been shoed," he finally pronounced.

"Seriously?" Isra glared at him. "That's all you can pick on?"

"According to the terms of hire —"

"If you want to take this to court, I'm happy to meet you there," Cristina said, finally out of patience. "But I think the magistrates will realise that you are considerably better off from this trade, and may even order you to pay compensation to us. So I suggest you accept these horses, then we can all get on with our lives."

The groom stared at Cristina, put two fingers on the side of his nose, turned away and exhaled sharply, sending a globule of phlegm from his nostril onto the straw-covered floor.

"I'll take that as a yes," Cristina replied.

As they walked home through the streets, Cristina felt a strange awkwardness edge out the trust that had grown between her and Isra over the past two weeks. On the road, it had seemed natural to share their thoughts, but now it felt as if the city was listening to their every word, and judging them.

Cristina turned onto Via di Pasquino and glimpsed her house on the corner. "Well, it's still here."

But Isra kept on walking.

"Where are you going?"

"To the market at Campo de Fiori. I need to get food for dinner."

"What are you talking about?"

"I'm still your cook."

"Isra, we have to focus all our attention on exposing the Evangelicals of Light."

"Is there a 'we' now that we're back in Rome?"

"Of course. Don't be absurd." Cristina moved forward as if to hug Isra, but the girl backed away. Cristina felt the rejection like a flicker of pain. "What's wrong?"

"It's probably best if I call you mistress again."

"Isra, don't do this. I wouldn't have survived out there without you."

"Then I'd better make sure you don't die of hunger now that we're back."

"But … I need you. To help solve this mystery."

"I'll only be in the kitchens, mistress." She turned and headed off towards the market. "Meat or fish?" she called over her shoulder.

"We're beyond this, aren't we?"

"I'll get whatever's freshest, then."

Cristina watched Isra disappear into the crowds, baffled by the ease with which she had become a seventeen-year-old housekeeper again.

55: CLOSER

Cristina didn't say anything; she just went straight for the hug. A big, tight bear-hug that sisters gave their brothers all the time … only Cristina didn't.

Domenico finally disentangled himself so that he could look at his sister's face. "What happened? Where have you been?"

Instead of answering, Cristina just pulled him close again and squeezed him tightly.

Domenico had never seen this side to her before. Even as children she never felt comfortable showing affection, and he realised that wherever Cristina had been, it must have been dangerous. "You're all right now. You're safe," he said quietly. "We can deal with this together."

Suddenly Cristina broke the hug and straightened herself up. "Better get Deputato Gilo in here. I've found the crucial lead."

"No, no. Wait a moment."

"We don't have time, Domenico."

"You can't just come in here and hug me like your life depends on it without telling me what happened!"

"What do you want to know?"

This was more like the Cristina he knew, impatient with anyone who couldn't keep up with her speed of thought … which was most people. But Domenico wasn't going to be brushed off. "Everything. I want to know everything."

"You'll need to be more specific."

"Where did you go?"

"South."

"To Naples?"

"Further south."

"On your own?"

"No. I went with Isra."

"The cook?" Domenico couldn't believe what he was hearing.

"You think strength is all about having an armed escort?"

"Actually, yes."

"Well, you might be surprised."

Domenico took his sister's hand, led her to the chair on the other side of the desk and forced her to sit down. "Now tell me exactly what happened out there."

Realising he wasn't going to accept a quick precis, Cristina told him about the journey and Isra, about Castro and the monastery, about dodging death at the hands of the feral gang, and about nearly drowning in the flash flood.

Domenico was astonished that his bookish sister had embarked on such a reckless trip. Part of him felt jealous that he wasn't there to protect her; he had been playing that role that all his life, and it was hard not to feel rejected. But more than that, Domenico felt an incredible sense of pride; his sister hadn't just survived, he could see that she was stronger for it.

"So, back to the case," Cristina concluded. "Do you want the good news, or the bad?"

"Good. Always start with good news."

"These boxes," Cristina said, sweeping her arms across the room, "are redundant."

"What?"

"The murderers are not among the Pope's enemies."

"Then who?"

"That's the bad news. They are among his friends. We need to look at those who move in the circles closest to the Holy Father."

"That doesn't make sense."

Cristina told him about Bartolo's radicalisation by the Evangelicals of Light, and the hermit's defection; crucially, she told him about the sect's ruthless modus operandi.

"If the Evangelicals are so dangerous, why have I never heard of them?" Domenico scratched his temples, where the first flecks of grey were starting to show. "We read intelligence reports from all over Christendom."

"Secrecy is their power. Anonymity is how they infiltrate."

"What if this hermit really is a madman? Have you thought of that? He could've told you a pack of lies."

"I'm convinced the Evangelicals are behind the terrifying attacks we've seen in Rome. They believe the world will end in 1500 and are determined to cleanse the city before Judgement Day."

"But where is your hard evidence?"

Cristina scooped up the mass of testimony documents from Domenico's desk and dumped them into one of the boxes lining the walls. "Forget evidence, this theory makes sense of everything. The Evangelicals would be violently opposed to the construction of a new basilica because they believe that betrays the teachings of Christ. They would hate the wealth and decadence of a Borgia Pope, and whilst waging war on him would love nothing more than the Ottomans getting blamed for all their atrocities."

Domenico started pacing the room, trying to grapple with the repercussions. "So you're saying all these testimonies we have, all this evidence … it's useless?"

"Completely."

"Gilo's going to go berserk."

Cristina slammed her hand on a pile of boxes. "These won't help us find the Evangelicals, because they are already in position, close to the Pope, waiting for their moment to murder him."

"Right now, that is a tiny number of people. The Pope's in tight seclusion."

"But not in complete isolation."

Domenico pulled a key from his pocket, unlocked the top drawer of his desk and took out a leather folio. "This is the full list of people authorised to have contact with the Holy Father until we know it's safe again. One sheet of paper, that's all." He opened the folio and started reading from the list. "Private secretaries … bodyguards … confessor … Cardinali Riario and Orsini … myself and Deputato Gilo… You see? Only the most trusted."

He handed Cristina the list for her to scrutinise, but she remained adamant. "My guess is that the Evangelicals infiltrated his inner circle a long time ago. Possibly years ago."

"Then we must warn His Holiness immediately." Domenico reached for his sword belt, but Cristina got there first and snatched it from the hook. "What are you doing?" Domenico exclaimed.

"Not a clever idea."

"We don't have a choice. It's our duty to warn the Pope."

"Right now, the Holy Father is in the perfect position. He is the bait in our trap."

Domenico looked at his sister in disbelief. "The Pope as bait? Are you insane?" He tried to grab his sword again, but Cristina dodged backwards.

"What use is sanity when the people we're hunting are insane?"

"Give me the sword, Cristina!"

"As long as we're ready to move quickly, no harm will come to the Pope."

"No! I won't take the risk!"

"The bigger risk is to let this opportunity slip through our fingers. For the first time we hold the advantage. Whoever the traitor is, he doesn't know that we know."

Domenico felt his mind swirling, trying to keep up with his sister's logic. "If there is a clear and present danger to the Holy Father, we have to act immediately."

"And we will. But not by warning him."

"What else can we do to keep him safe?" Domenico said, exasperated.

"I need to be taken through the daily routines inside Castel Sant'Angelo. Everything. The security arrangements, the routines for work and prayer, all the domestic details, how the Pope eats and washes and bathes."

"I can describe that."

"No. I need to see it for myself. I need to walk in the Evangelicals' footsteps, imagining that my greatest desire is to murder the Pope. That is the only way of breaking this case."

Domenico studied her. He desperately wanted to overrule her, to play a safer game, but he knew that his sister's logic was faultless. As usual.

"Can I at least have my sword back?"

"Of course," she smiled.

56: TIME/MOTION

Locals unkindly called it Hadrian's Mole, but even the most cynical had to admit that Castel Sant'Angelo was an imposing building. It was certainly difficult to ignore.

A towering cylinder of stone on the banks of the River Tiber, the castle had been built in the second century as an imperial mausoleum, but had fallen into disrepair after the city had been sacked during the collapse of the Roman Empire. It was the enterprising medieval Popes who'd set about converting the massive relic into a high security private castle where they could hide in times of crisis.

Cristina met Domenico and Gilo at the main guardhouse that was built into the fortified walls surrounding the castle.

"Did you write everything down?" Cristina asked Gilo as he approached. "The entire security schedule?"

"No. I didn't."

"But I need to study every detail and find points of vulnerability."

"Patience, patience," Domenico urged. "Hear the man out."

"I'll gladly tell you everything," Gilo said, "but as soon as the protocols are written down, we run the risk of them falling into the wrong hands. So it's all in here." He tapped the side of his head with a chubby forefinger.

Cristina smiled. "Forgive my impatience."

"One of the key safeguards of the Pope's security is that he is never left in the company of just one other person," Gilo began. "Whenever the Holy Father is not alone (sleeping or praying), there are always two other people present, so one is always watching the other."

"Yes. Good," Cristina nodded. "That makes sense."

"Unless there are two traitors," Domenico pointed out.

"That's not how the Evangelicals think," Cristina replied. "They work as lone wolves. The hermit was a loner, Bartolo was a loner. That is the true face of fanaticism."

"And far harder to detect," Gilo added. "If two traitors had infiltrated the Pope's most trusted circle, they'd naturally try to protect each other, and people might notice."

"There is nothing more dangerous than a single, driven fanatic," Cristina said.

Domenico led them into the guardhouse, where their papers were checked. "To get beyond this point, you need an access warrant, double-sealed by the Pope and Cardinale Riario." He handed an official document to Cristina. "We had to get this issued even for your brief visit."

"So the Pope knows I am here today?" Cristina said.

"He does."

"I'm surprised he agreed."

"If he is ever to lead a normal life again, the Pope knows the traitor must be found. And that requires the best minds in Rome."

They left the guardroom and crossed a short walkway into the cylindrical body of Castel Sant'Angelo itself, then ascended a long, straight ramp and entered a room where the Pope's personal bodyguards were on standby night and day. Domenico and Gilo unbuckled their swords, took off their daggers, and put them on an inspection table.

"No weapons past this point," Gilo explained.

"Not even for you?"

"No exceptions," Domenico said, then he and Gilo stood legs akimbo, arms outstretched while the bodyguards frisked them.

Cristina glanced at her brother. "Can't you vouch for me?"

Domenico shook his head. "Don't worry, they're very professional."

Cristina adopted the same pose and stared into the middle distance, trying to blank out the young soldier as he ran his hands over her body. She could feel herself gritting her teeth, hating every moment of physical closeness.

When the ordeal was over, she followed Domenico and Gilo onto a wide ramp that spiralled lazily up the inside of the castle, giving access to all floors. On the second level, Gilo ushered them into the kitchens, where three cooks were busy preparing the Pope's evening meal.

"To eliminate the risk of poisoning, each cook prepares a separate meal, and all three are served to the Pope, who only decides what to eat when the food is actually in front of him."

"You could still poison all three dishes," Cristina pointed out.

Gilo shook his head. "Each meal goes through double testing, with individuals randomly selected from those people authorised to be in here. So a would-be poisoner could end up killing himself."

They left the cooks braising and parboiling, and climbed further up the spiralling walkway until they came to a pair of bodyguards who seemed to be doing nothing. "The last line of defence," Gilo explained. "If an intruder got this far, he would not get any further."

Cristina looked sceptically at the guards. "They've only got fists to fight off an attacker?"

"Fists. And this." Gilo pulled an iron pin from the wall and a heavy chain rattled up into the air, releasing an eight-foot section of floor that dropped away. "We call it the traitor's trapdoor."

Cristina peered down into the gloomy shaft that receded into blackness. "What a way to go."

The bodyguards hauled on the chain, swinging the lethal section of walkway back into place so that Gilo could lead Cristina and Domenico up to the fourth floor, which opened out into a large chamber with smaller rooms leading off it.

"And these are the temporary papal apartments." He pointed to each chamber in turn. "Bedroom. Study. Dining room. Audience chamber. Private chapel."

Cristina's eyes took in the space: rough-hewn walls slowly turning black from numerous flickering torches; a huge floor covered in narrow herringbone tiles typical of ancient Roman construction. It was strange to think that these rooms, built to guard the dead, were now protecting the living.

"His Holiness is visited daily by the same priest who takes his confession and administers the Eucharist."

"Who is it?"

"Padre Gabriel, the inquisitor."

Cristina shuddered. "He is a violent man. He shouldn't be anywhere near the Pope."

"But his loyalty is beyond question," Gilo replied.

"I don't like Gabriel either," Domenico added, "but he was the Pope's choice."

Gilo opened the door to the Pope's study, revealing a large desk with various quills, inkpots and sticks of sealing wax, and a small bookshelf. "Documents are delivered to the Holy Father by his private secretary, who holds them at all times."

"The Pope doesn't even touch any documents?" Cristina asked.

"In case there's poison on the paper," Domenico explained.

"You seem to have thought of all eventualities." Cristina looked around the room and her eyes settled on the sparsely populated bookshelf; all it contained were three large financial ledgers and a solitary bible. "Hardly impressive," she mused.

"The Holy Father is not a great reader," Domenico replied. "His inspiration comes from God."

"So it would appear." But Cristina couldn't hide her disappointment.

It was a relief to get away from the smoking torches and out into the fresh air on the roof of the castle. There were commanding views across the entire city, with one bodyguard positioned at each point of the compass, keeping watch for any suspicious activity in the surrounding streets.

"And this is where the Holy Father takes his exercise." Gilo led the way towards the stone parapet. "Here, or along the passetto." He pointed down to the arches of a raised walkway that strutted for half a mile over streets and houses, providing an emergency corridor between the Vatican and Castel Sant'Angelo.

"That looks like a weak point," Cristina said. "How well guarded is the passetto?"

"Two sets of locked gates on each level, manned by guards day and night," Domenico replied.

"And how long has this system been in place?" Cristina asked.

"Two weeks. We set it up shortly after Bartolo's execution."

"And there have been no changes? No irregularities?"

Gilo shook his head.

"Then that will be our alarm system," Cristina said. "When the assassin decides to make his move, something in this carefully constructed routine will change. I don't know what that will be, and it may appear trivial. But it will be a signal for us to react."

"Then we need to put some kind of warning system in place," Domenico said.

"Exactly. Like a messenger," Cristina replied. "Have a runner on permanent standby. Whenever there is a change, I need to be told. It could be changes to the Pope's daily routine, or new access warrants being issued, or something going wrong with the castle itself, like a flood or a fire. If anything changes, I need to know immediately."

Before the day was out, Domenico had arranged a system of three runners who worked around the clock, taking reports filled with minutiae and trivia from Castel Sant'Angelo to Cristina's house on the Piazza Navona, where she combed through the details, searching for anomalies and ripples.

Days passed without incident.

Then early on Saturday morning, a message arrived that the Pope's confessor, Padre Gabriel, had been taken ill and a replacement was being sent to the castle.

Cristina felt her heart race. This was it. This was the trigger. The assassin was making his move.

57: POLLEN

"Don't … don't…" The messenger was gasping so hard he could barely speak.

"Don't what?" Domenico demanded.

The man could see how annoyed his commanding officer was, but pain was stabbing his lungs and he was starting to feel sick. Cristina had told him to run to the Vatican as if his life depended on it, but now his heavy breakfast of fried lucanica sausage was about to make a second appearance, and he belched loudly. "Sorry."

"Just speak!" Domenico yelled.

The messenger focused on his breathing. "Don't let … the new … confessor in, sir."

Domenico blinked as he tried to make sense of the message. "My sister said that?"

"Yes, sir."

This must be the warning. Gilo had sent over the daily list to Cristina, and she must have identified a new confessor as the irregularity, the weak link. "Who is he?"

"Don't know, sir … didn't say."

"Get three men from the guardroom and come with me," Domenico instructed as he grabbed his sword.

"Now, sir?" the messenger could feel his stomach churning again.

"Now!"

Cristina was also breathless as she arrived at a discreet house overlooking the secluded Malandrino gardens in Trastevere, just on the other side of the river. The house had no name, but she recognised it from the large, black double doors at the entrance; this was where visiting inquisitors lodged when they weren't torturing confessions out of people.

She glanced impatiently along the street. Where were they? She couldn't do this on her own. She had sent Isra to summon the City Watch, but if they didn't arrive soon, it would be too late.

Finally she heard the clatter of boots on cobbles as four guards emerged round the corner, followed by Isra.

Cristina beckoned to the troops, urging them to be as quiet as possible, but as they approached she was dismayed to recognise their leader as the sergeant from Collatino Tower, the one who she'd clashed with while investigating Barberini's crucifixion. Judging by the expression on the sergeant's flabby face, he remembered the encounter as well.

"I think a murder may have taken place. In there," Cristina whispered urgently.

The sergeant looked at the tranquil house. "Why?"

"The Pope's confessor is inside. But someone has taken his place without warning."

The sergeant narrowed his eyes. "Have you tried knocking?"

"Really? That is your best suggestion?"

He glared at her, then strode towards the shiny black doors, raised his fist and hammered on the wood.

Silence.

"And for your next trick?" Cristina said.

The sergeant ignored the barb and turned to his men. "Right, let's do it."

THWACK! CRACK! The 'enforcement pole' was driven into the doors. The device looked crude, a four-foot length of heavy iron with handles on either side, but it was effective.

"Again!" the sergeant commanded.

The Watch took a few steps back, tightened their grip on the enforcement pole, then rushed forward.

SMACK! The lock was punched out, the doors flew open with a loud clatter, and the Watch stormed into the building.

"City Watch! Don't move! Don't move!" the sergeant bellowed as he rushed from room to room, sword drawn. But as he entered the study overlooking the garden, he held his hand up to pause the raid. Cristina pushed her way forward to see what he'd found.

"So much for your dead body." His tone was withering.

Cristina peered into the gloom and saw Padre Gabriel cowering in the corner. He wasn't dead, his throat wasn't cut, but his eyes were streaming and his nose red. Then he sneezed loudly, six times in quick succession.

"Have you been poisoned?" Cristina demanded.

Padre Gabriel shook his head. "Hayfever. Terrible Hayfever." He looked up at the City Watch towering over him, weapons drawn. "Is that illegal now?"

Wearily the sergeant signalled his men to retreat. "Better check the rest of the house while we're here."

Left alone, Cristina offered her hand to help Gabriel up. "Is this why you sent a replacement? Hayfever? Nothing more serious?"

He nodded. "I cannot sneeze and sniffle all through the Holy Father's confession." By now, shock was giving way to irritation as Padre Gabriel realised how his privacy had just been violated, but every time he tried to show his indignation, hay fever cut him down.

"Who did you send as a replacement?"

"Padre Umberto. He's a colleague."

"How well do you know him?"

"I'd trust him with my life. Do you think I'm a fool? I know there is a threat against the Pope's life."

"Yet still you gave your access warrant to a stranger."

"Umberto is my right-hand man." Sniffle. "A brother inquisitor. A man beyond reproach."

"Let's hope you're right." Cristina left the room and came face to face with an unhappy sergeant.

"I assume that will be all." His smirk was maddening.

"Actually, no," Cristina replied. "You need to deliver a message to the guardhouse at Castel Sant'Angelo."

"We're not errand boys."

"Tell my brother, Domenico Falchoni, Capitano della Guardia Apostolica," she said pointedly, "that the replacement confessor, Padre Umberto, is cleared for access to the Pope. This was a false alarm."

"So you were wrong."

"I was doing my job. As we all are."

The atmosphere became even more strained after the City Watch had left. Cristina didn't want to spend a moment longer in the inquisitor's presence than was necessary, but after the violent intrusion of his lodgings, she felt obliged to try and make amends, so she asked Isra to find a broom and sweep away the wood splinters from the smashed doors and generally tidy up.

Trying to re-establish his authority, Padre Gabriel sat at his desk and continued going through a large pile of dossiers. Cristina noticed how thin and white his fingers were, like studies in cruelty.

"Would it not be better to rest?" she suggested. "So that you are well for tomorrow?"

"Heretics do not rest, and neither can I," Gabriel replied, before a loud sneeze undermined him.

Cristina couldn't resist peering over his shoulder to see what was in the documents, and was surprised to recognise the stamp of the Guardia Apostolica at the bottom of each one. "Is my brother working with you now?"

"They need my expert knowledge to identify suspects." He turned and looked at Cristina. "So your rude interruption may actually have put the Holy Father's life in more jeopardy."

"Domenico sent you those files?"

"Your brother is too stubborn. But Deputato Gilo is more pragmatic." Suddenly Padre Gabriel was gripped by a sneezing fit which sent snot flying down his cassock, and he hurried from the room to try and limit his humiliation.

Isra appeared at the doorway. "All done," she said. Then she noticed some dirt on the floor around the desk and stepped in to clear it up. But as she swept it away, Isra noticed that the dirt on the floorboards smeared as if it was some sort of powdered ink. She bent down and dabbed her finger in it, then hunted across the floor to trace the source: it seemed to be dropping from the bottom of the filing box containing the documents Padre Gabriel was working on.

"That's strange." Isra showed her stained fingers to Cristina. "What do you think it is?"

"I don't know." Cristina lifted the dossiers out and discovered that the bottom of the box was covered in the same powder. She dabbed her fingers into it, sniffed and immediately sneezed, then sneezed again.

"It's pollen," Isra realised. She leant into the box, breathed in deeply, and gave three loud sneezes. "Why is there so much pollen in the bottom of a box of documents?"

The realisation hit Cristina like the enforcement pole smashing into a door.

Gilo had sent this trunk over.

He had incapacitated Padre Gabriel.

The replacement confessor was being detained for questioning, which meant that at this very moment, Gilo was alone with the Pope, informing him of the developing situation.

Alone.

The one thing that should never happen.

Circles of the astrolabe spun in Cristina's mind, then clicked into place in a startling chain reaction…

Gilo.

It was Gilo who'd taken control of the murder scene after Barberini's crucifixion. *He'd* gathered the evidence and interviewed witnesses.

Gilo had organised the covert surveillance of the monastery and exposed Brother Bartolo as a Muslim.

Gilo knew which church Cristina used for meditation and when she would be there.

And it was Gilo who had organised the security detail to protect the Pope in Castel Sant'Angelo.

He'd been there at every crucial moment, nudging events to fit his plan without anyone noticing.

The hermit had warned them to look for the traitor among those who are closest.

It had to be Gilo.

58: ROSARY

Gilo waited respectfully in the large outer chamber of the papal apartments in Castel Sant'Angelo. From behind a closed door in the far wall he could hear the splash of water as the Holy Father washed in preparation for confession; as soon as the priest arrived, Gilo would accompany them both to the private chapel and stand guard. This was the routine he had put in place to safeguard the leader of the Church … but today it would safeguard the Church against the monstrous corruption of its own leader.

Gilo looked at the imposing statue in the centre of the chamber: St Michael slaying Satan. How appropriate for what was about to happen, and definitive proof that God condoned the spilling of blood to eradicate evil.

So many times Gilo had imagined what this moment might feel like; he'd imagined rage, fear, guilt, or even paralysing anxiety. Yet now the time had arrived, he felt a strange calmness. He had drawn strength from all the sacrifices of the other Evangelicals, and inspiration from their brilliant execution of Divine Justice.

Barberini's crucifixion had been beautifully choreographed to shock and confound.

Bartolo had blinded his friends without hesitation, then maintained his cover right to the sacrificial end, despite the unimaginable agonies of torture and immolation.

Suffocating claustrophobia did not weaken the fireball-bomber's resolve; he had waited patiently for the perfect moment to cause maximum fear.

Then just when everyone had started to breathe again, the bold and bloodthirsty flourishes of Giovanni Borgia's murder, with nine savage stab wounds and a slashed throat, had once again terrorised the city, the Church and the Pope himself.

The Evangelical brotherhood had made their sacrifices. Now it was Gilo's turn. The honour had fallen to him to strike the definitive blow and cleanse Christendom of a man who should never have been elevated to become Pope. The End of the World was imminent, but if that Day of Judgement dawned with a corrupt fornicator sitting on St Peter's throne, then the whole of mankind would be damned.

Gilo's fingers tightened around his rosary beads; as soon as the confessor arrived, the violence could begin.

Cristina had never run so fast in her life. Hurtling through crowded streets, pushing aside dawdlers and dodging round shopfronts that spread greedily out onto the road, she ignored the angry cries of protest in her wake and focused on getting to Castel Sant'Angelo. It terrified her to think that Gilo was roaming free inside the security cordon of his own design; the Holy Father would never see the mortal threat coming.

She practically threw herself into the guardhouse and demanded to be let inside, but slammed straight into the pedantry of protocol.

"Access warrant, miss," the guard demanded.

"What? No!"

"I need to see it."

"This is an emergency!"

"No warrant, no entrance." He was as solid as the stone walls he guarded.

"Wait." Cristina fumbled in her pocket, pulled out the crumpled document she'd used the previous week, and thrust it at the guard.

He read it and tutted. "This is out of date."

"I was here! A few days ago! My brother is Domenico Falchoni."

The implacable guard handed her back the warrant. "This was only valid for one day."

"The Pope's life is in danger!" she yelled at the guard.

"Which is why these measures are in place," he countered.

This was useless; she was trying to reason with a man who would rather march into damnation than disobey an order. She changed tack. "Is my brother here?"

"I cannot reveal details of —"

"Tell me!"

The guard drew a deep, contemptuous breath. "Yes. He is."

"Then summon him. Please."

The guard didn't move.

"Look, I understand why you are being strict." Cristina struggled to muster some charm. "You are following protocols that I personally approved. But I beg you, for the love of God, for the sake of the Pope's life, please get my brother down here immediately."

Finally Gilo heard footsteps approaching up the stone ramp. He glanced across the chamber to make sure the doors to the Pope's rooms were still shut, then pulled his shoulders back and clipped on an easy smile as Padre Umberto stepped into the lobby.

"You're late."

"Apologies." Padre Umberto was breathless from the climb up the ramp and was clearly feeling the effects of carrying too much weight around his midriff. "There was some concern about admitting me, but Padre Gabriel is unwell today."

Gilo shrugged. "No matter. Once you've met one inquisitor, you've met them all."

"I … I don't follow."

"Well, you're all sadists, revelling in cruelty and torture. Isn't that so?"

Umberto gave a nervous smile, unsure whether or not Gilo was trying to make a joke. "Take me to the Holy Father, please."

"Of course." Gilo beckoned for the priest to go first.

One step. Two steps. Now he was in front of Gilo.

Now was the moment.

Gilo whipped his rosary around the priest's neck and pulled hard.

A shocked gurgle.

Padre Umberto tried to claw the rosary away, but it was useless because a leather cord didn't hold these beads together; this was a razor-wire garotte threaded with ebony beads to hide its deadly purpose.

The priest gasped, desperately trying to cry out for help, but Gilo tightened his grip, focusing his gaze on the back of Umberto's neck, watching the skin go blotchy and the blood vessels swell.

Umberto started to writhe as panic took hold, but the more he struggled, the more energised Gilo became. Finally, after all the years of deceit, the cheerful deputy could live as he truly believed: a Warrior for God. As he listened to the death agonies of the priest, Gilo knew that he had finally made a direct connection to the Divine. This humble deputy would achieve greatness and salvation by channelling His will through the garotte.

A desperate gurgle, then Umberto's body went limp. His knees buckled and his entire weight dropped so that it was held only by the garotte.

Gilo grunted with exertion as he pulled one final time to make sure there was no way back.

He waited, counting silently … no man could survive this long without air.

Finally, Gilo loosened his grip and watched Umberto tumble face down onto the stone floor.

Job done.

Gilo straightened his back and massaged his fingers to restore the circulation.

But when he looked up, he was staring directly into the stunned eyes of Pope Alexander VI.

59: GILO

The instant Domenico entered the guardroom, Cristina grabbed him. "It's Gilo! Where is he?"

"What do you mean?"

"Deputato Gilo is the traitor!"

The blood drained from Domenico's face. "No. That's impossible."

"He sabotaged the files you sent to Gabriel to make him fall sick."

"You're wrong. You have to be wrong."

"Why else would he do that?"

"But you sent word the new confessor could be trusted."

"Gilo created confusion so that he could find a way to be alone with the Pope."

Domenico struggled to take in the enormity of what she was saying. "I would trust Deputato Gilo with my life."

"Which is precisely what makes him so dangerous."

Four floors above them, the Holy Father backed away from Gilo, hands raised in contrition. "Please, think about what you're doing."

"I've thought about nothing else since you became Pope."

"You will be damned for all eternity."

"But I am not the guilty one."

The Pope screamed for help, desperately trying to raise the alarm, but Gilo loomed towards him, rosary swinging from his hand. "No-one can hear you, Holy Father. The walls are too thick. The nearest guard is down the ramp."

"I beg you! Think of your immortal soul!" Alexander stumbled as he tried to scramble away.

"Oh, I am." Gilo had backed the Pope into a corner. "There is a simple yet shocking story I will tell the world to explain this tragedy."

"Money? Is it money you want?"

"Unbeknown to anyone, Padre Umberto was the traitor all along. His first loyalty was not to the Church, but to a fanatical sect called the Evangelicals of Light."

"I'm a rich man. Name your price!" the Pope begged.

Gilo raised the rosary and dangled it in front of the Holy Father's face. "When he was alone with you, taking confession, Umberto wrapped a garotte, cunningly disguised as rosary beads, around your throat."

Gilo's hands moved with deadly speed, looping the garotte around the Pope's throat.

Alexander tried to fight him off, but he was no match for Gilo's hardened strength. The deputy pulled the garotte tight, watching calmly as the Pope's mouth gaped open and his tongue lolled out.

"I heard your pitiful cries," Gilo continued as he strangled the Holy Father. "I rushed in and attacked the black-hearted Umberto, killing him with his own weapon. But tragically I was too late… You were already dead."

The Pope's limbs thrashed and twisted as he tried to shake Gilo off.

"You will be dead. Umberto will be blamed for your murder. And I will live on." Gilo tightened his grip, listening to the Pope retching his final breaths. "You are an abomination, Holy Father. A stain on the Church. A fornicator, a thief, a corrupter of innocent men. You are the Devil himself."

A scream of unalloyed hatred erupted from Gilo's mouth as he pulled the garotte even tighter, relishing the feeling of the Pope's life slipping away.

Gilo was no longer the cheerful deputy, passed over by everyone, never taken seriously. Now God would see his true strength and be in awe. In this one defining moment, his life would finally become heroic.

THUNK!

A searing pain tore through the side of Gilo's head.

He was flung sideways. His head hit the cold stone floor.

He swivelled his eyes, trying to understand what was happening. He saw the Pope scrambling to his knees, coughing and retching.

He looked up and saw Domenico looming over him, fury and hurt twisting his face into an ugly grimace.

"I trusted you!" Domenico screamed. "I trusted you!"

In his right hand was a heavy silver candlestick from the chapel's altar … a bloodstained candlestick.

Now Gilo understood. This was the weapon. This was why his skull was fractured.

"How could you do this?" Domenico cried. "You were my friend!" Tears of incomprehension and hurt ran down his cheeks.

"Kill me," Gilo whispered.

"*Filo de putana*!" Domenico spat furiously.

"Kill me now."

Domenico raised the candlestick above his head like a club, his hands trembling with rage. Yet he hesitated.

"Do it," Gilo groaned.

Domenico howled as he channelled all his rage into the heavy candlestick.

And then another voice commanded, "No!"

Domenico turned and looked at the Holy Father as he stood up and composed himself. "Do not stoop to his level."

Cristina waited anxiously, the gaping chasm in the ramp blocking her passage to the Pope's rooms on the floor above. She had refused to wait in the guardroom, and releasing this trapdoor was the only way Domenico could force her to stop. But now that she heard shouting from above, she knew that Domenico was in trouble.

Cristina turned to the guard manning the trapdoor. "We must help him. Raise the trap."

"He gave strict orders —"

"Listen to him! He's in danger!"

The guard just shook his head and looked at the open trapdoor. "Whatever Gilo's done up there, he can never escape as long as that chasm is in the way."

"*Testa di cazzo*! Why are you all so obedient?" Cristina exclaimed.

"Because we're told to be," the guard replied.

Suddenly they heard footsteps at the top of the ramp. Cristina peered into the gloom … and saw two figures moving in the shadows. As they approached, she could make out Gilo, his uniform soaked in blood, hands tied behind his back, being frogmarched down the ramp by Domenico.

"Is the Pope safe?" Cristina called out.

"No thanks to him." Domenico jabbed Gilo in the back.

They stopped on the far side of the open trapdoor. The hurt and confusion on Domenico's face contrasted with his deputy's cold contempt.

"What happened to you?" Cristina asked.

Gilo stared back at her without a flicker of remorse; it was as if his soul had shrivelled up.

Cristina realised that this was what it meant to come face to face with extremism: eyes dead to humanity, mind closed to reason. "Do you feel no shame?"

"I answer only to God," Gilo replied in a strangely flat voice.

"You think God is a murderer?"

"I do not recognise the legitimacy of a corrupt papacy, or the fools who serve it."

It was chilling to see a man she thought she had known turn into this unreachable presence. "You were a good man. Once," Cristina lamented. "Now you have betrayed everyone and everything."

"Who are you to judge? You blaspheme every time you pick up a book."

The comment was intended to hurt, but Cristina suddenly felt a deep sadness for this lost man. "You could have had a full life, Gilo. You could have enjoyed grandchildren and love. Yet you chose madness."

He gave an indifferent shrug. "There can be no salvation without sacrifice."

"Is that what you've destroyed your life for? A slogan? Doggerel for the mindless?"

But Gilo wasn't listening anymore; he closed his eyes and started humming a tune. A simple folk tune, something remembered from his childhood, perhaps. And as he hummed, he rocked back and forth, as if putting himself into a trance.

The tune echoed off the stone walls of the corridor, resonating with Gilo's voice, creating a strange cacophony.

Without warning, Gilo leaned forward and threw himself, head-first into the black void in front of him.

"No!" Domenico reached out to Gilo but only managed to grab his shirt, which ripped in his fingers.

Cristina screamed as she saw the traitor's body plummet into the darkness of the chasm.

And as he fell, Gilo kept on humming the strange tune, without even skipping a beat.

Moments later they heard a dull thud of dreadful finality, as Gilo's body hit the rocks fifty feet below.

60: FALLOUT

Beneath the disused dungeons of Castel Sant'Angelo was the grimmest level of all: the ossuary, a dark and soil-damp place where the bones of hundreds of forgotten dead had been stacked in neat piles. Some said they were victims of the plague that had torn through Rome in 590 AD; others said they were the remains of priests who had died in scandalous circumstances. No-one really knew.

Domenico led the way, his passing torch flickering warm light on gaping eye sockets and rows of white teeth, making it seem as if the skulls were smiling a welcome to these unexpected visitors.

Cristina stuck close to her brother until they came to a heavy metal door at the far end of the chamber that was rusted from disuse.

"We don't have to do this," Cristina whispered in the gloom. "That could be Gilo's final tomb."

"I need to look at him one last time." Domenico handed the torch to Cristina then took his dagger and started to scrape away the rust from the hinges. The shrill, wincing sound of metal on metal set Cristina's teeth on edge, but there was no other way to loosen the mechanisms. Finally, Domenico slid the bolts back and swung open the door.

This was where the bottom of the chasm emerged.

And there was the body of Gilo, twisted into grotesque absurdity by his fall.

Domenico flinched at the pitiful sight, but Cristina was fascinated by the physics of impact. Judging from the way Gilo's skull was smashed and his brains had been forced out through the many fissures, he had hit the bottom of the shaft head-first, without even trying to reach out and break his fall. His arms were twisted awkwardly across his body; one leg had been dislocated by the impact and now rested next to his head as if he were a contortionist. It was a bizarre and gruesome sight, redeemed only by the knowledge that death would have been instantaneous.

"It is my failure that he is dead," Domenico said quietly.

"You must not blame yourself."

"Why didn't he confide in me, rather than turn to a cult of fanatics?"

"Because that's not how it works."

"The one good thing, maybe the only good thing to come from war, is loyalty to your comrades. Soldiers have each other's backs." Domenico looked at the broken body of his deputy. "I thought he understood that."

"Listen to me." Cristina swung the heavy door shut, hiding the mangled body from sight. "When someone turns away from reason, they put themselves beyond reach. There was nothing you could have done to save him."

Domenico covered his face, trying to hide his failure. "How could he have fooled me? I am supposed to be the one who sees danger before everyone else."

Gently Cristina lowered her brother's hands so that she could look into his brown eyes. "Domenico, if you lose faith in yourself now, if you give into fear, they will have won. Even from beyond the grave. That is what these people try to do, undermine who we are. But they must not win. We must not let them."

They found the Pope kneeling over the body of Padre Umberto where he had been murdered, praying earnestly for his soul. But when he stood up and turned around, there was anger in the Pope's eyes.

"How could you have let the traitor get so close?" he demanded.

"We did everything we could to protect you, Holy Father," Domenico stuttered.

"Clearly not!" Alexander touched the painful red marks around his own neck. "Does this look like protection?"

Cristina had never been so close to the Pope in person, and she was surprised at what she saw — more angry old man than divine presence.

"I've always had my doubts about you, Domenico," the Pope said accusingly. "Lack of imagination. Poor insight. Too obsessed with trivia."

"Forgive me, Holy Father —"

"They murdered him!" he yelled. "My son would still be alive if it weren't for your incompetence! And *your* deputy, *your* man was central to the conspiracy."

Domenico fell silent.

Alexander's hands trembled with rage, his face flushed. "Someone must pay for this grievous loss of life," he pronounced as he sat in his great carved chair.

Cristina glanced at her brother and saw his world falling to pieces. This job was his life, and now it was being stolen from him. In his heart Domenico knew it wasn't his fault, yet he didn't have the words to defend himself.

"May I speak, Holy Father?" Cristina asked.

The Pope glared at her. "Do you have anything to say that is worth hearing?"

"The investigation of these terrible crimes took me far away from the civilisation in which I have spent my whole life. And in those places, on the very edge of meaning, I saw how fanaticism is born. Violent reactions provoke violent responses. Hurt is nurtured into anger and passed down from mother to son. And once the cycle of conflict is running, it becomes a vortex, drawing in the damaged and the vulnerable. The only solution is Christian love, Holy Father. Forgiveness and love can break the chain reaction of hatred. And as supreme pontiff, that example must always come from you." Cristina lowered her head, hoping that a display of humility would hide the sharpness of her reprimand. She braced for papal anger, but it didn't come.

"Is it finally over?" Alexander asked. "Have all the radical elements been eliminated? Is my life safe? Is Rome safe?" He didn't look to Domenico for an answer, but to Cristina.

"What you do in this room, in this moment, will answer those questions. Because what the Pope does echoes across Christendom. Your actions affect people you will never meet, and influence hearts you will never know. It is over if you want it to be over, Holy Father."

Alexander considered her words. "Leave me." He waved his hand to indicate that the audience was over. "I have much to think over."

61: REFORM

Anticipation in the Curia was running at fever pitch. From the moment the Pope summoned the cardinals into 'special session', rumours began to swirl around the Vatican. Some cardinals shared what they knew, some shared what they wanted to be true, and others just made mischief with disinformation.

The Pope had taken the unusual step of instructing Domenico to escort him into the meeting chamber; he said it was to look after his personal security, but Domenico suspected there was another agenda at play. In the Vatican, there was always another agenda.

Domenico followed close behind the Holy Father as he swept into the hall; the cardinals stood and bowed, then Alexander gave a blessing and everyone sat down. All eyes locked on the papal throne.

"The traitors who terrorised Rome have been exposed and executed, one way or another," the Pope began. "They challenged our authority in the most violent way possible. They tried to undermine me as a Pope, as a man, as a Borgia, and most painfully of all, as a father."

The cardinals nodded gravely, acknowledging the Holy Father's grief, even though few of them had personally mourned the death of his dissolute and corrupt son. But it was important to be seen to grieve.

"The crucial question we now face, is which path should we follow in order to put these terrible crimes behind us and move forward stronger than before?" The Pope studied his cardinals closely. "Some believe we must show the world we refuse to be intimidated, that we must reaffirm who we are and what we stand for by forging ahead with the construction of the new St Peter's. A monumental basilica will glorify God, and shine as a beacon across Christendom and the dark lands beyond."

Domenico tried to read the cardinals as they listened. No doubt some were calculating how they could enrich themselves from such an enormous feat of construction, while others were calculating how much moral authority Alexander would lose by squandering vast sums of money on a vanity project. All the cardinals were wondering how it would affect their own chances of one day wearing the papal crown.

The Pope reached into his robe, pulled out a silk handkerchief and slowly dabbed his mouth, relishing the way he held everyone in the palm of his hand. He folded the handkerchief and put it back into his robe.

"I have decided to choose a different path," he said quietly. "These terrible events have made me reflect deeply. I have prayed and searched my soul, and I must acknowledge my own failings as well as the personal weaknesses that have clouded my judgement."

Domenico could see confusion crease the faces of the cardinals; were these the words of a Borgia Pope? What game was he playing? Surely he could not be sincere?

"Starting today, this very hour, I am instituting a sweeping programme of reform that will touch every corner of the Church. I will root out excess and banish corruption from the Vatican. Henceforth, the Church must focus not on self-aggrandisement, but on serving the poor and helping the weak. I want my papacy to be remembered as a time of spiritual renewal, and it is for this reason that I am abandoning all plans to build a new basilica. We must serve the Church, and the Church must serve the poor. That is all. And it is enough."

The outcry was immediate. Cardinals started talking over each other, giving vent to their surprise and confusion.

"Holy Father!" Orsini stood up and bellowed above the commotion. "Whilst I applaud spiritual renewal, as do all the cardinals, I feel compelled to question the wisdom of bending to the will of fanatics. The Evangelicals of Light may have been eradicated, but by effectively giving in to their demands, are you not inviting every other radical sect to wage war on the Church?"

There was robust agreement from all the cardinals who stood to lose by the Pope's decision, but the Holy Father just raised his hand for silence. "No-one applauds their fanaticism. But remember, these men were acting from Christian motives. And the conviction they displayed was beyond the comprehension of mortal men. When people are willing to sacrifice themselves in such a way for God, should we not be asking whether God may indeed be speaking through them?"

"God works through us!" Orsini thundered. "Not through madmen!"

"And did not the Romans declare much the same sentiment as they nailed Christ to the crucifix, Cardinale Orsini?" the Pope replied.

Now everyone joined in the commotion. Even those cardinals who had been silent up to now started to argue with each other. Perhaps what worried many was that a Pope who was truly pious, who wanted to do penance through spirituality, would be extremely hard to topple.

Domenico blurted out the news as soon as he entered the hallway. He had planned to be more subtle, but in the end was too agitated to hide his anger.

Cristina listened in silence. What could anyone say when a capricious leader snatched away your dreams? Shock gave went to a heavy emptiness that seemed to drain away joy and hope.

Her silence made Domenico angrier. "We did everything right! Everything! We exposed the whole conspiracy. We proved the crimes were nothing to do with Divine wrath, yet still the Pope scraps the new basilica. It makes no sense!"

"Maybe we are partly to blame," Cristina replied flatly.

"Us? Why? No! How is any of this our fault?"

Cristina walked across the hallway and gazed out of the window beside the front doors, trying to find solace in the bustle of everyday life. "It was by playing on the Pope's guilty conscience that we managed to get the new basilica approved; now that same conscience has brought our plans crashing down. We played with fire, and we got burned." She closed the shutters and started to climb the stairs.

"That's it?" Domenico called after her. "That's all you have to say?"

"I'm going to reflect. And to study."

"What's the point? The dream is finished." He watched her cross the landing and vanish behind the heavy mahogany doors of her library.

"Would you like some wine, sir?"

Domenico turned and saw Isra emerge from the kitchens. "Did you see that? After everything she's been through? She just calmly accepted it."

"I don't think she's accepted anything, sir." Isra poured a tumbler and handed it to Domenico. "More likely she's just thinking of another way forward."

62: ONWARDS

Professor De Luca strode briskly along Via di Pasquino, his leather shoulder-bag heavy with books, but when he looked up to the library window of the corner house, he could see no candlestick signalling that today's lesson was on.

He glanced at the clock on a nearby church; this was definitely the time he had agreed with Cristina. Perhaps she was too depressed at the turn of events to continue studying. It was a dark day indeed, De Luca lamented to himself, when someone of Cristina's calibre gave up. He sighed and turned to make his way back to Sapienza University, but had only gone ten paces when he came face to face with his student. "Cristina! What are you doing here?"

"Greeting you."

"But, but … the candlestick."

"No longer required." She took De Luca's arm and led him towards the front doors of her townhouse.

"But the servants' entrance is the other way," he protested.

"I genuinely believed I was protecting my family's honour by keeping my studies secret," Cristina explained. "Many times I was told, 'Academia is not for the daughter of a respectable merchant.' But I was wrong. Now I realise that knowledge should never hide its face." She flung open the front doors of her house. "*Sapere aude*, Professor. Dare to be wise."

De Luca peered into the hallway, then looked at his student with pride. "Indeed."

It was a relief to put his heavy bag down on the long library table, and De Luca rubbed his shoulder to ease the cramp as he studied Cristina's latest move on the chessboard. "Hmm. Interesting."

"Checkmate, I believe."

"Check. But not mate." De Luca slid a cunningly hidden rook across the board to rescue the king.

"Damn," Cristina muttered. "I didn't see that."

"My condolences about the basilica. A bad day's business. Such a disappointment."

"What a time for a Borgia to discover humility," Cristina replied.

"These books —" he patted the leather bag — "I acquired specifically for our architectural research. Perhaps I should send them back to Florence?"

"Absolutely not." Cristina pulled the bag towards her, undid the buckles and looked inside.

"But if the new basilica has been scrapped —"

"Scrapped *for now*. So we must wait until the forces are better aligned."

De Luca watched how avidly Cristina inspected each of the books and read the titles. "Maybe the Pope is right," he suggested. "Maybe spiritual renewal is more important than shiny new buildings."

"The Pope is scared," Cristina said, still absorbed with the books, working out how each one would fit into her intellectual map. "That is why he has taken this decision. He has given in to his fears. In truth, a brilliant new cathedral is needed now more than ever. But just as with the astrolabe, one cannot force the rotations."

De Luca gave a half-smile. "Patience never used to be one of your strong points, if you don't mind me observing."

Cristina looked up at him. "The Pope is old. I am young. If we have to wait for the next Pope, so be it." She divided the books into two piles. "In the meantime, we must press on with our architectural studies, so that when the day comes, we are ready."

It was well past lunch when Professor De Luca left, and Cristina's stomach was grumbling as she made her way to the kitchens in search of food. But instead of preparing a meal, Isra was getting ready to go out.

"What's happened?" Cristina asked.

"I'm treating you to lunch."

"But I have a lot of studying to get through."

"I think you'll find all that much easier after lunch," Isra said with a mysterious smile.

"Really? What are you going to feed me?"

"It's a surprise." Isra went to fetch Cristina's cloak.

It wasn't long before they were standing in front of Baker Yusuf's newly refurbished shop, where his family had put on a lavish spread to celebrate their grand reopening. The baker and his wife had fused Ottoman and Roman cuisine to create a feast of delicacies, and the hours slipped past in good food and lively conversation.

Late in the afternoon, Halil and Nubia arrived with a parcel that had just been delivered from Venice, containing a jar of African coffee beans. Everyone watched, enthralled, as Nubia got to work, roasting the pale green beans in a skillet until they were a rich brown; grinding them into a powder which she boiled in water, simmering and straining the mixture repeatedly, until the most delicious new aroma filled the small bakery: fresh coffee.

But the smell was nothing compared to the energising euphoria everyone felt after the first few sips. The coffee transformed afternoon drowsiness into laughter and debate, and everyone demanded that Nubia get to work on brewing a second pot.

Hours later, Cristina's mind was still racing. Feeling too restless to go home, she insisted on taking Isra for a long walk along the banks of the Tiber.

"I really think coffee could be the greatest aid to studying yet invented," Cristina enthused. "My mind feels so sharp and quick."

"Then you're definitely retreating back into your library?" Isra replied.

"It's not a retreat. And it won't be forever. But yes."

"You're not tempted by our adventures in the real world? Too messy, perhaps?"

"That was what I liked about it. But right now, I need time to process everything." She took a piece of paper from her pocket and handed it to Isra. "This is for you."

Isra unfolded the paper — it contained a handwritten number. "What does it mean?"

"It's what I'll be paying you from now on."

Isra's eyes went wide. "No, no. This is too much. The going rate for a housekeeper —"

"But you're going to be so much more than that, Isra."

"Going to be?"

"What makes you such a powerful asset is not just your courage, your ingenuity, or even your knowledge of the real world; it's that in Rome, no-one pays attention to the humble housekeeper. And that will be the key to our success."

"Success at what? We don't have anything to investigate."

Cristina gave a knowing smile. "The new basilica will be constructed. Eventually. And when that process starts, it will unleash a tidal wave of greed across this city. Nothing good ever came from greed, Isra. It is the Original Sin. We will have to fight hard if we are to prevent the new St Peter's from being devoured by greed." She pointed to the scrap of paper. "You will earn that money, Isra. Every last ducat. Believe me."

A NOTE TO THE READER

Italy at the dawn of the 16th century — what an incredible time to be alive! Thank you for diving into this adventure with me, and I really hope you enjoyed the story.

This was a world in transition as the Medieval gave way to the Renaissance, and through that ushered in the modern world. While some parts of society were clinging to the past and centuries-old traditions, other factions were surging ahead with new ways of thinking. At the same time, huge swathes of society were just trying to survive, put food on the table and avoid being killed in war or enslaved by hostile armies.

It made for turbulent and unpredictable times and was the perfect opportunity for an intelligent woman like Cristina to cast off traditional expectations and forge her own path.

Although Cristina is a fictional character, the inspiration for her comes from real women whose stories are only now starting to be appreciated … women like the artist Artemisia Gentileschi (1593-1656), who has only recently been recognised as one of the most progressive painters of her generation. I will never forget standing in front of her painting of Judith Slaying Holofernes for the first time and being blown away by the single-minded determination on Judith's face; how modern her wilfulness felt.

This sense of modern characters wrestling their way out of the medieval world is something I hope to capture on every page of all the books in the Basilica Diaries series. As the magnificent St Peter's Basilica rises from the dirt, stone by stone, our characters will wrestle with problems that still resonate with life in the 21st century — religious extremism, corruption, gaslighting, the abuse of learning, the search for fulfilment.

I would love to hear your thoughts on these novels!

If you have time to post a review on **Amazon** or **Goodreads**, that would be great, or if you'd rather give me feedback through social media, here are the links.

Website: www.RichardKurti.com

Instagram: RichardKurtiWriter

Twitter: @Richard_Kurti

Either way, I hope you'll join Cristina and Domenico on their next thrilling investigation in *Palette of Blood…*

SAPERE
BOOKS